Flight of the
Wild Swan

Flight of the
Wild Swan

MELISSA PRITCHARD

Bellevue Literary Press
NEW YORK

First published in the United States in 2024
by Bellevue Literary Press, New York

For information, contact:
Bellevue Literary Press
90 Broad Street
Suite 2100
New York, NY 10004
www.blpress.org

The illustration on page 389 was originally published in *Notes on Matters Affecting the Health, Efficiency, and Hospital Administration of the British Army* and sent to Queen Victoria in 1858.

Cover photograph by the Everett Collection/Shutterstock.com

This is a work of fiction. Characters, organizations, events, and places (even those that are actual) are either products of the author's imagination or are used fictitiously.

Library of Congress Cataloging-in-Publication Data
Names: Pritchard, Melissa, author.
Title: Flight of the wild swan / Melissa Pritchard.
Description: First edition. | New York : Bellevue Literary Press, 2024.
Identifiers: LCCN 2023003089 | ISBN 9781954276215 (paperback ; acid free
  paper) | ISBN 9781954276222 (epub)
Subjects: LCSH: Nightingale, Florence, 1820-1910--Fiction. | LCGFT:
  Biographical fiction. | Novels.
Classification: LCC PS3566.R578 F58 2024 | DDC 813/.54--dc23/eng/20230523
LC record available at https://lccn.loc.gov/2023003089

Bellevue Literary Press would like to thank all its generous donors—individuals and foundations—for their support.

This project is supported in part by an award from the National Endowment for the Arts.

This publication is made possible by the New York State Council on the Arts with the support of the Office of the Governor and the New York State Legislature.

Book design and composition by Mulberry Tree Press, Inc.

Bellevue Literary Press is committed to ecological stewardship in our book production practices, working to reduce our impact on the natural environment.

♾ This book is printed on acid-free paper.

Manufactured in the United States of America.

First Edition

10   9   8   7   6   5   4   3   2

paperback ISBN: 978-1-954276-21-5
ebook ISBN: 978-1-954276-22-2

For my husband and heart's companion,
Dr. Philip Thomas Schley

Here and there a cygnet is reared uneasily among the ducklings in the brown pond . . .

—GEORGE ELIOT, *Middlemarch*

Flight of the
Wild Swan

Delirium

35 South Street
Mayfair
London
1877

S HE WAKES IN STALE DARKNESS, sweat-soaked, freezing. The same nightmare, always. A common grave, hundreds of the dead, their arms tightening around her, pulling her down. An indistinct murmur of voices. Some still in uniform, most writhing, naked. She cannot save them. Cannot save herself.

This time the waking is different. This time she is dying. She is sure of it. The nurse, Anna, will find her in the morning.

Then what?

Vultures descending. Family first. Spying. Searching through her things. Then the press. Speculating. Digging. She hasn't much. Papers. Paperwork, journals, letters. As she likes to say, enough writing to cover Australia.

Some things should never be read.

I stand at the Altar of these murdered men and while I live, I fight their cause.

Let them read that.

God spoke to me and called me to His service. What form this service was to take the voice did not say.

That, too.

Kindness to sick man, woman, and child came in with Christ.

The beginning of my story.

Three things all but destroyed the army in the Crimea—ignorance, incapacity, and useless rules.

A tragic fact.

But it all takes too long. She becomes confused, feverish, rummaging through papers, journals, letters, unable to decide what and how much of herself to burn. Until the sky lightens, until the nurse puts her to bed and goes to find the doctor, she will feed more and more of herself into the fire. Stupid pieces, damaging, irrelevant. Ravings. Infatuations. *Master*—imagine having called him that! Bitter outpourings against God, men, men's government, men's wars, all of it. Bile that had to come out, put where she put everything, saving every word. On paper. To be used against her once she is gone.

Keep the scientist, the statistician, the nurse. Preserve the myth. History a jumble of half-truths anyway. Let the fire eat her rage, her failures. Let her become what each generation needs her to be.

A light to lead others.

The rest worthless.

I must strive to see only God in my friends, and God in my cats.

My favorite.

PART ONE

I Am Educated

Lea Hurst

Derbyshire, England
1827–1836

Ensnared

I RUN TOWARD THE PITEOUS CRIES, my boots weighing me down, small stones I've collected for Papa clatting against one another in my pocket.

It had not been my intent to rescue a thing. In the library this morning, Papa had let me hold a new fossil from his collection, an ammonite from Lyme Regis. When I'd asked how I might find fossils of my own, he suggested I first scout the woodlands, develop an eye for unusual stones. Father's library, an oak-paneled room smelling of tobacco, cloves, and bergamot, of dust and dead insects clinging to heavy folds of maroon drapery, is a shadowy, crammed place where rare books are piled up, haphazardly shelved, left open on glass-topped naturalist's cabinets. Besides the nursery I share with my sister, it is my favorite of the many rooms at Lea Hurst. Setting the ammonite back in its precise place amid a neat row of labeled fossils, Papa added, "After you've found your stones, Flo, bring them to me; then you may choose from among my Midlands brachiopods."

I have collections of coins, seashells, wax dolls. I've a cemetery trove of harvest mice, a baby wren, pink-skinned and naked of feathers, a blackbird, two halves of a grass snake, a natterjack toad, a striped brown lizard. Papa collects hundreds of rare books, plant and insect specimens, fossils. I covet his Jurassic ammonite from Lyme Regis, its green-tinged, coarsely pitted spiral.

So, on the governess's day off, when Parthe and I are meant to be resting before tea, I get up. Making as little sound as possible, clutching my boots to my chest, I steal down the back stairway, servants' stairs we are never to use, drag open the iron-studded door, slip into the bleached glare and chapel-like hush of a Sunday afternoon in Derbyshire. On the granite steps, I lace up the iron-lined boots—because my ankles are weak, I am made to wear them—and set off down one of several footpaths winding deep into Lea Hurst's woodlands.

Searching the ground among oaks, birch, sweet chestnut, and spruce, I choose three gray striated stones, drop them into the pocket of my day dress. Once I show him these, I will be able to choose from among Papa's brachiopods, mollusks millions of years old. Pushing strands of hair back from my hot cheeks, I hear it, a cry of injury. Hear it again. A creature, in distress, not far from me. The cries are high-pitched, monotonous. For an instant, I long for the somnolent peace of the third-floor nursery, the large open windows overlooking the river Derwent. But the sound draws me on.

Its injury is worse, more fascinating than anything I have seen. A hare, fully grown, caught in a poacher's snare. Sensing my presence, it goes still. Even in its agony, it wants not to be found.

Dropping to my knees, I stare into its amber eyes, stretched wide with fear. We regard each other. Though I am only seven, I see its creature soul.

"Shhh. Poor thing."

Twine, wire-thin, hardened with wax, has torn the skin off its back legs, cut into its flanks, torn open the white-furred abdomen. I study, as if dreaming, the bloody muscle, white bone, sinew. The hare kicks once, with little force. Sinks onto its side, unmoving, one slightly protuberant eye steadily regarding me. A wild creature with tall, tapering ears and tawny, stippled fur, powerful hind legs meant to bound at great speeds across fields and woodlands, unharmed until now.

I work to free him from the sharp twine, drag the petticoat from beneath my dress. Wrapping the maimed animal in its muslin (a use for the stupid thing!), I struggle to my feet, return to the footpath. Papa's stones, the size and weight of chestnuts, shift against one another in my pocket.

Blood, red and warm, seeps through the petticoat. Stepping out from the woodland's edge, I see my sister running toward me. Farther off, standing in the kitchen doorway, arms crossed, scowls our nurse and Sunday cook, Mrs. Gale.

Parthe dashes up, her blond hair plaited into two skinny ropes.

"What have you got, Flo? Gale is very angry. You have run off and frightened us."

"I found him in a snare. I'm going to save him."

Screwing up her face, Parthe lifts the blood-soaked hem of the petticoat. A hard little expression of disgust.

"Flo. It's dead. Ugh, your petticoat! Mama will be so mad with you."

Mrs. Gale trundles up, panting.

"What have you got, naughty child? I nearly sent one of the gardeners after you. Oh my. If you haven't got Jack Rabbit! Poor thing, snared, was it? Good as finished. Give him over; I've still time to turn him into Mr. Nightingale's favorite supper. Come into the house, wash your filthy hands, change clothes before tea. A blessing it's Miss Christie's day off. If she saw you looking like some dirty little heathen, she'd faint away, wouldn't she?"

Before Gale can pry the bundle from me, I cradle the hare, nuzzle its warm brindled fur, stroke the rounded place between its tall, dusky ears. It smells of wild grasses and sunlight. *A film slips over its eyes, a glassy, distant look. Gone.*

Deep Time

Take your Hare when it is Cas'd. Cut it into little pieces, lard them here and there and with little slips of bacon, season them with a very little pepper and salt, put them into an earthen jug, with a blade or two of mace, an onion stuck with cloves, and a bundle of sweet-herbs; cover the jug or jar you do it in so close that nothing can get in, then set it in a pot of boiling water, keep the water boiling, and three hours will do it; then turn it out into the dish, and take out the onion and sweet-herbs, and send it to table hot.

—Hannah Glasse, The Art of Cookery (1747)

"AH, *LEPUS EUROPAEUS*, MRS. GALE. Blood sauce as well?"

"Your favorite, sir."

"Indeed. High season for hares. How did you come by it?"

"It was Flo!" Parthe shoves her plate away. "She thought to save it!"

"Florence?" Her father looks with curiosity at his younger daughter, tucks a large white napkin down into his shirt collar. "You are responsible for my favorite dish?"

Mrs. Nightingale speaks kindly. "Flo dear, tell us. And Parthenope, a bite at least. Mrs. Gale has gone to great trouble."

Briefly, because it is painful, I describe freeing the hare, Mrs. Gale's taking it from me. Wonder what to do about the petticoat, stuffed beneath my bed.

"Poor thing," says Mama. "You tried saving a wild creature's life. I am sorry you couldn't."

"I'm not," Mr. Nightingale says, waving his fork. "Parthe, try a taste with the blood sauce. Mrs. Gale has peppered it to perfection."

"I won't!" Parthe sobs. "I won't drink blood!" She slides off her chair and runs from the room.

I chew on a nip of hare's meat in dark red gravy. Delicious. Not for the first time, I wonder what is the matter with me, why things that cause my sister to cry do not bother me in the least.

Mrs. Nightingale excuses herself to go ask Mrs. Gale to fix a simpler supper for Parthe.

"I found stones on my walk, Papa."

"Excellent. Bring them to the library after supper, and we'll have a look."

⁓

He examines my ordinary bits of rock, sets them aside, holds out three small fossils. I choose the largest.

"A brachiopod, dug from a limestone quarry in Roade. How many years are you now, Florence?"

"Seven since May, Papa."

"Well, that mollusk in your hand is millions of years old. You must imagine it coming into your possession from a place called Deep Time."

"What is that?" I ask.

"Not a place so much as a way of looking far outside the limits of human time. Not that long ago, it was believed the world was no more than six thousand years old. Today science tells us it is far older, a fact that disturbs a great many people."

"Why?"

"They fear science will challenge the existence of God. Call into question the truth of the Bible. Threaten all Christian civilization. I hardly agree. Science helps us know how God made this world. It is glorious inquiry, not witchcraft. Here, have all three. The others are echinoids found in glacial beds from the same quarry."

With Parthe, Papa talks of simple things. With me, it is as if I am some creature he must pour all his man's knowledge into. As if to change me into the boy, the son he will never have.

∽

In the nursery, I pull the notebook from under my pillow. Fashioned from Mama's and Papa's old letters, each page is folded into fours, the folded pages neatly stitched down one side. I write in the blank spaces, down the sides, at the very top and bottom. When one notebook is full, I put it in an old glove box of Mama's and make a new one.

Beneath a pencil sketch of the mollusk, I copy the description Papa has written down for me. *Brachiopod. Jurassic Age. Found by William Nightingale, 1825, limestone bed in Roade.* Turning the page, I sketch the three echinoids, then, from memory, the ammonite, named after the Greek ram-horned god, Ammon. Papa has promised to take me to Dorset one day to dig for fossils. He forgets most of his promises to me; it is doubtful he will remember this one.

Beneath the spiraled ammonite, I print:

Monster
Latin: *monere,* "to warn"
I am unlike other children.
I may be, as Miss Christie says,
a monster.

Sickroom

A Drama

by

F. Rossignol (English trans: Nightingale)

PLAYERS:

Nurses: Florence and Parthenope

Grave diggers: Florence and Parthenope

Rx:

Rosalie: one tsp. sarsaparilla syrup, fourteen grains of James's powder

Margery: two liver tonic pills taken before bed

Mai: green liniment rubbed on arms thrice weekly

Lucy: ginger plaster on chest

Ada: ginger plaster on back

Jane: beef tea, amputation right leg

Abigail: tonic pills, one every other day

Isabella: rhubarb powder with water, one tsp. every half an hour

Emily: steam vapor bath

Harriet I: green liniment

Harriet II: yellow liniment

Alice: herbal salve on flannel, to be wrapped around throat

Rebecca: flannel eyeshade for sick headache

Julia: bed rest

Amanda: cold-water bath for hysterics

Charlotte: bath with tincture of hyssop, dusted with rhubarb
    powder
Florence: jasmine tincture for scarlet fever
Parthenope: a tragic, terrible death

—The End—

Eighteen patients on doll-size mattresses, lying under squares of
old crinoline. Eighteen heads of poured wax with hard glass eyes
and stiff tendrils of brown or blond hair, eighteen pairs of miniature wax feet with painted-on black slippers, pointing heavenward.
Carrying a cobalt-edged porcelain platter pilfered from the kitchen,
I move from one to the next, reading each prescription aloud. On
my medical tray are pills made from bread, spat on and rolled into
balls, liniments and salves made from vegetable skins, lard, kitchen
spices. Behind me, Parthenope holds a pewter spoon and a brown
bottle of foul-smelling syrup made from soured milk and molasses.

"Today all are dreadfully ill. Jane must have a leg removed. Two
will die within the hour."

"Why, Flo? Why must they die?"

"Because God wants it."

We administer salves, liniments, syrups, bread pills. Pretending to saw off one of Jane's sawdust-stuffed, muslin-covered legs
with a paring knife, I bandage the pretend stump with a bit of
linen, stick my finger with the knife point, smear blood on the
bandage, suck my finger clean.

Sixteen of our patients, buttoned into nut brown flannel robes
sewn by Kitty, sit straight up in their beds, staring at nothing.

"These we have saved."

My sister points to the last two, crinoline blankets drawn over
their faces.

"For those, we must put on mourning bonnets."

"Why? What did they die of?"

"Scarlet fever took Florence. Parthenope tumbled down a well and split her head in two."

"That's cruel!"

"Death is cruel. One day, a child is eating gingerbread; the next, she has dropped down a well."

"I'd rather play battledore, Flo."

Wearing black caps borrowed from the servants' closet, carrying a doll apiece, we creep downstairs and out to the back end of the vegetable garden to "bury" Florence and Parthenope beneath handfuls of torn grass, "skirts" of pink hollyhock, white umbrels of water parsnip.

"May we unbury them after tea?"

"Of course. We can be like Lord Jesus. Bring the dead to life."

Urchin

"HURRY, POP, WILL YOU? This morning, Miss Christie asked to know how your essay on Christian martyrs could have been so free of mistakes. If you do not cut my hair off this instant, I will tell her why. That I wrote it for you."

"Nasty thing, you wouldn't!"

"I certainly would."

"But these scissors are so heavy."

"You're afraid of Miss Christie, that's all."

"Does hair grow back?"

"Dunce. Quick, before she comes in."

Two hard, grinding bites of the shears and Parthe finds herself holding the cook's jointing scissors in one hand, her sister's braid, a red-gold tail detached from its bossy animal, in the other.

"What shall I do with it?"

"Throw it out the window—what do I care?"

Miss Christie glides into the nursery, a love letter from the German bank clerk tucked into her pocket. Staring from Florence to the braid, swaying like a long, fat snake in Parthenope's hand, she shrieks.

"God's mercy, what have you done? You look like a street urchin!"

"Not an urchin, Miss Christie. A boy. Francis. Francis Nightingale."

Silva Rerum

SEIZING THE BRAID, STILL WARM and smelling of chamomile rinse, Miss Christie wads it into her other pocket, the one without Werner's letter. She hasn't the first idea what to do with it.

"Sit on that chair, Miss Nightingale. Not a word until you have got the spirit of obedience."

A snort of laughter from the far end of the nursery, where Parthe is working a sampler. "Enough from you, Parthenope."

Miss Christie, who is young and pretty but understands nothing of children and dislikes being a governess, turns to the worst thorn in her side. Francis, for heaven's sake.

"What is the first rule of girlhood, Florence? Obedience. And the second? Silence. Parthenope, read your sampler aloud to us. I believe it is called 'The Danger of Delay.'"

> *Why should I say "'Tis yet too soon*
> *To seek for heaven or think of death?"*
> *A flower may fade before 'tis noon,*
> *and I this day may lose my breath.*

Miss Christie allows the association of childhood and early death to deepen the springtime chill in the large unheated room.

"Florence, stop pulling a face. Parthenope, turn away from your sister."

Scraping her chair around, Parthe bursts out laughing. Miss Christie, clenching her fists against her skirts, comes close to weeping with frustration. Florence, who is not rude so much as truthful and iron-willed ("You were not born like other children," her father teases; "you marched, full of fire and inquiry, from under your mother's skirts"), feels a slight twinge of remorse.

"Sorry, Miss Christie, but I really must go my own way. You say girls must obey first and be silent second, but that would mean to stop thinking. I like thinking. I like speaking, too. There lies the trouble between us."

That morning, Miss Christie had had to abandon a classroom exercise she set great store by, assigning a single virtue to each letter of the alphabet, having Florence make up a phrase to fit that virtue. They had begun with *A, Avoid Lying, It Leads to Every Other Vice*, and gotten as far as *E, Elevated Thoughts Energize*, when Florence had laid down her pencil and balked. Pointless, she complained, adding that her hands hurt. Suffering from weakness in her wrists, she is still unable to write in anything but a childish hand when she should, like her sister, be writing in cursive. Her unfinished sampler, with its hopeless tangle of threads, (*Now that my journey's just begun, / my course so little trod, / I'll stay before I'll further run, / And give myself to God*), lies in a troubled heap on the music room floor.

Every day brings a new affront to Miss Christie's conventional sensibilities. Florence's disgusting caterpillar "farm" in one corner of the nursery, her objection to instruction, her obstinacy in getting dressed. And now her hair all shorn off, what's left sticking up every which way. Miss Christie herself has never rebelled. Having neither the will nor the spirit for defiance, she views her job, educating these sisters and punishing their least disobedience, as one and the same. In a letter to her mother, she admits to preferring the elder Nightingale girl. Parthenope reminds her of herself as a child, docile, eager to please, content to be doted on by adults. A butterfly nature, dilettantish, with a gift for drawing. The other, one year younger, is a monster, and on more than one occasion, Miss

Christie has said so right to her sour, set little face. "Stand straight.
Keep still. Don't make that face when I speak to you. Not another
word. Mon Dieu, what a little monster you are!"

⸞⸞

Miss Christie's little monster, I sit up late, finishing stitchwork on
a new notebook fashioned from Mama's and Papa's discarded letters. Unlike Parthe, eager to sketch whatever she likes—her affections so broad and shallow as to be meaningless—I am compelled,
despite the ache in my wrists, to write down every smidgen of life
going on around me, every thought boiling up within me. Nothing
is real unless I take it down, pin and straighten what I see and think
into measured words, solid sentences. I have filled dozens of note-
books, each no larger than my palm. Saving them in an old glove
box of Mama's, I keep the box in my little cemetery, along with
dozens of crickets and caterpillars, two grackles, a nuthatch, a baby
squirrel fallen from its nest. My private thoughts, hedged round by
Papa's and Mama's faded sentences, decaying in the earth.

On the day Mama surprises me with my first grown-up "commonplace" journal, bound in blue morocco leather and accompanied by a note: *Dear Flo, at last—your very own* cahier *or* silva
rerum—*(Latin for "forest of things")*. *All my love, Mama*, I will write
on its inside cover: *CAHIER DE F. NIGHTINGALE. Is the Lord
not with thee, wherever thou art?*

Mother Twitchett

WEARING SERVANTS' GLOVES, I polish each seashell in my collection with oxalic acid. A copy of Woodarch's *Introduction to the Study of Conchology* lies open to an illustrated description of the spiral operculum (Kingdom: Animalia; Phylum: Mollusca; Class: Gastropoda; Binomial name: *Turbo marmoratus*—Linnaeus, 1758), a sea snail shell I purchased for four pence in a local shop, along with a Bulla "brown bubble shell" (Kingdom: Animalia; Phylum: Mollusca; Class: Gastropoda; Binomial name: *Bulla australis*—Gray, 1825) for two pence. In the commonplace book Mama gave me, *dans mon cahier*, I have made an alphabetized list of each of forty shell specimens. I intend to collect one hundred. My coin collection is tucked away in a cupboard. Money, man's creation, is of less interest to me than God's fantastical sea creatures. Each seashell has its own perfect symmetry, its unique colors and patterns through which to glimpse the mind of God.

The nursery windows are flung wide to the gray-green roar of the Derwent below. Behind me, on the Turkey carpet, Pop lolls on her stomach, flipping through *A Choice Collection of Riddles and Charades*.

"Flo! What about this one?" She reads the lines aloud.

> Old Mother Twitchett had but one eye,
> And a long tail which she let fly:
> And every time she went over a gap,
> She left a bit of tail in her trap.

I hold a dog whelk up to the light, admire its pink-and-amber roundness. "Don't know, Pop."

"Needle and thread, dull wit! What about this?"

> *Hoddy-doddy,*
> *With a round black body!*
> *Three feet and a wooden hat,*
> *What's that?*

How interesting. The muted stripes on two tellins are alike, yet not. "I give up."

"Iron pot, silly! Cutting your hair and pretending to be a boy hasn't made you one dot smarter than me."

Mad Peter's Cabinet

WITH A SLIGHT SHUDDER, Miss Christie takes the slippery braid from the pocket of her dress and hands it to Mr. Nightingale.

Coiling his daughter's plait into a large handkerchief, William Nightingale goes into his library and places it in his cabinet, a new curiosity in an exotic miscellany of inherited objects: a five-inch crocodile tooth from the Nile, a dried seahorse, a miniature female anatomical figure from Bologna, a narwhal's tusk mislabeled "unicorn horn," a glass phial of twin animal embryos preserved in spirits, a mandrake root from the Orient, a string of amber beads from Africa, the shell of an armadillo, a wampum belt made by Indians of North America, ivory sewing tools from China, a vial of red liquid collected when a terror of "blood" rained down on the Isle of Wight on June 19, 1177.

The cabinet and its contents originally belonged to William's great-uncle, Peter Nightingale. A solitary bachelor prone to sodden bouts of drunkenness that led to flogging his horse over fences and across ditches in the dead of night, earning himself the local name "Mad Peter," he had deeded his entire estate—2,200 acres, lead mines, cotton mills, and a sum of 100,000 pounds—to his great-nephew so long as William agreed to change his surname from Shore to Nightingale. The moment his great-uncle died, William Shore, now Nightingale, became a wealthy country gentleman free of any need or incentive to earn a living. Devoting his life to the quiet accumulation of knowledge for its own sake, he retreats into his shadowy libraries, a sea snail gone into the richly brined depths of its shell.

Iron Cage

WHAT A FINE SON FLO WOULD HAVE MADE. He watches his daughter, crouched on the dirt footpath to Cromford, absorbed in the workings of a busy anthill. Except for Mrs. Nightingale, who refused to indulge Flo's whim, they had all called her Francis until the pretense grew tiresome and everyone forgot. Even Florence stopped badgering them. She had drawn the wrong sort of attention to herself, the amused condescension of her parents and her sister's obnoxious teasing.

"Goodness, Flo. What if I insisted on being called Percival? Or Horace? Algernon? It's too silly. Cutting your hair and changing your name did nothing but hurt Mama's feelings. I wonder where it went, your pretty braid?"

In the dark, lying beside Parthe, I run my hands through the stiff tufts. Why must everything be about sparing the feelings of others? What an iron cage life is turning out to be!

"Might as well give me all your hair ribbons, since you can't use them."

"Have them. You fiddle about with bows and curls. I'd rather go on walks with Papa."

⟋⟍

Removing his cap, Mr. Nightingale squats beside Florence, who is intently focused on a rivulet of ants. She pokes at them with a twig.

"See how they persist despite every obstacle, Papa? I have counted eighty-seven so far."

"Determined little fellows. Do you know how to say *ant* in Latin? *Formica.* For-mee-cah."

"See that one? How it carries its dead comrade on its back?" She looks up at her father.

"Ants have intelligence; I am sure of it."

"All living things have intelligence, Florence."

"Francis, Papa."

He ruffles her sun-warmed, unruly hair. "Francis. Time to leave the kingdom of *formicae* and carry on to Cromford."

Jumping to her feet, she opens her palm to show her father a tiny ant, scurrying directionlessly.

"Look, he wants to come with us!"

"Put him back where he belongs, and don't forget your mother's basket."

Hattie Moone

IF ANY LIVING CREATURE IS ILL OR INJURED, I must do my best
to nurse it well. I do not think Parthe or Cousin Hilary, Aunt
Mai, Mama, or anyone else shares this feeling. I am drawn to sickness. Gale says I am "a queer little creature." Mama wonders how
a family of ducks could have possibly hatched a wild swan like me.

Last week at Cromford, after I begged, Papa let me go with
him into one of the tenants' cottages. I brought the family a loaf of
bread, drippings, black tea, and sugar, all packed in Mama's wicker
basket. The tenant, Albert Moone, was away at the lead mines in
Wirksworth. Two of his daughters were away, too, apprenticed to
the cotton factory in Lea Mills. The youngest, a boy of six, had died
in an explosion at the mines the year before. Only Mrs. Moone,
heavily pregnant, and a girl my own age were at "home," a smoky,
windowless room with a floor of hard dirt. The girl, Hattie, lay
curled on a straw pallet in one corner. As Papa stood with Mrs.
Moone, telling her that her husband's debt of six months' rent
was forgiven, I sat beside her. Huddled under a sprawl of rags, she
clutched a black tomcat, which hissed as I reached over to pet it.

"He only loves me. No one else dares touch him."

"He's awfully fat."

"He's a good ratter."

"Tom the cat, fat on rats."

When she smiled, I saw the purplish line along her gums, above
her rotten teeth. When Papa asked about Hattie, Mrs. Moone
sighed. Dead tired all day, bent in half with stomachaches, never

more than a bite or two of stirabout. I could see for myself that her arms and legs were matchsticks, her great mass of black hair tangled and unwashed. Her large brown eyes wandered around the room, as if unable to find what they were seeking. But I petted her cat, made her laugh, said nothing about the purple line above her stubbed black teeth.

Walking home, Papa told me Hattie's trouble was lead poisoning. When I asked when I might visit again, saying I had a picture book to give to her, he said books were of no use; the child's mind was enfeebled, her body sick from the breathing in of dust off her father's mining clothes, clothes it had been her task to shake out and wash. Hattie Moone, he told me, had not long to live, adding he didn't know if it was a blessing or a curse that another child was to be born into such poverty.

When I next went to visit, Mrs. Moone let me hold her newborn, a scrawny mite with wild ginger hair named Albert, after his father and dead brother.

Letters Going Here and There

Grandmother Shore,

Answer me my letter if you please! Do you have any solution for rats that are eating holes in our drawing room carpet? Last month, Papa and I made a visit to the new Zoological Society, where I saw: 2 leopards, 2 bears, 2 parrots, 2 emus (very large birds), 2 rabbits, 1 lion, and 2 cockatoos. Except for the lion, Papa says it was a perfect Noah's ark.

How is Nelson? He is such an amusing dog. Please tell him hello from me.

Write me!

Affec yrs,
Florence Nightingale

Dearest Mama,

Shall you come back Wednesday or Thursday? We are all of us better, though Parthe coughs, and Miss Christie keeps to her room with fever. The music room carpet is down, *the curtains are* up. *We read our daily chapter today, the seventh of Luke, and said our prayers. I have done my music, my flower, and my point. Last week, Parthe bought a skein of blue thread, and Gale and Kitty bought us flannel and some cambric to make petticoats and nightgowns for our dolls—plus yards and yards of scarlet ribbon.*

Ever your affectionate child,
Florence Nightingale

P.S. Cousin Hilary sent silkworm's eggs, which I intend to educate, as she included all the particulars as to how to bring them up. Good-bye.

Dear Cousin Hilary,

We have lost a tomtit. Parthe found him on the garden path, his little black cap and golden feathers so quiet and still. I buried him near the wild plant garden I am cultivating with Kitty—what do you think of Parthe's and my epitaph:

Here lies Sir Tomtit
a tiny golden bird
his song no more
his wings no longer flit.

I think it very bad.

Your affec cousin,
Flo

Dear Mama,

I pinched my finger, so could not write until today. Do you think I need wear my steel boots now that it is getting so hot, and could you send me a pair of walking-out shoes, as my boots are getting so very hot I can scarcely wear them? I am just come from church, where Mr. Green preached from Luke 15:10, "There is joy in heaven over one sinner that repenteth."

Repenteth what?
Good-bye, dear Mama.

Your affectionate
Flo

Commonplace

YESTERDAY, PARTHE AND I CAPTURED a green caterpillar. We have tried everything, but it does not eat. After church, Miss Penton, the clergyman's daughter, told us it feeds on privet. Now it is alive and well, eating its privet. We keep it under a sieve in the garden.

Today's text at church: "I am the good Shepherd." Saint John 10:11.

We happened upon the two Miss Cooks as we neared home. I bought from them two buns, three hard biscuits, and two little round ones. I will make a receipt for Mama, as she likes to see how I spend my allowance of six pence a week.

Dearest Mama

Gale has cut me out a new cloak and put a green ribbon on my bonnet. Miss Penton tells us that when our caterpillar turns chrysalis, it plunges into the earth, so yesterday I made it a bed of earth and, above that, a bed of leaves. This morning, I found a leaf half-eaten and our caterpillar gone. Miss Christie sends her love and says she is sorry she cannot locate Mr. Gimbernat's letter. I have found my misplaced bag for Embley—in it I put my prayer book, a pair of gloves, a volume of L'Ecolier, a backbone of cuttlefish, some of my work, your stockings, some paper, and another book. I shall use the powder from the backbone of the cuttlefish to dry this letter. Tell Papa we are very happy and everyone is well again, except poor Gale, who has a headache. We come by gig to Embley in eight days' time. Will you be there or away in London? I enclose a receipt for my week's spending.

Votre petite fille,
FN

Two buns: 1 pence each
Three biscuits: 1 pence each
Two little round ones: ½ pence each

Mademoiselle F. Rossignol

SOMEONE HAS BROUGHT A CHALKBOARD and packet of white chalk up to the nursery.

"Choose a word, Pop; arrange the letters into new words. As many as you can."

"Parthenope."

"Not your name, goose. Watch." Chalking *breathe* on the board, I write underneath it: *beat, bat, the, at, be, heat, hat, he, brat* . . .

"Boring. Let's play ghosts."

"No. I'll finish *La Vie.*"

I'm calling my life's story *La Vie de Rossignol.* It is marvelous how much can happen in twelve years of life. My wrists, for instance, have strengthened. My ankles are stronger, too, I almost never wear the horrid boots, and yesterday, after measuring me and finding I had shot past Parthe by two centimeters, Miss Christie said I was certain to be very tall and have suitors. "Do suitors prefer tall women?" I asked. *Sometimes. Especially pretty ones.* Miss C. has a suitor who sends twice-daily letters. Whatever is contained in those square packets must be extraordinary. Opening and reading them, she goes pink, acts giddy, ignores our schoolwork.

"Miss Christie said my essay on Alexander the Great was the utmost. It's not, Flo; it's rubbish. I stuck mistakes in it on purpose. She didn't notice a single one."

"It's because of her beau. His letters."

"Her what?"

"Beau. Someone who might marry you."

"No! She cannot. What about us?"

"If Miss Christie marries, Papa will hire someone else."

"Let's steal her letters while she is asleep. If we read them, we'll know everything."

"Parthe. Letters are private."

"But Papa employs Miss Christie, which means she belongs to him. Which means her letters belong to him, too. Which means we can read them."

"There's not an ounce of logic in anything you've said. No one belongs to anyone. Let's go down to the library. You can read one of Papa's books instead of Miss Christie's letters."

"Reading is hard. I'd rather play ghosts."

At Lea Hurst, their father's library has a bookshelf with a secret door that opens into a little-used garden room. The door is cleverly painted to look as if it has real shelves, with books titled *Leather on Woods*, *History of Moroccan Leather*, *Optical Delusions*, *Tales of the Doorway*, and *Oaths Not Binding*. His game of "ghosts" involves creaking open the secret door, slipping into the library covered up in a white bedsheet, and calling woo-woo-wooo while flapping after his shrieking girls. It is one of the few times they see him other than preoccupied, buried in one of his books. His mornings begin with a book propped against a milk jug. Warned never to interrupt, the family talks around Mr. Nightingale as he turns pages, moves his lips, loose crumbs of toast, blobs of jam, threads of cream spilling down his breakfast robe.

"No ghosts. I want to finish *La Vie*."

"Pish." Parthe flops onto a chair. "No fun, you. I'll get my sketchbook and draw an amazing party of ghosts. A parliament."

"Don't put me in your parliament."

"I should think you'd like seeing yourself as a spook."

"I wouldn't. Besides, portraits are vain."

Hoping the story of someone's life isn't just as vain, I begin to imagine my last day on earth. What it will be like.

Death of Hattie Moone

"SHE SUFFERED CONVULSIONS," Papa said. After a day and a night, she slipped away, her father, mother, little Albert, and two older sisters, come home, gathered around her. "She is in heaven," he added awkwardly.

"What about her cat?" I asked.

Commonplace

WHILE SHAKING OUT MATTRESSES in one of the little-used upstairs bedrooms, Gale came upon five mouse babies in a nest. Their mother, it seems, had run off.

"Have you ever seen such a wee one?" She drops it in my palm, a pink snippet of raw meat. Four tiny paws, a long tail and largish head, bits of skin over its eyes. "Horrid," Parthe whispers. Even as I cup it in both hands, it stops breathing. Gale takes it by the tail, flips it into the fire as Parthe dashes, shrieking, from the nursery. I wrap the other four baby mice in wadding, place them in a basket beside the fire, set a drop of milk to each of their mouths. Queer hairless things, stretching out spindly legs!

Three others die during the night. I move the last one closer to the fire, give it milk. I should like to rear this bit of mouse, make a pet of it.

Miss Christie Is Married

BUTTONED INTO A BROWN TAFFETA PELISSE, their governess is saying good-bye. Two travel trunks sit by the front door.

"My dear [*spoiled-to-the-teeth*] children," she says. I shall miss you [*not a bit*]."

"How shall we get on?" Parthe sniffs.

"Who is to be your husband, Miss Christie? Where will you live?" (*Little monster gets straight to the point.*)

"In London, near Russell Square. Mr. Leipzig is from Berlin. He has an important position in a bank. [*A clerk, my precious Werner, clinging by his teeth to a back desk.*] Enough, girls. My carriage is late. *Allons dehors.* Let's go outside and walk a little. Parthenope, I'd like you to name in Latin any flower we pass by. Florence, after I am gone, you must feed that curious [*nosy*] brain of yours and do something useful [*other than snooping*] with it."

"Miss Christie!" Parthe runs up, waves a magenta bloom with a piercing yellow eye. "*Primula vulgaris!*"

"*Très bien.* My carriage, girls. Hurry! You must help me with my trunks."

Dearest Mama

This morning I walked to church with Aunt Mai. It is a fine day, though blowy. Gale is sick with another headache; she says she can scarcely talk it hurts so. Her right foot is very much swelled and has no feeling even after Mr. Winter came by and causticed it.

The text in church was Isaiah 12:3. I cannot recollect it, but it was followed by a long sermon about cholera, the uncertainty of life, and the necessity to always be prepared for heaven.

Coming home, I found the last mousie dead, poor pet. It had such velvet pink paws! I pray it has gone to mouse heaven, since its life here was not nice at all.

This paper is so rough, I can hardly write on it.

Do you know if my goldfish have arrived?

Your affectionate child,
Flo

Commonplace

Does God love His mice and snakes any less than His humans? I cannot think so.

Once we are at Embley for the winter season, Papa has promised to take me to the Zoological Society's gardens in Regent's Park so I can see the porridge-eating hippopotamus and the elephant family from Calcutta.

This morning, when I asked if I might bathe her sore, swollen foot and bind a salve of comfrey leaves on it, Gale snapped, "Mad thought. A body heals if God wants it to."

Which made me think of Hattie Moone, how she cannot have wanted to be dead.

PART TWO

Further Educated

Embley Park

East Wellow, Hampshire
1837–1846

As with the commander of any army, or the leader of any enterprise, so is it with the mistress of a house.

—MRS. ISABELLA BEETON,
Book of Household Management

122 dinner plates
21 "best" tablecloths
20 mince pie pans

—Items in Embley House
kitchen and linens inventory

Commonplace

On the first day of January 1837, I resolve to:

> run to the gate & back before breakfast each morning
>
> take ½ an hour's walk before dinner & a long walk after
>
> perform twenty arm exercises before I dress
>
> practice the pianoforte one hour a day, draw ½ an hour regularly
>
> go to bed in proper time, read the Bible
>
> pray before breakfast & at bedtime
>
> visit the poor & care for the sick
>
> take medicine when I need it
>
> go to church on Sundays when there is someone to go with me
>
> read the books put out for me
>
> read *Robinson Crusoe* aloud to Grandmama this afternoon as Parthe walks her about the drawing room
>
> remember to thank Mama for the gilded smelling bottle she gave me
>
> give in to fewer temptations this year than last

Grand Wash

Four times a year, Frances Nightingale hires half a dozen village women to come to Embley to sort, wash, and iron the soiled household linens. For days, the lawns surrounding the house turn into a snowy patchwork of bedsheets, pillowcases, linen kitchen towels, linen bath and hand towels, luncheon and dinner tablecloths, napkins. And clothes—underclothes by the dozens, sleeping shirts, men's shirts and pants, women's chemises and day dresses, all stretched and drying in the sunlight, human shapes in congress, missing their living forms.

Four times each year, on these "Grand Wash" days, Mrs. Nightingale puts her daughters to work, just as her mother had done with her. One day, they will manage large households of their own. How will they know a thing is done well unless they do it themselves, under her supervision?

Frances gives her favorite daughter an easy task. Parthenope, at seventeen, is slow-moving, averse to chores (overindulged, in Mr. Nightingale's opinion), so Frances has her sorting Embley's china services, separating out what is chipped or cracked, recording and numbering each piece in the Household Accounts ledger. Checking on her progress after an hour or so, Mrs. Nightingale finds Parthe, forehead pressed against a window in the dining room, staring dreamily down at a group of women folding linens into great wicker baskets. As she stares, an expensive gravy boat dangles from her fingertips—Davenport's "Flying Bird," the pattern Lord Palmerston and his wife, distinguished dinner guests, had once eaten from.

"Parthenope! Give me that gravy boat before you break it."

"Sorry, Mama. I've finished, actually."

"Then you may sort the silver. Where is your sister?"

"Upstairs, I think. At the linen press."

Setting the gravy boat in a safe spot on the sideboard with the other pieces of Davenport, Frances sighs, knowing she will have to ask one of the kitchen servants to redo Parthenope's work, and heads upstairs. At least Florence is dependable. By nature, she does things right, efficiently. Then why is her younger daughter so difficult to like? Frances can feel Florence's silent criticism of her inadequacies, vanities, social ambitions. Those gray eyes, narrowed against her. She prefers Parthe's pleasanter, pleasure-loving nature, even if she never will lift a finger. Her children can never understand what it was like, growing up the daughter of a wealthy merchant and member of Parliament, spoiled with every luxury and advantage, to find out while she was on her honeymoon with William in Italy, that her father had lost his entire fortune overnight. She would return home to find him as politically active as ever, an idealist defending the poor, an abolitionist fighting to end the slave trade, a dissenter fighting religious prejudice, dragging his family into a degrading new life, leaving her mother to put a good face on diminished circumstances, selling off property and possessions, fending off bill collectors, forced to seek financial help from her own children, including Frances. Her mother's humiliation haunts her to this day, her parents' fall from material grace, and she has vowed, sworn, it will never happen to her. With William's head in the clouds (and to Frances, a book might as well be a cloud), the Nightingale fortune, the holding on to it, is up to her. Every day of her life she feels that burden. And a second burden, just as heavy. Since they have no son to inherit William's wealth or his two estates, if he should die before her and if neither daughter has married and produced a male child, a direct heir, all will be lost by law, all will go to William's nearest male relative, his sister's son, William Shore, and Frances will end up like her mother, standing in the ugly doorway of a reduced life, dependent on the good will of relatives. Her daughters, Florence especially, will never understand or sympathize with the battles she faces, never understand the reason for her headaches, her need to "be seen," to entertain those who "matter," the importance of finding good husbands for them both. And unfortunately, Florence, the more rebellious of the two, the one least interested in money or status and most like her grandfather, possessed of an exaggerated spirit of Christian idealism, is the prettier and more graceful of her two girls, the more attractive to the opposite sex. Were it not for Florence's aloof, obstinate personality, her mother would have placed her best hopes in her.

Drowned in Bedsheets

I STAND PARALYZED BEFORE MY MOTHER'S prized linen press, all three of its long, deep drawers pulled out, stocked with newly washed sheets, smoothed, folded, smelling of sunlight. Tomorrow, Mama's servants will make up all Embley's beds from these dozens of sheets and pillowcases.

My useless life. Drowned in bedsheets, swallowed up by linens.

I shove each of the drawers back in, slam shut the two doors, rubbed and gleaming with beeswax and linseed oil. The sound rings like a gunshot down the long hall. *Such a satisfying violence—* then I hear her, laboring up the stairs, willingly enslaved to her possessions.

"Finished, Flo dear? Whatever was that noise?"

Breathing in her sweet, familiar fragrance of orris root and Parma violets, I watch my mother open the carved doors of the press as if they were church doors, slide out the first of the long, scented drawers, caress the stack of sun-brightened sheets with manicured white hands. Cleanliness calms her. Order reassures her. Excess, too. Especially excess. I sometimes suspect she has a terror of ending up like her mother. Reduced.

"I've folded the strong sheets and pillowcases the way you like, Mama. The tablecloths and napkins are counted and folded as well."

"Good. Go help your sister with the silver and glassware. That child is as slow as pond water."

Why must my natural efficiency result in having to do Parthe's chores as well as my own? Better to pretend to be a stupid ninny, like her.

"Remind me to order three dozen footed wineglasses from Fortnum's. Heaven knows why I torment myself so. Twelve dinner parties, this season alone!"

Commonplace

WHAT EARTHLY POINT, owning two estates, two mansions, each with its sets of silver and dinnerware, goblets by the hundreds, bed linens stacked to the roof—while the poor (as if some less worthy, negligible species) sit starving by the roadside and begging outside of church on Sundays? The few times Mama visits Papa's tenants in the villages, she distributes scraps from our table, leaving these families, after they have gorged on the stale liberality of our crumbs, no better than before. How can such poor-peopling please God? Mama is lavishly kind to family and friends, fair with servants, yet I swear she cannot see past these suffocating circles of domesticity. She keeps constantly busy, managing Lea Hurst and Embley, entertaining "socially important" guests, hosting endless rotations of relatives. That she expects me to marry into wealth and live as lavishly, as mindlessly, as she does, makes me want to smash everything in sight. Beat my head against a wall. I may not know why I was born, but it cannot be to wage war on dust and broken crockery. It cannot be to put down in a house ledger, as I do now, meaningless columns of tweedly this, twaddly that.

Murder!

HAVING HIRED MISS ADA HAWKINS, a spinster with acceptable letters of reference, to instruct his daughters in the female arts of music, drawing, dance, and social intercourse, William takes it upon himself to ladle rich spoonfuls of his own Cambridge education into his daughters' hollow, impressionable heads. Latin, Greek, chemistry, geography, physics, astronomy, grammar, philosophy, history, subjects he knows are intended for the stronger minds of men. But William's mind is lonely and wants an equal. A companion.

One afternoon, as Florence sprawls on the divan rereading Plato's *Republic*, and Parthenope slumps over her father's desk, twirling a strand of loosened hair and yawning over Walter Scott's *The Talisman*, Mr. Nightingale opens the library door.

"Girls."

At his tone, they raise their heads.

"I'm afraid I have distressing news. Your former governess, Miss Christie, has died."

Running over to her father, Parthe presses her head against his chest, sobbing. Florence calmly marks the place in her book.

"How, Papa?" she asks coolly.

"While giving birth."

"Did the child live?"

"I'm told the child, a boy, will be fine. But our Miss Christie—Mrs. Leipzig—is gone."

↬

Next morning, Mrs. Nightingale addresses a black-bordered note to Mr. Leipzig, poor man, widowed, with a child to raise. Tucks it into a bouquet of Persian roses from Embley's greenhouse, has it delivered to his home in Russell Square.

In a fit of clarity, I scrawl in my commonplace book:

If Miss Christie had not married, she would not have borne a child.

If she had not borne a child, she would not have died.

As I see it, Miss Christie was murdered.

How?

By the society that made her.

Permanent Truths

B LOWING ON THE TIPS OF MY FINGERS, I am glad for the woolen gloves Gale has knit me, leaving off the fingertips so I may turn pages and write in my exercise books. On the nightstand, a whale-oil lamp illumines the Greek grammar book propped against my knees. Beyond the double flame of the glass and pewter lamp, the room is pitch-black, freezing cold.

Noble-looking, the Greek letter A, alpha, derived from the Egyptian hieroglyphic for the head of a horned ox. Here is B, beta, the shape of a house having two stories, then gamma, Semitic for "camel." I trace the G with my finger. It is indeed a camel's head! Do all alphabets originate with pictures? Who decides on such shapes, how does a people or a nation agree on their meanings? Delta—D meant to look like a door—is Daleth in Semitic. Its triangular shape tilts, rounds on one side, turns into our English D. The story of each letter becomes a larger story when the letters are strung together into a word. Alphabet: the Late Latin alphabetum, from the Greek alphabetos/alpha beta, from the Phoenician aleph (trans: ox) and bet (trans: house).

Suddenly, I have slipped into another of my dreams. "Trances," Mama calls them. They can occur any time, during dinner, in the drawing room, listening to Parthe drone on from a novel—or even now, studying the Greek alphabet.

"Leave her," Papa once said, defending me. "There is a great deal going on in that head."

"A great deal of nonsense," Mama shot back. "A pleasant nature, fine manners, perfect posture, that is all my daughters need know."

(And how anxious I am to see Florence give up her ambition to grow a "great head." Of what use is intellect when it is a proven fact that excess intelligence endangers a woman's ability to bear children?)

Take a single Greek letter, dig down to its source, unearth a universe expanding into other universes. Alphabetos! *Sweep me in your current, back to the Semites, back further still to the Phoenicians, so that I may rise up from your roiling sea of words and walk among the most ancient of peoples!*

Parthe sighs, turns in her sleep. Though she has her own bedroom, she creeps in beside me most nights, saying she is frightened of burglars. Fast asleep, she is oblivious to the sounds of my lighting the lamp at 3:00 A.M., doesn't hear the rustle of pages turning, the eager scratching of my pen.

The only way I can be alone in this house is to rise before the servants begin cleaning grates, building fires, heating water for breakfast. Awake before anyone. Memorizing my Greek letters, their shapes loyal, like permanent truths.

Sickness, Wellness

Dear Pop,

Naughty thing!! Why don't you write from Lea Hurst? Or from Aunt Elizabeth's? I write such long letters and receive only one from you—with two sentences! Here, all in the house are down with influenza or ague, bad colds or coughs. I rush from patient to patient, thus far killing no one with my senna teas, spirits of nitre, saline mixtures, castor oil, and doses of ipecacuanha (syrup made from a Brazilian plant, thought to be an emetic). All of my ten lives worn thin as playing cards. I have not had a minute for needlework (of that I will not complain!) or for reading "books of entertainment combined with instruction," as Papa disparagingly calls novels. He asks that you carry on where you left off in Dante, and is anxious to see your translation of the particular canto he gave to you.

All the parish in Wellow is ill of influenza, three hundred people—ditto at Romsey. I am told they have used up the leeches and cannot get more in Hampshire for love or money.

Good-bye from your sister, blue-deviled until you return. Papa leaves for London on the morrow to join Mama at the Burlington.

Dearest Mama,

Gale's cough is troublesome, her pulse high, but she had a good night and insists on getting up today. She is obstinate as ever about not taking her medicine and inquires every day as to when Parthe is to return from Aunt Elizabeth's. Even ill, she goes on airing your shifts! I shall see you very soon.

Your child,
Flo

Pop,

Mama has returned from London, and with all gone but the servants, we potter about in solitude. Each night we sing an imaginary duet to the sleepy tune of nod, nod, nodding, then creep upstairs to our beds before TEN O'CLOCK!!

We have had two lovely days, most welcome after a hurricane of pelting rain and high winds. The surrounding fields are underwater; yesterday, I noticed three unhappy ponies stranded on a bit of land scarcely big enough to hold them. Gale is well again, Kitty recovered from an attack of ague. For three days I managed the entire household, held the reins, galloped from room to room, administering the medicine bottle to all and sundry.

Astounding, what a person's industry can perform! Up at 3:00 A.M., producing enough pages on the lives of British notables to smother Papa when he returns. Manuscripts sprout like mushrooms from beneath my pen, even as I am nurse, governess, student, curate, doctor—curing none but murdering none, either!

Your letters are my breakfast companions. Last night, Gale made bread sauce, followed by a jelly cake crowned with bay leaves. She has given me an old working apron of Mama's, since mine, much used, is falling to rags.

Papa writes of influenza being everywhere, though he is in fine health. His news of Cromford: Little Renshaw is no better, Yeoman's man had a hurt at the quarry, and George Flint has died.

Your affec sister, careering about with mustard plasters, spirits of turpentine, and great spoonfuls of castor oil.

Dearest Mama,

Gale has suffered a lapse. She lay in bed all this morning, then exerted her strength to get up and dress. By the end, she was trembling with exhaustion, and I made her lie down again. The maids are all gone to church this morning, after a storm of buffeting wind and cold rain.

Yours affectionately,
Flo

Commonplace

How to be ten people and everywhere at once! How to care for Kitty, Gale, and the other servants, all of them down with influenza, while finishing Papa's assignments—*ipso ipsimus tempore*—at the same time?

With no one to walk to church with, I stayed at home, read my Bible.

> *Do not neglect to show hospitality to strangers, for by doing that some have entertained angels without knowing it. Remember those who are in prison, as though you are in prison with them; those who are being tortured as though you yourselves are being tortured . . . do not neglect to do good and to share what you have, for such sacrifices are pleasing to God.*
>
> —*Hebrews 13*

Cracked in Half

The voice of the Lord breaks the cedars; the Lord breaks in pieces the cedars of Lebanon.

—Psalm 29:5

INNER DISQUIET, GROWING UNEASE, during an ordinary lunch-time at Embley. Turtle soup, roast guinea fowl, one of Gale's egg custards. No appetite, only hollow satiety, the sense, too, of being unable to breathe even while taking in great drafts of air. I had occupied the morning working on a translation of Dante's *Inferno*, Canto V, then helped Papa, deep into his design for "the Diligence," a coach seating twelve passengers that is to carry our family and a few servants on an eighteen-month journey across Europe in the autumn. Calling it "Nightingale's Grand Continental Tour," Papa has tasked me with collecting facts about roadways in Italy and France. My mind is as usual; I have no illness. Still, my disquiet grows, a peculiar fluttering sensation in the region of my chest. At the dining table, I turn pages of a book on French medieval history, but the words swim, as if they have tails and fins, before my eyes. After an eternity, lunchtime ends, and I announce I am going for a walk.

The afternoon is fine, but cold. By now, I am trembling, not from weather, but from a sense of being towed by some invisible force to the place where four great cedars of Lebanon form a sheltering grove. Slipping into the grove, I sit on a simple bench of granite. The trees are very still. Sunlight glints between the needles of every branch. Arrows of light say they point to God's grace.

By now I am panting; my lungs fill with silt or sand. My fingers and feet are numb; vertigo assails me. I close my eyes to pray but am pitched into some lightless shaft, where I fall and fall and fall. Just as I seem about to plunge to some terrifying destruction of body and soul, I force open my eyes. An immensity of light penetrates the majestic cedars, turns white the dark, swooping boughs. Then I see nothing but Light; the trees themselves have vanished. I sit on an immaterial dais in a hall that stretches to infinity, made of dazzling Light. From a core place deep within me, timeless, not of this earth, I hear God.

You are to end the world's suffering.

With sudden, shattering force, I feel the hard stone bench, the dark, freezing air. Trembling. Myself again.

Stories of the saints—Joan of Arc, Saint Teresa, Saint Francis, Saint Catherine of Siena—ordinary persons summoned by God from their ordinary lives. Lives cleft in two. Never the same.

Light glinting through the cedar grove is sunlight again. Plain light. A westerly breeze causes the trees to murmur in dark, vernal voices. Wrapping my cloak around me, I return, dazed and shivering, to Embley.

In my bedroom, I open my new commonplace book, a Christmas gift from Mama, to its first page. In my best cursive, I press upon the blankness.

7 February 1837:
God spoke to me and called me to His service.
Called on me to end the world's suffering.

In days to come, I will find it odd that my family notices no change in me. They are stupid to the truth I am no longer their daughter or sister, but a creature hunted down, ensnared by God. Cracked in half.

I am not yet seventeen.

Poor-Peopling

"**M**RS. FERNSBY?"
Taller than both my mother and sister now, I must bend down to enter the lightless, dirt-floored room. In the shadows I find a woman of middle years on a pallet of horsehair. Covering her with a scrap of wool cloth, I find the ashy hearth, rekindle the fire. Magnus, Mrs. Fernsby's husband, has died in a lead mining accident; their three young children were taken by cholera in one week. I locate the slop pail by its stink, lug it outside. Turning my head, holding my breath, I spill out its foul contents, bile rising in my throat. I can find no water, so return the pail to the cottage, uncleaned.

When Mrs. Fernsby is awake, I help her stand, note the shuffling gait, the swollen, discolored ankles. I prepare a plate of cheese and bread, a cup of beef tea, and promise to return.

The next cottage down from widow Fernsby's teems with life—an infant squalling, little ones wandering naked, their mother heavily pregnant. The room is all noise and chaos, with a nauseating, viscous smell of soured, spilled food. Young Mary Hogg, her face mottled with exhaustion, malnutrition, and gin drinking, her belly swollen, the unborn child sucking the marrow out of her, snatches at the bread and cheese, the box of tea I have brought her, with a look of sly, darting greed. Poverty turns the gentlest creature desperate. Handing out drippings, bread, medicines, I note the falling-in thatched roof, the dirt floor, the few tattered blankets, the filthy, callused feet of Mary Hogg, not yet twenty and looking twice that. The stink of unwashed bodies, urine, brown waste, the musk of armpit odor, the animal smell of fear, too, all in one dark, windowless room. Dipping a square of flannel in water, I try to clean the infected cut on the knee of a girl who stares up at me, mute, wild-eyed, until she breaks away and tears outside to chase after other children, all of them naked, rail-thin, with swollen, wormy bellies.

In the last cottage, Charlotte Villin. It is known that her husband, a lead miner and heavy gin drinker, beats her. The children are underfed, neglected. This visit I bring her a clean shift, a bar of soap, an old linen towel begged from Kitty. I make stirabout, oats and water, for the children, put a kettle on the fire, brew a tea of nettles, comfrey, goldenseal. I am glad the husband is nowhere to be seen, but I know as well as Charlotte does that he will be back to hurt her more.

Of an Age

Mrs. Nightingale hurries down the weed-choked lane, trying not to slip in the mud and animal manure everywhere. Rapping on the doors of cottages, most of which stand open, she finds Florence feeding bread and porridge to a filthy, shouting brood, squeezed like sardines onto a single broken bench. Fuming, she waits outside.

"This obsession with helping the poor, coming home late every night, must stop now." Mrs. Nightingale is striding fast, swinging her lantern to throw a wider light.

"Mama, how am I to sit down to seven o'clock supper when I am only too aware of the desperate hunger in families ten minutes' walk from our home? How can you, how do we, a wealthy family, allow it?"

"Our Bible instructs us. 'The poor you have always with you.' We do what we can, Florence. If we gave all we have to the poor, we would have nothing ourselves; then we should be just like them, and whom would that benefit? Your father's tenants are thankful for what care we do show them. Many of the other landowners in Derbyshire do nothing at all. Imagine if we were that heartless."

Imagine if we did far more. Imagine bringing everyone to sit among us, dine with us at Embley. Old Mrs. Fernsby, sucking the sweet marrow out of a chop bone, grease shining her chin; pregnant Mary Hogg, breasts leaking, crumbs and stains on her belly's rounded shelf, her husband chugging Papa's best port, skinny Adam's apple riding up and down, temper rising. Charlotte Villin, coughing blood, bearing her husband's bruises. No doubt Mama would faint and Parthe run weeping to her room. Papa would vanish into his study, his selfish, solitary pursuits. What of Jesus? Would he not sit with these people, would he not break bread with them? Love them? I would prefer to live among the poor, or at least be like Aunt Julia, Mama's sister. When she visits, Aunt Julia goes straightaway into the villages, writes down every complaint and illness, make notes of needed foods, remedies. Small, practical acts of mercy. Tossing a few coins, scattering bits of leftover food, then rolling away in her carriage, as Mama does, is a shallow imitation of Our Lord. She will attend church, be seen in church, but what Jesus asks of her is too hard. She will not do it. Will any of us?

Still, I adore Mama, predictable as she changes the subject to one more pleasing to her.

"Next week Rebecca and Kitty must help you pack for the London season. You are of an age now to attend winter balls, so you will need three trunks. And Flo, scrub your hands with lye soap before you come in to supper. God only knows what vermin those wretched people have crawling on them."

Commonplace

DEAREST MOTHER, HAD I THE COURAGE, which I do not, I would show this to you:

But when you give a banquet, invite the poor, the crippled, the lame and the blind. And you will be blessed, because they cannot repay you, for you will be paid at the resurrection of the righteous.

—*Luke 14*

I would tell you that whenever I step inside one of their cottages, I want to stay the whole day, wash the children's faces, relieve the mother, care for the sick ones. I long to live with them.

Yet are not a hundred families just as unwell, just as poor within half a mile?

The Moones will know me. They have lost Hattie. What if I can be like a new daughter to them?

Your Daughter, Sir

CALLED AWAY FROM THE DINNER TABLE, Mr. Nightingale stands in the open doorway of his home, looking into the coal-blackened face of Albert Moone. Holding Mr. Moone's hand is Florence.

"I've brought your daughter home, sir. Mrs. Moone and I thought you might be wondering where she was."

"We didn't yet know she was missing, Mr. Moone. We'd just sat down to dinner, thinking she was late." He looks at his younger daughter, wearing one of Gale's old house aprons, her hair undone, mussed. "Florence. What's all this? Why have you troubled Mr. Moone to bring you home?" It is as stern as he has ever sounded with her.

She darts past her father, runs up the stairs.

"It's all right, Mr. Nightingale. The 'little squire' told Mrs. Moone she wants to live with us. To replace Hattie, she said. Be of help. I wouldn't be harsh with her. She means well."

"Well, I'm sorry for the inconvenience. Wait a moment. I'll see you are given some roast quail and vegetables to take home with you. I believe there may be fresh bread and rhubarb, too."

For this trouble, for bringing the Nightingale girl home, Albert is able, for one night, to feed his family "like the rich ones do."

And for the trouble she has caused, Florence is made to write an apology to her parents. Mrs. Gale brings dinner to her room, and after a scolding that includes a grisly account of what happens to runaways and thieves in this world, demands her apron back and stomps downstairs.

71

A Grand European Expedition

Excerpts from Travel Diaries 1837–1839

A T HALF PAST THREE ON THE AFTERNOON of 8 September 1837, Papa, Mama, Parthe, our French maid, Therese, Mrs. Gale, and myself depart Southampton aboard *The Monarch*, a solid old steam packet. Our first stop is Le Havre de Grâce. We are to be gone eighteen months, and Papa has arranged everything so that while we are away, Embley will be greatly enlarged, changed from its sober Georgian self into what Mama says will be an Elizabethan "monstrosity."

Our Nightingale itinerary is book-thick, mostly researched by myself. We have also brought Mr. Baedeker's red guidebook. From Le Havre, we will travel on to Rouen and from there ride in Papa's Diligence, the traveling carriage built to his design.

I write from a cramped position in my tiny *Monarchian* berth. Too excited to sleep, I stayed on deck long after the others retired, and talked with one of the crew members, Mr. Towsey. He told me the story of his tragic experience on board the *Amphitrite* four years before. A female convict ship bound for New South Wales, the *Amphitrite* wrecked near Boulogne. All 108 women and 12 children perished within plain sight of shore. Only three crew members survived, one being Mr. Towsey. Their captain, Mr. Hunter, refused help offered from shore, fearing if the women convicts reached land, they would escape. He assumed, too, that the rising tide would free his ship. It didn't, and as the *Amphitrite* groaned and broke apart, the women convicts were heard crying out, weeping, shrieking as they and all the children drowned. Mr. Towsey helped bring their bodies ashore. He said people came all the way from town to gape and marvel at the beauty and perfection of the drowned women's bodies. Four years after, he still suffers nightmares and repeats his story to anyone who will listen.

As we cross the English Channel, I think of those women and children, how the same sea that drowned them rolls and surges with watery indifference beneath me.

To my travel journal I say *bonne nuit*. I have brought nine such journals, one for every sixty days, as well as three sketchbooks. Drawing is my sister's provenance, but there may be an architectural or natural wonder that will inspire me to try my own skill, though I question the human impulse to imitate badly what God has already made so fine.

Time of Arrival in Le Havre de Grâce: 5:30 A.M.
Time of Departure for Rouen: 8:00 A.M.
Distance to Be Covered: 57 miles

One Week into Southern France

Thus far, we have rumbled and pitched down a great many nearly impassable roads, crossed a monotony of treeless plains, slept in lodgings with verminous beds and food so scarce or rotten as to put our party in danger of starvation. I picture our little caravan halted by some desolate roadside, our skeletons in various attitudes of reading, drawing, or sleeping.

The Diligence can travel thirty-five miles in a day, its six horses ridden by six postillions. Mama assures Parthe and me, as we take turns riding with Papa in the open-air seat, that once we reach Nice, our adventure will improve. Thus far, I have no understanding why I am jolting along horrid roads, my stomach where my heart should be, my heart where my brain should be, staring at miles and miles of nothing. Whenever we approach a new town, our little party grows overexcited, then cross. I will not say who (though her name starts with *P*) has been especially disagreeable. Mrs. Gale, whom we nearly forgot to bring with us, is an anchor of cheer and resourcefulness.

Nice, France
Arrived: 15 December 1837
Population: 33,811
Government: part of the Kingdom of Piedmont-Sardinia
Geography: on the southeast coast of France, on the Mediterranean Sea
Newspaper: *Gazette de Nice*

Twenty years ago, Mama and Papa spent the early days of their honeymoon in Nice. Some English people here still remember them, so we find ourselves invited to parties and dances. But it is the Advent season, band music is not permitted; for accompaniment, there is only one badly tuned pianoforte. My sister, having "set her cap" for a certain Mr. Hugh Plunkett, came to last night's dance resolved to claim Mr. Plunkett, only to find he had forsworn dancing and was nowhere to be found. Today, she is, as Gale calls it, "fit to be tied."

Genoa, Italy
Arrived: 13 January 1838
Population: under 300,000
Government: Kingdom of Piedmont-Sardinia
Geography: on the Gulf of Genoa; occupies a narrow coastal plane on the western slope of the Apennines
Newspaper: *Corriere Mercantile*

Parthe and I have gone to see Donizetti's *Lucretia Borgia* three times. I would go every night of my life if I could. The balls in Genoa are splendid, all waltzes and quadrilles. Parthe declares it an *Arabian Nights* dream. To my surprise, I am sought after and danced off my feet.

Pisa
Arrived: 11 February 1838

I attended a court ball hosted by the grand duke of Tuscany. The next day, as a guest at the duke's private luncheon, I am led into the garden by the duke himself to admire his trio of humped, mangy camels imported from Cairo.

Florence
Arrived: 26 February 1838

Florence, city of my birth, city I was named after. In our rooms at the Albergo del Arno, overlooking the Ponte Vecchio, Mama insists on weekly "At Homes," inviting elite Florentine families to meet her marriageable daughters. It is a trial of the first water to me, though Parthe, preening and simpering, takes to it like a duck.

I have seen *Don Giovanni* twice, am reading Sismondi's *History of the Italian Republics in the Middle Ages*. A book to rival the *Iliad*, Papa jokes, best employed as a brick.

∽

Bologna, Venice, now Geneva, where I meet the exiled author himself, Jean Charles de Léonard Sismondi. Married to one of Mama's friends, he is the ugliest, most stunted little man I have ever seen in my life. When I called on him in his study this afternoon, I found him feeding bread to the mice who live tamely among his books and papers. Last night, at a party given by his wife, he ended the evening sitting ON the dining table, giving an impromptu lecture on Florentine history. He has invited me on daily walks around Geneva, teaching me about the dehumanizing effects of industrialization, the brutality of competition, and the unfair distribution of profits. As we make our way around the poorer parts of the city, he stops to give a coin and a kind greeting to every beggar he sees.

Paris
Arrived: 14 October 1838
22 Place Vendôme

On the verge of an endless melancholy, Parthe and I take warm vapor baths, talk of music, mostly Mozart. We long for the sunlight and warmth of Italy. A thick, dispiriting fog hides Paris from us; we see nothing.

Mama takes ambitious care to introduce us to the city's finest families. If only she knew how determined I am to know what it is God asks of me. Still, I am absurdly vain about my hair, and will have it done and redone two and three times in a day, until it suits me. And if I could, I would dance every night until dawn. I drift even further from God since meeting Mary Clarke. "Clarkey" hosts stimulating salons in a set of apartments above Chateaubriand, one of her many male admirers. Known in Paris as "*la jeune anglaise*," she takes Parthe and me to galleries, concerts, and evening gatherings of scientists, artists, politicians. Her "intimates" are Claude Fauriel, a medieval scholar, and a much younger man, Julius Mohl. Calling himself an Orientalist, Julius hands out cups of weak tea and stale biscuits at Clarkey's soirées. She is the cleverest woman, wears her hair in short, wild tufts, much like a Skye terrier, and goes about half naked in a loose style of her own design. Forty-five, refusing marriage ("*patriarchal imprisonment*"), she fearlessly puts forth any bold opinion that comes into her head. Her praise of Elizabeth Fry, the Quaker preacher who visits imprisoned women, for instance. In Mrs. Fry's work, she says, lies women's way to power and influence—not through encouraging the ridiculous passions of men, but by intelligent action and use of one's moral force. With Mary Clarke, the twaddle that passes for conversation among most Englishwomen cannot live. She says and does as she likes. I do find it peculiar that Mama approves of her, since she would die a thousand deaths should I attempt such liberties.

After reading *Théorie des Signes* by l'Abbé Sicard, former director of the Institut National de Jeune Sourds-Muets, I visited the free public school for the deaf on rue Saint Jacques. Its cleanliness and near religious care of its pupils impressed me.

6 April 1839

Our "Grand Continental Tour" has come to a tired end. Mama declares it a "grand failure," since she has found no eligible bachelor for myself or Parthe, though Pop still warbles on about the "divine" Hugh Plunkett in Nice. My sister's romanticism, her callow fantasies, encouraged by silly novels, irritate me no end. Though glamour is seductive, I admit. It is lovely to be admired by dinner companions and dancing partners, yes, but for me, it ends there. Even as I admit the sin of vanity in myself, I feel deep aversion to what Mama calls "an advantageous marriage."

In every city we came to, I quietly made inquiries as to hospitals, orphanages, and asylums. Visited when I could. Walked out on my own when I could manage it. Went down streets, turned corners, ducked down alleyways and into neighborhoods I knew were forbidden to me.

One morning in Rouen, I came upon a group of old women, survivors of Napoléon, huddled for warmth against a sunny wall, too weary to brush away the flies that crept over their old, worn faces.

On a side street in Paris, I watched workers pick up a dead man from the street, sling him by his arms and legs into a cart piled high with trash.

In an alleyway in Pisa, I emptied my purse, giving all of my pocket money to a street prostitute covered in yellowing bruises. Her front teeth, when she tried to smile, were black with decay.

I sought out others' sufferings, degradations. Who can understand my strange compulsion to look upon horrors, tableaux of suffering? Who can cure this gnawing hunger to know God's will?

No one.

Not even myself.

Silence

THE SOUGHING OF THE TALL CEDARS, their clean, sharp scent in the winter air. Above me, a peregrine falcon circles, dives, kakking.

Another day, seeking Him.

Another day, climbing the steep, bitter slope back to Embley.

Pure Thought

HENRY NICHOLSON, ONE OF OUR FIRST COUSINS, stops at Embley on his way back to Cambridge. According to Papa, he is the most brilliant of the Nicholson children and has a passion for geometry and algebra. He is afflicted, though, with an extreme shyness, which shows itself in clumsy manners, a constant stammer.

Walking the grounds with him after luncheon, I am tempted to turn from God's silence and concentrate my mind on mathematics. My awkward, gentle cousin lives in a world of numbers, thinks of little else, and quotes from Plato's *Republic*. It is not lost on me that he never stammers when quoting the words of others.

"'The highest form of pure thought is in mathematics.' Not my words, dear cousin, but Plato's."

"Will you teach me what you know, Henry? While you are here?"

He laughs. "That, d-d-dear cousin, would take a dozen fortnights."

"Begin with the smallest thing, then."

"All r-r-right. I can try. Which do you prefer, geometry or algebra?"

"Both."

"No t-t-time for all that. We'll begin with algebra, and when I visit next, we shall g-g-grapple with geometry.

For a fortnight, we spend our days in Papa's library, going over more and more complex equations—if x equals $y-2$ $(x+8y)$, et cetera.

I astonish Henry with my quick grasp of formulae, nearly equal, he says, to that of his Cambridge classmates.

Sometimes Parthe slips into the library, hovering near us until she tires of being ignored and goes in search of Mama, who has been teaching her to arrange flowers. Botanical math, if one is generous.

On the day he leaves, my envy of Henry, his freedom, is so great, I feel ill with it.

"A farewell g-g-gift, cousin Flo."

From his carriage, he hands down a small wrapped package.

"Practice your e-e-equations; next time you'll learn g-g-g-geometry. 'The laws of nature are but the mathematical thoughts of God.'"

"Plato again?"

"Euclid. F-f-father of geometry."

When he has gone, I unwrap his gift, my fingers fumbling to untie the string. It is the book he taught me with, an inscription in tight handwriting, as if he'd prefer letters to be numbers, on its first page.

> *Dearest Flo,*
>
> *God ever geometrizes*
>
> > *—Plato*
>
> *Greatest affection,*
> *Henry*

Hysteria

I HOLD MY COUSIN'S BOOK, for courage, over my heart.

"Papa?"

Night after night, they sit in the drawing room in their same chairs, facing the hearth. Papa and Parthe reading, Mama doing point. A passage deemed of interest might be read aloud. All wait for the clock to chime ten before rising from their chairs and retiring to their rooms.

"Papa?"

He peers over his reading spectacles.

"May I have a mathematics tutor? Henry says he has never known anyone so quick to grasp algebraic principles. He is certain I have a genius for numbers."

"Well, Flo, I . . ." Papa gets no further.

"William! No. Of what use is mathematics to Florence? To any woman? You must stop encouraging her in this ridiculous quest to grow a great head. Parthenope, what is the matter?"

Pop twists her handkerchief, her lower lip trembling. "It isn't fair."

"What isn't fair? Don't tell me you wish to study mathematics, too?"

"Hardly. I detest numbers."

"Then whatever is the matter?"

My sister shuts her book, another of her silly popular novels, with exaggerated care.

"In case no one has noticed, Florence gets all the attention these days. She demands a thing until she gets it. Even then, she is never satisfied. She pretends concern for the poor, but anyone with eyes can see she cares only for herself. Now she has Henry sighing after her like a great sick mooncalf."

The image makes me laugh. "Parthe, how can you say that? Henry is our cousin. A first cousin at that."

"I don't care what he is; he is in love with you."

At this, Papa removes his glasses, his tone firm.

"I fear your mother is right, Florence. You have no need of a tutor. Mathematics is a subject meant for men's stronger minds. Parthenope, you must not be envious of your sister; surely you exaggerate your cousin's feelings for her. Henry has gone on to Cambridge; he simply took a few days to indulge Florence's curiosity."

I burst from my chair, my voice shrill with anger.

"I should like to know, Papa, why you have taken such pains, since I was eleven years old, to educate me on every subject, following the exact curriculum you studied at Cambridge. You have overeducated me, educated me into a half man, and now you don't know what to do with me. You are proud of my intelligence; you say you relish our conversations on history and philosophy. Now what am I, at age twenty, to do with all that? Take up flower arranging with Parthe? Read romances? Tinkle out pretty tunes? Shrink my brain to the size of hers?"

With a wail of fury, my sister bolts from the room.

No one speaks.

What is my mother likely thinking? That a mathematics tutor is sure to be a penniless young man—why else be a tutor? That by poring over equations with him, I will encourage a ruinous attraction.

What can Papa be thinking? I can guess at that, too. Of escaping to his men's club in London, fleeing this pack of hysterical women. I could try persuading him to hire a tutor when Mama is not in the room, but I know he will not go to battle for me. History, philosophy, the sciences do not weep or fall in a faint on the divan as my mother is capable of doing. Indeed, these are her preferred forms of argument. He will take refuge in his mute fossils, his books and journals. Their impotency. He is unwilling to speak up for me. He will always be too weak.

I turn back. "Why is it that Henry goes to Cambridge and I cannot? Why have you bothered to overeducate me? To what end? And Mama, I say it plainly: I have no interest in marriage. I am grateful that my cousin, at least, appreciates an intelligent woman. Good night."

Commonplace

LIKE THE MOON AROUND THE EARTH, I orbit these people. Turn cool, silent, inward. The earth sees one side of me; the other side forever unknown.

I miss my cousin, his faith in the divine order of numbers.

From my window, I see the high black crown of cedars.

God withdraws. I am utterly alone.

Black Crown

MEN GO OFF TO SCHOOL. *To Oxford or Cambridge.*
I am left with a book.

Men go on expeditions. Cousin Fred went to Australia and died, doing what he wanted.

Florence? A freak, an ornament in a room. A useless thing, broken, gathering dust.

I throw a cloak over my nightdress. In the work kitchen, I shove my feet into a pair of men's boots. The leather boots are too long, too wide; they rattle and scrape against my bare shins and ankles. I head across the bare, wintry grounds of Embley, the frost-whitened lawns, toward the cedar grove. I hate them all. How can I hear God in the din and clang, clang, clang, the cheap, awful noise of possessions and busy habits, their thoughts mundane enough to be identical to any number of interchangeable, shallow English brains? Why was I born to them? Why born at all? My own brain feels like bursting. Sinking onto the cold granite bench, I feel the great cedars press around me with their shaggy, tarry-smelling arms.

"I hate them. I murderously, evilly, *hate them.*" Spoken aloud, my words sound melodramatic. False. I don't hate them. I hate myself.

The cold of the stone bench cuts through my thin cloak. Throwing off the boots, I stumble from the cedar grove in the direction of the woodland Parthe and I often walk near, a wild, sharp-thicketed place where roe deer and foxes live. Owls, grouse, pheasant, snipe, as well. I think of the hare I found, how it died in my arms. I drop to the earth, fling my arms wide against a soft, decaying drift of leaves translucent with ice, burrow beneath a freezing cover of leaves. Let the deer find me, the ravenous foxes and vultures, the devouring insects. Let the earth turn me into some better form of life.

❧

"Mercy, child. Take my hand. Get up now. Where are your shoes? Up, that's it, hold on to me."

"Don't tell. Please don't tell anyone."

"I won't, poor mad thing. Why are you out here? You'll be lucky if you haven't caught your death."

Tripping on numb feet, quaking with cold, I listen as Gale tells how a new servant, bringing hot water up to my room and not finding me, had gone downstairs and told her I was not in my room, not in my bed. How they both went searching the house, quietly, so as not to disturb anyone. How Gale took a lantern and went outside.

Warming beside the kitchen fire, I cannot tell the truth. I thought it might help me sleep, I tell her, to walk outside awhile.

"Foolish girl," Gale scoffs. "What if we had come upon you in the morning, frozen to death? Your mother would never recover. No one would."

"It was foolish. I'm sorry." *But had I died, wouldn't they regret their treatment of me?*

"You saved my life."

"Nonsense. Let's get you upstairs and into bed before anyone finds out."

Marriage, Bah

"I NEVER COULD PICTURE YOU as Lady Wyvill. Thank heavens you were at Aunt Elizabeth's when he came to call."

"Marmaduke Wyvill? Isn't he one of two brothers we met in Nice?"

"Both wicked as sin. What matter which one?"

We scuff along in our boots, wade through rotten, damp leaves of beech, oak, chestnut, a musty smell rising from the stirred leaves, leaves I had laid down in one night, hoping to die. Veils of afternoon sunlight float among the bare trees, settle like golden squares of silk over the distant, empty pastures.

"He was overdressed, even for the occasion of asking Papa for your hand. Vain, too, to the point of arrogance. His chin was weak and his calves bowed."

"Who noticed he'd been drinking? Mama?"

"Who else? After finishing off a decanter of wine and two plates of oysters, he declared that on first seeing you in Nice, he'd been struck dumb as Zacharias by your beauty."

"Bah."

"By your feminine grace."

"Twice bah."

"Your ready wit."

"Better. At least he had the wit to know wit. What is his scandal?"

"Mama made inquiries through Aunt Julia and her set of

friends. The Wyvill brothers are fortune hunters, gamblers, seducers of women."

"A narrow escape, then."

"A needle's eye. Cousin Henry, you've rejected him, too."

"Of course. He's our first cousin. I'm fond of Henry, that's all. I wonder why no one seeks your hand?"

"I have no idea. I adore the thought of marriage."

"Shhh, look."

A roe deer steps out from a barren copse of trees, followed moments later by an antlered buck.

"What beauty," Parthe whispers, making a subtle movement. The deer, wary, melt back into the woods. "I saw a kit fox coming out from these same woods last week. May we turn back, Flo? My feet are freezing."

On the way to the house, we talk of my most recent and persistent suitor: Richard Monckton Milnes.

"Entertaining," I begin.

"Charming."

"Plain."

"Terribly."

"A bit too old."

"Short. Shorter than you."

"His forehead is large."

"To contain a great mind."

"His legs are twigs."

"To prop up his stomach."

"Have you seen how it jiggles, like calf's foot jelly?"

"Seriously, Flo. Monkton is a well-regarded member of Parliament. His views, like yours, are liberal. He is well connected, wealthy, and even writes poetry. Mama says no one in London has any social importance until they have been invited to one of his famous breakfasts. You could do worse than Monckton Milnes."

"Now you sound like Mama."

"Admit you like him a little, Flo. He makes you laugh more than anyone, and his politics are yours."

"True. He votes from his conscience, is against the death penalty and for the reform bill. He even traveled to Ireland to see for himself the horrors of the potato famine."

"But could you be his *wife*, Flo? Preside over his famous breakfasts, hostess elaborate dinner parties, shrink to nothing in the man's great shadow? I do not see it."

Parthe has seized on the true obstacle—my self.

"Do you know what you will decide?"

I lie. *"Je ne sais pas."*

"He returns to Embley next week."

"So I'm told."

Haven't I considered it multiple times? How marrying such a man would satisfy my family? Perhaps if I let Parthe think I might say yes— as anything I tell her goes directly to Mama—would that not buy me time to think about what I must really do with my life?

"Monk is a fine man. I will consider it."

"So now you must tell me. Has he kissed you?"

"Only once. It was awful. He had such thin, dry lips. Like pecking a piecrust."

In the house, we find the newest cook, Hannah, in the kitchen, a linen cloth flung over one shoulder, thumping out pastry dough.

"Hannah, might we have tea early? We are chattering with cold."

"Piecrust!" hisses Pop, pinching my arm on our way out of the kitchen.

Rough Office

Dropsy. Mrs. Gale's old complaint, though it is far worse this time. Mama gives me permission to care for her. Hers will be the first death of someone I love.

To lie on her side is painful. On her back, she is suffocating. I walk her to her chair. Pressing gently against her work apron and heavy skirts, I feel her abdomen—drumlike and hard with fluid. Her ankles are swollen, her feet puffed to three times their size. Pure agony, she groans, to put the least weight on them. Her good, kindly face is slick with sweat. Dipping a cloth in a water basin, I wipe the sheen from her broad forehead. All week she has insisted on working. Now her breathing is noisy, labored, air harder and harder to come by.

Her face relaxes a little, soothed by the cool cloth. Her legs splay out, her feet too big to wear the black felt slippers Mama sewed for her.

Mrs. Gale has always set the world right, kept my childish secrets, known what to do. She has loved me my whole life. Yet I can give her no comfort other than to press a damp cloth to her lips and forehead, the back and sides of her neck. I feel helpless.

When Hannah steps in, Gale speaks with a shade of her old authority.

"Nothing is needed. Go back to your work."

These are her last words. She dies sitting up, her hands in mine. When I start downstairs to ask Hannah to bring the midwives, I find them already at the bottom of the stairs, two old vultures, an ugly black satchel by their feet.

They follow me into the tiny bedroom, walk over to the chair. One roughly shakes her to make sure she is dead, grasps the body beneath the arms. The second takes hold of the legs. Together, they lug the body across the room, heave it wrong wise onto the bed, the feet landing at an unnatural angle on the pillow. Using iron scissors, they cut away the clothing, toss everything onto the wood floor. Stripping off the neatly mended stockings, they snip away the old chemise, the fouled pantaloons, until she is flat on her back, a bloated doll, slack breasts, huge, slightly haired abdomen, glass eyes staring up, mouth open, gaping.

A crude rite. Pitiless and swift.

Before these two witches appeared, I had held Mrs. Gale's work-callused hands in my own, gazed at her stilled face, almost beautiful in death. As I prayed for her soul, a sensation crept over me that the real presence in the room, the true presence, was Him. That it was we who were ghosts. Apparitions.

Taking a stick wrapped in blue cloth from the satchel, one of the women props one end beneath the chin, props the opposite end against the breastbone, shutting the slackened mouth. The second grotesque yanks apart the heavy legs, plugs a lump of coal into each lower orifice. The other turns the head to one side, wipes away an oozy black substance trickling from the mouth. Thumbs shut the eyelids.

Slapping bits of rag into the basin of water, they start, one on either side, washing down the trunk with its fish-belly skin, the limbs, misshapen by disease, overuse—wipe off death sweat like fat from a roasting pan. They tear strips of linen, binding the wrists and ankles, tug a long, filthy shroud over the head, covering the body, knotting it at the feet. These creatures cackle and gossip during their rough office; their hands brusque, unfeeling. They earn a paltry sum, pulling life from between a laboring woman's legs, plugging coal into that same dark cavity when she dies.

Progressive Animal

Up to my chin in linen and glass—counting, noting breakage, ordering replacements, sorting, stacking, folding. Putting up preserves, supervising meals. Since Mrs. Gale's death, the little comforts and kindnesses she always provided have come to an abrupt end.

"Do explain, Pop, why anyone needs the possessions we Nightingales have. Do reasonable persons need all of this? Do excessive goods make a Progressive Animal?"

Parthe, who has perfected the art of evading tasks, makes a sympathetic sound as she folds and refolds a pillowcase until I snatch it from her and fold it properly.

Flo is a workhorse. She pretends she hates it, but she knows better than anyone how to manage and fix everything. She likes being in charge.

"Isn't it obvious, Flo? The more one has, the higher one ascends in society. A wealthy wife and mother can do such good for her family. She can better the world in so many little ways."

"Rubbish. You parrot Mama. Would Christ live in two grand homes surrounded by those with nothing? Would He count water goblets and table linens?"

Oh, my sister and her tiresome comparisons to Christ!

Commonplace

WHAT WAS DONE TO MRS. GALE'S BODY—the indignity of it—haunts me. Some degree of training, practical midwife and nurses' training, is needed. So far as I know, midwives and nurses are thought to be disreputable, condemned as little more than drunks and prostitutes. I have begun to put my pocket watch on the floor before bed each night so when Kitty brings in a pitcher of hot water in the early-morning darkness, I am forced to spring out of bed to keep it from being stepped on and smashed. Awake, I can begin my studies. Not Greek or mathematics or history. Something more useful. Friends in London, France, and Germany, sympathetic to my interests, send me government "blue books." These contain census numbers, diagrams, long descriptions of hospitals, workhouses, orphanages. I underline and take notes, memorize details of hospital systems, percentages of illness, causes of illnesses and deaths. I am convinced the key to reform lies in facts, in averages, diagrams, reports. Statistics! The true measure of my purpose.

Last month, Dr. Fowler, chief surgeon at Salisbury Infirmary and a friend of Papa's, came to dine with us. A tall, long-legged man in his eighties with a mane of iron gray hair, he walks three miles a day, sets himself daily brain exercises, toils away at his life's work, a book on the history of medicine. Since his visit, I have written to him with a plan. If I could spend three months with him and train to be a nurse, I could then establish a house near the infirmary for gentlewomen like myself, all trained as nurses.

Dr. Fowler's reply is terse. Discouraging. Even so, I intend to present my plan to my parents on Christmas Day, hoping the "Christ spirit" will move them to give permission.

I cannot go on like this. Imagining great achievements, accomplishing nothing. Lost in dreams of heroism while standing in front of cupboards with pencil and paper, tallying up pots, platters, and jars of preserves. Mathematics is a sacred language. To put numbers to such banal use is killing me.

Christmas Dinner

"**W**HY SPOIL CHRISTMAS?" Mrs. Nightingale frowns at her slab of roast beef, prepared to complain of its toughness.

"Mama . . ."

"No, dear. Your 'little plan' is preposterous. Work with Dr. Fowler at Salisbury? That pit of filth? There are a hundred reasons why you must never do this. The infirmary is notoriously infested with rats; you would be exposed to disgusting sights, forced to touch unclothed people—men—of low birth. God knows what diseases, what indecencies and blasphemies you would be exposed to. What on earth has Hannah done to ruin this beef?"

"Mama's right, Flo. You spoil everything." Parthe glares at me. "Even Christmas."

I ignore their predictable outbursts. "Papa, what do you say? Mr. Fowler is your friend. Surely you trust him to protect me."

Mr. Nightingale chooses his words with care.

"Florence, no, I cannot agree to this. Salisbury—any hospital, for that matter—is no place for a young woman from a good family. I remind you that your own health is not strong, and to care for those who are ill and poor, with no other place to go, puts your own life at risk. As for sharing a house near the infirmary with other young women like yourself, I can assure you that you will find no support from any of the other fine families in our area."

Mrs. Nightingale, surprisingly gentle, adds, "Why not be content taking care of us, Flo? Our household is large enough, you will always be needed, and our tenants in East Wellow and Lea Hurst have need of care, too."

Parthenope is bitter. "I'll tell you why. She reads stacks and stacks of stupid books about hospitals, orphanages, and lunatic asylums. She has no heart and means to leave us. Sometimes I hate you, Flo. Hate how you act the saint, put yourself above us."

With a martyrlike sigh, Mrs. Nightingale stands.

"No more talk. I suggest we go into the drawing room so that your father may read Luke's story of Christmas aloud to us, as he does every year."

A Widening Gulf

18 January 1846

Dear Papa,

I write because I cannot bear to have my little hope talked at. Mother has nothing to say on the matter; she treats me as a child. Parthe thinks me selfish, unfeeling, et cetera. At Christmastime, I opened my soul to you in vain. Papa, try to listen. I cannot remember a time when I did not live in a world of my own, a world peopled with visions, spirits, dreams. I was judged a matter-of-fact, stubborn child; no one troubled to ask about my inner world. Now I have spoken of it, and for that offense, I apologize.

That said, can you find it in you to consider a second plan? Would you consent to my going to the Sisters in Dublin who run a hospital there? I do not see how you could raise the same objections to St. Stephen's as you did with Salisbury.

If you find it impossible to consent to this second plan, let me know at once.

I shall never speak on the subject again.

Yours,
Florence

No reply. I keep my word, speak no more of Salisbury or St. Stephen's. Instead, I rise every morning, study an ever-accumulating stack of books from Berlin, Paris, London, Dusseldorf. Memorize, and even like, the dry, crucial language of administration.

Statistics stack up in my mind, as neat as Mama's silverware and plate. The gulf between the world of family and the realm of my ambitions grows wider each day.

The Poetic Parcel

Lea Hurst
1846

1. Manage a semblance of normalcy.
2. Walk to Cromford, nurse the sick.
3. Complete tasks at home.
4. Act pleased to see Mr. Milnes when he comes, as he soon will, to propose yet again.
5. Put him off, saying neither yes nor no.

❧

"How are you and Monk getting on?" my sister asks on our daily walk. She would marry him today if he asked. If only he would.

"The Poetic Parcel? I find him amusing."

"Each time he visits, I find him nicer than the last."

Marrying Monckton Milnes would free my family from the burden of myself. But how would it benefit me? I am fond of Monk, more so since he admitted his own insecurity about love. He would like to love, he says, longs, in fact, to love, but whether he is capable of love is another matter. How well I understand! I, too, am a creature of less heart than ambition and intellect. Emotions are the enemy.

"Did you know he visits George Sand in Paris? I am plodding through her novel *Gabriel*, about a girl raised to be a boy. Remember when you made me chop off your hair and insisted we call you Francis?"

"A childish solution that fixed nothing."

"Monk knows so many brilliant people. As Mrs. Milnes, you would know those people, too."

"Honestly, Parthe, wouldn't you rather *be* a brilliant person than brush elbows with one?"

Commonplace

Madness. Every day I descend further, while Parthe chirps her one happy note, dabbles in the shallows of flower arranging, dish painting, sewing, light music, inoffensive reading.

I am of no use to anyone. Increasingly the thought: Why live at all?

Wild Swan

"How grateful I would be to you! Dr. Fowler from Salisbury has diagnosed her with depressed spirits, a lack of blood circulation. You saw for yourself this morning how lethargic she is, how weak. He prescribes fresh air, meat broth, pleasant distractions. A winter in Rome is exactly what she needs."

Mrs. Nightingale sits in the drawing room across from Charles and Selina Bracebridge. A wealthy, childless couple in their forties, longtime friends of the Nightingales, they have seen for themselves Florence's alarming decline.

"We would welcome her company. I am in perfect health, but Charles has his little complaints, mainly gout and an unreliable stomach. It will be a help, having Florence on hand."

Watching the Bracebridges' hired carriage take the long curve down the beech-lined drive, Mrs. Nightingale feels a fleeting guilt. How rashly she has thrown Florence at them! But Flo wears them all flat. No one knows what to do with her, how to make her happy.

It is possible, once she returns from Rome, she will see the sense of accepting Mr. Milnes's proposal. With one daughter wed, Frances could turn her attention to a suitable husband for the other. With both daughters married, chances for a grandson, a male heir, would increase—as would the possibility of keeping William's two estates, his wealth, within the immediate family. A long, fragile chain Florence seems determined to break.

Commonplace

TEN YEARS SINCE HE CALLED ME to His service. May a winter passed in the heart of Christendom provide direction I cannot find here.

PART THREE

Rome and Beyond

November 1847–May 1848

Blood of Beasts, Gold Leaf

ASSAULTED BY THE WET, COPPERY STENCH, I step into a doorway, let the cart piled with slaughtered cattle pass by. Jostled along cobblestone streets, the carcasses slip and shift as if still alive. The driver wears his butcher's apron untied, smeared with gore. After the cart has rumbled by, I walk through the meat market, pass game birds, like an avian valance, strung the length of several stalls—pheasant, dove, grouse, partridge, geese. On the counters are blood puddings, blackened "top skins" congealed, feathery hills of dead larks, sparrows, quail. A few stalls offer whole chickens, where market women sit plucking off feathers before slinging them up on metal hooks. Others sell legs, wings, necks, breasts, gizzards, a scarlet jumble of coxcombs. Everywhere are huge netted baskets crammed with live, gabbling birds, while from abattoirs behind the stalls come the bellowing protests of cattle, terrified bleatings of sheep and goats. One stall sells only wild game—a spotted deer, porcupines bristling with black-and-white quills, a wild boar hung up by its hind legs, its curved tusks in a permanent snarl. Everywhere, men sluice off wood counters with tin pails of water. A foul paste of blood, feathers, and manure accumulates on the cobblestones. I nearly stumble over a bundle of rags piled against one of the stalls. The bundle stirs, sits up, becomes a man. On a street opposite the market, slaughtered pigs and sheep are neatly hammered onto the doors of butcher shops and decorated with holiday frills of gold leaf. Everywhere, the panicked braying of animals, the stench of blood and offal.

Death is a reality, I tell myself. *And people must eat.*

Lifting my skirt above pools of blood, feathers, waste, I continue down the narrow street toward the gleaming dome of the Pantheon, the Piazza della Rotunda, until I reach the bird market. Sparrows, gray thrushes, nightingales, green finches, ringdoves, yellow canaries, parrots—the song and feathered screech of hundreds of captured birds mingles with the plashing of the central fountain. Sunlight turns the fountain's spray to diamonds, sets green fire to Amazon parrots, gilds the yellow feathers of the black-eyed finch. Half a dozen mournful owls are chained by leathery talons to crude wooden stands, while a hooded raven, imprisoned in a wire cage, shivers, listless and sick.

A cruel lie—human superiority.

The Bracebridges

T HIS MORNING, WHILE I WAS AT the animal market, Charles fell down the stone stairs leading to our third-floor apartment. Pollock, an English doctor living near Piazza di Spagna, diagnosed him with a major concussion and ordered him to remain two weeks in bed. "Your husband was protected by an angel," the doctor tells Selina. "He should have died from such a fall." ("Pio Nono saved me," Charles jokes, as soon as Pollock leaves.)

In a wall niche opposite Charles's bed is a small white bust of Pius IX. Made of bisque porcelain, "Pio Nono" seized his interest on his first day in Rome. He bought three, one for himself, one for Selina, a third for me. This newly elected Pope supports the Italian people in their fight for independence from Austria. The busts are the only ornaments in our sparsely furnished, poorly heated apartment.

Pushing up from his rumpled bed, Charles leans against a soft mash of pillows, his head wrapped in linen bandages. He is restless, irritable.

"This cracked noggin wants news, Florence. What did you see on your morning walk?"

"Yes, dear, tell us." Selina places a ribbon marker in the book she has been reading, the first of three volumes, *History of Manners and Customs of Ancient Greece*. Redoing Charles's "turban," soothing him as he complains, she finally says, "Hush now. Listen to Flo."

I describe the meat market, causing Charles to recall a dish of *cibreo*, boiled coxcombs, he had relished on an earlier trip to

111

Rome. *Like soft, salty mushrooms. Italians are wonderfully resource-ful; they'll eat anything—cats, songbirds, dormice. Even cheese with jumping maggots.* When I describe the bird market, he recalls a pair of finches he once bought and set free. Selina asks if I had seen Rome's famous *mendicante.* When he isn't begging, he sleeps under the stalls of the meat market. "They say he never changes his clothes and gives all his money to the poor. There is talk of Pio Nono making him a saint."

I had not seen such a person, I tell her. *Surely not that bundle of rags?*

The Bracebridges are indifferent, trusting chaperones. On occa-sion, they ask about my day, but their own interests and devotion to each other are so absolute as to preclude anything but the most fleeting curiosity about me.

Mrs. B., Selina, studies Greek and Roman history, Etruscan art. A handsome, heavyset woman, she wears shapeless aubergine and plum-colored dresses made from the finest silks and wools. For jewelry, she wears her wedding ring, an engraved pocket watch, and a pair of jet earrings that had belonged to Charles's mother. She claims no denomination of faith and has an acid view of religion, calling it a man-made prison that fails to contain the Uncontainable. Her chief talent is pencil sketching, and since she and Charles travel constantly, her drawings are mostly town scenes and portraits of local people. She has one peculiar lack. She rarely smiles and almost never laughs. As if to compensate, Charles turns everything into a joke. He wakes humming, whis-tles his way to breakfast, and by noontime is in full, cheerful roar. Less than fastidious, he endures his wife's grooming—dabbing stains off his cravat or waistcoat, pressing down his cowlicked hair, unruly and salted with gray.

His frequent boast is that he is the last surviving male in a family tracing itself back to Lady Godiva and the earls of Mercia. I give you this morning's exchange over breakfast.

"A woman who protests taxes by riding through town naked on a horse—now there is a woman I should wish to meet. Though I know my ancestor well enough by way of her bloodline coursing through my veins."

"You haven't enough of Lady Godiva's blood in you, Charles, to cause you to ride naked anywhere on any beast, horse or camel, thank God."

He splutters over his baked, parsleyed eggs. "Fully agree, Sel. But you must admit the picture of my pretty ancestor, stark naked on a dobbin, is a charming one."

Charles writes, publishes, and distributes pamphlets no one reads, fires off opinionated letters and windy editorials to newspapers. Easily inflamed, his political ire is just as quickly doused by his amused take on life and the many pleasant distractions of his wealth.

This morning, peevish, rebelling against Dr. Pollock's instructions, Charles struggles out of bed as Selina writes Mama, no doubt saying how well I look, how much they are enjoying my company. By late afternoon, he insists his brain is recovered enough to attend Lord and Lady Minto's Christmas Eve dinner. When I say I first wish to visit the Christmas market, he sketches a little map for me, which, in my haste, I abandon on the table in the foyer, pinned beneath one of the little busts of Pio Nono.

Are Not Two Sparrows
Sold for a Farthing?

NEAR THE FOUNTAIN OF FOUR RIVERS, I rummage through rows of books and prints. I have already purchased a red silk handkerchief for Charles and a tortoiseshell comb for Selina, but I would like to find a Christmas gift for them both to share. After looking through dozens of engravings of the Vatican and choosing one, I watch as the seller carefully rolls it up inside heavy brown paper. Leaving Piazza Navona, pleased with my gift, I hurry down side streets, trying to recall the details of Charles's map, when I am stopped by the sight of a child huddled, sparrowlike, on the bottom step of a flight of stairs leading up to a neighborhood church. Her ribs jut like staves through a too-big cotton dress; there are crescents of exhaustion beneath her large sunken eyes. She has on no shoes or stockings, her scabbed legs are purple with cold, and her long hair is a wild mane of greasy black knots. Seeing me looking at her, she springs up, tears open the front of her dress, revealing a pitifully concave chest with two tiny flat nipples. Holds out an upturned palm.

Digging through my carpetbag, I pull up a jumble of loose coins, press them into her hand. Before I can ask her name or where she lives, she darts, little minnow, into the surging crowd of shoppers.

The disparity between the English envoy's elaborate Christmas Eve supper, as I envision it, and the awful life of this child turns the rest of my walk to Lord Minto's into one of bitter reflection as I compare the Christmas story to my own insufficient actions in this world. What if I had brought the girl, as my guest, to dinner with me, introduced her to the warmth of a luxurious English residence in Rome? What if, for once, I had had the courage to bridge these two worlds? Raising a gloved hand, I bring the ornate brass knocker down against the English envoy's door, thinking, *My life is one great hypocrisy.*

A butler takes my cloak. Untying my bonnet, I hand that to him as well, along with my carpetbag and the rolled-up engraving. From the dining room comes a murmuring rise and fall of voices, a woman's jarring peal of laughter, the bright clink of cutlery on bone china. The room, when I enter, is stifling. It smells of roast meat, cinnamon, melting beeswax, rosewater.

Selina waves me over, pats her hand on the seat she has saved. At least thirty guests, all of them English, line each side of the long linen-draped table. I know no one.

"I've put you between us, Flo. I have been telling Mrs. Herbert about your interest in hospitals and nursing."

Elizabeth Herbert looks up, smiling. She has luminous dark blue eyes and chestnut hair, fastidiously arranged. A face of sheltered goodness.

"I've saved your soup, Flo, though you needn't bother. If warm eel soup is dreadful, cold eel soup is sheer punishment."

I lean to one side so a servant can remove the dark, oily soup and replace it with cold guinea fowl in a clear aspic. I am still thinking of the child.

"I am sorry for being late. Something happened, you see."

"What, my dear, are you all right? I'm afraid Charles had to turn back on our way here, his head hurt so. I told him to send for dinner from Luigi's. You weren't robbed, I hope? Rome is sadly overrun with pickpockets and thieves at Christmastime."

"I was on my way from the book stalls at Piazza Navona when I saw a small child by herself."

"A Gypsy, no doubt." Selina takes a too-generous bite of fowl.

"She was trembling through her scrap of dress. She looked badly treated."

"Gypsy parents starve their children, then force them to beg on the streets. If they return with nothing, they are beaten and sent out again."

"True," Elizabeth Herbert murmurs. "A horrible fact."

"Many of our English friends shrug it off as performance, a way the parents save themselves from honest work."

"Hunger is never a performance."

"Of course not, but people go to astonishing lengths to escape feelings of guilt. But why this child, Flo? There are thousands like her, common as starlings, all over the city."

"I can't say."

Elizabeth Herbert turns. "Perhaps God wanted you to help this one particular child."

"I gave her what was left of my money, but she ran off before I could speak with her."

"Would you like me to introduce you to the mother superior of the convent at Trinità dei Monti? The Sacré-Coeur nuns run an orphanage in Travastere. You could speak with Madre de Sainte Colombe about how you might help these children. Perhaps even this one child."

"Excellent thought, Liz! As I told you, Florence has a strong calling to nurse the sick and help the poor. Her parents neither understand nor approve. Forgive me, Flo, but your mother was desperate to be rid of you. She was at her wit's end."

Elizabeth turns to me again.

"Is your interest in nursing or teaching?"

"Nursing."

"I may be able to help with that as well. How wonderful to have met you, and on Christmas Eve!"

Beginning to slice into the cold fowl and suddenly recalling the meat market, I set down my knife and fork.

"I would be grateful for your help, thank you."

"I was first introduced to Madre de Sainte Colombe as a child. She has been my spiritual counselor for many years."

I start to ask about the times of Christmas Day Masses at the Vatican, when half a dozen gentlemen at the far end of the table stand up and begin singing "God Rest Ye Merry Gentlemen." A solo tenor sings the third verse, his voice perfectly pitched and pure. *From God our Heavenly Father / a blessed Angel came, / and unto certain Shepherds / brought tidings of the same . . .*

Selina leans toward the singer, squints. "Liz, isn't that Sidney?"

"You know the soloist, Mrs. Herbert?" I ask.

"A little," she smiles. "We are on a late honeymoon."

As she turns to answer the gentleman on her opposite side, complimenting her husband's singing, Selina whispers, "Sidney Herbert is an MP with a stellar career ahead of him. The younger son of the eleventh earl of Pembroke, he is expected by many to be our next prime minister."

Pollock's Turban

"SHE HAS TAKEN AN INTEREST IN YOU." Selina, who doesn't see well at night, tightens her grip on my forearm as we pick our way down the maze of dark streets. "Liz is sympathetic to Catholicism. She would convert were it not a disadvantage to Sidney's career. I tell her she is an outward Anglican with a popish heart. I must see to it you meet Sidney Herbert. He is that rarest of politicians, a man who serves his nation before himself. He was secretary at war under Sir Peel, and before he married, he had a long, scandalous affair with Lady Caroline Norton. Have you heard of her, Lady Norton? A famous beauty trapped in a dreadful marriage, she ended the affair when she realized that Sidney needed to marry and have a son, a legitimate heir. He and Liz are friends since childhood."

"Not a love match, then?"

"More of a tender bond."

Halfway up the stairs to the apartment, Selina stops to catch her breath.

"I was remiss, dear. I did not introduce you to your hosts. Lord Minto is pleasant enough. Lady M. is a dragon. I have never known anyone or anything to satisfy her."

Having thrown off Dr. Pollock's linen turban, Charles is on his back, snoring, arms and legs akimbo. Unraveled strips of bandage lie on the floor near the bed, beside a plate of half-eaten spaghetti Bolognese from Luigi's.

Selina gazes at her disheveled, sleeping husband. "Charles and

I have had many marvelous experiences, but love surpasses every adventure we have enjoyed."

I feel the sting of that sentence. I live without love, by choice, but suddenly feel the misery of someone who has rejected convention with nothing to replace it. Later that night, old demons of self-loathing and doubt keep me tossing, awake in my shuttered bedroom.

Nun

Pop,

Tomorrow begins my ten-day nunship, thanks to Madre Laure de Sainte Colombe. She is head of an order of French nuns at Trinità dei Monti, a church at the top of the Spanish Steps.

Sacré-Coeur nuns are dedicated to the education of girls. They run boarding schools for upper-class girls and "free schools" for the unfortunate. I met Madre through Elizabeth Herbert. (Have I mentioned the Herberts to you? I think I have.)

Imagine your little sister's face trapped inside a wimple, wearing a habit of black. These nuns, very chic, sport habits in the style of Parisian widows. Even the religious in France are slaves to fashion!

My days have been taken up with tours of orphanages and hospitals that Liz arranges for me. San Giacomo, a hospital for incurable disease, is the grimmest place imaginable, crowded, filthy, full of indescribably foul smells. Santo Spirito, a general hospital on the Tiber River, is as bad, though the foundlings section, run by another order of French nuns, is very clean.

I attend Mass daily at St. Peter's, though my fascination with Catholicism stops at their insistence that Pope and Church are the one true path to God. Why would God be so stupidly restrictive? I do not even believe churchgoing necessary! Tied to a stake, I would signal through the flames that to bring relief to the poor and those who suffer is more pleasing to God than rote prayers in church pews on fancy-hat Sundays. But who am I if not an elite hypocrite, protected by privilege? Who am I to speak on such things?

Adieu, Flo

Cell

I PACE BACK AND FORTH TO KEEP WARM, try to recall Madre de Sainte Colombe's guidance. Once you are "removed from the world," she advised, "you must exchange vanity for new life, anchored in God. Who cares if others are difficult, make us desperate? So long as you do His will, nothing else matters." That morning, I had sat for a good hour in her study, confessing my long, bitter resentment toward my family. I spilled out my anger, loneliness, lack of direction, even told her about the cedar grove at Embley, how I had heard God's voice, how my life, like kindling, had been split in two. How miserable I have been ever since.

Eleven years of silence and here I am. Desperate enough to close myself in a cell, its whitewashed walls bare but for a crucifix crudely fashioned from two sticks and a bit of string. A straw pallet, a blanket of nut brown wool, a pillow hard as stone. I pace ten steps this way, ten steps that, gaze up at the round barred window, its gray light. *The dark hallway outside this cell smells of vinegar and lye, of virgin women vanished into Christ, growing old.*

In the pocket of my dress, I find the spiritual book Madre had given me, its pages softened, the ink blurred by others who have shut themselves away in this same freezing cell. I am only the latest in a line of desperate seekers. "Let the words of Saint Ignatius transform your soul," she had said. "As for your family, none of us lives with angels. We must learn to put up with human nature and forgive it."

Daily Exercises

—Discern God's will for you.

—Observe the "motions of the soul."

—Learn to see God in All Things.

—Conquer self.

—Make no decision under influence of attachment.

—Hear the Call of the King.

—Serve Him.

—List every one of your sins.

—Follow Christ as if you are one of His disciples.

—Do His work in this world.

I have no pen, no paper on which to list my sins. There is nothing. A hard bed, a crucifix, this small, fanatical book. I pace the stone floor, count steps by the dozens, by the hundreds, my sins outnumbering them.

✑

On the eleventh day, I sit in the convent's formal parlor, light-headed from hunger. Madre sits across from me, her hands folded in her lap. Small, mannish hands.

"Did God speak to you? Did He ask anything of you?"

"To surrender my will."

"To whom?"

"To all that is upon this earth."

"Then God calls you to a very high degree of perfection. Take care, child. If you resist Him, you will be very guilty."

Lady Minto's Parterre

THE WEATHER, UNSEASONABLY WARM for early February, changes abruptly. The temperature plummets, clouds darken overhead, a northerly wind whips the ribbons of the ladies' bonnets, tosses the hems of their skirts. They push on, touring Lady Minto's parterre, walking down paths of oyster shell, passing between severe patterns of low, clipped boxwood. In the center of the garden sits a massive fountain of pink marble, three dolphins sculpted to look as if they are leaping from the circular pool. Sitting on the broad lip of the fountain, near a floating carpet of dead leaves, I remember an afternoon last winter at Embley, when a cloud of robins, red-breasted, swooped with soft rushes of sound in and out of the cherry laurels, tearing at the dark fruit with sharp yellow beaks. Beneath my feet, thickly layered with fallen leaves, the earth began seething, rustling as startled robins, by the hundreds, burst up from the ground, a whirlwind of wings around me. The surprise of it, the terror, was nearly sublime. At the crunch of footsteps nearby, I turn to face Sidney Herbert.

"Miss Nightingale?" He bows slightly, as if amused by his own elegance.

My cheeks flush hot.

"My wife speaks of nothing but you. She says you would turn every Catholic church in Rome into a hospital."

"Heretical, I know."

"But I agree! Why should hospitals not be churches and churches hospitals? When we return home to Wiltshire, Mrs.

Herbert and I intend to improve tenants' conditions on our estate. We will build a new cottage hospital, add refinements to our little church. Perhaps you would like to visit and advise us?"

His large dark brown eyes gaze as a child's might, full of trust, into my own. I start to answer, but a rising wind takes my words, tearing them into thin, inarticulate sounds. Behind him, I see Lady Minto and Liz Herbert strolling toward us. Farther off, Selina sketches the pink fountain, its leaping dolphins.

"What is it, do you suppose," he carries on, half-shouting against the wind, "that compels a person to reshape nature into such lifeless geometries? I prefer a garden half wild. Good afternoon, Lady Minto. I see you practice an austere horticultural art. When we are back inside, you must explain the differences between the French and Italian philosophies of parterre."

Though he has just insulted both her taste and her garden, Lady Minto beams. In time, I will come to know these two sides of Sidney Herbert, the natural man who speaks without guile, with irresistible optimism, and the shrewder, more politic man who knows exactly what to say and how to gain people's favor. His is a charismatic, ruthless diplomacy. He has an inborn charm I cannot emulate, and in his career will attract few enemies, while I, lacking his tact or the unassailable power of his gender, will draw to myself too many.

Tell Us of Your God,
Miss Nightingale

"TELL US OF YOUR GOD, MISS NIGHTINGALE. Liz informs me you have made a narrow escape from a convent, and were nearly suffocated in the black folds of nuns' habits. Did you live on brown bread and Pope's water? Is it a fact that nuns never sleep? That they flagellate one another all day and night? One hears such strange, shocking things about the religious. I cannot understand why any woman should want to bury herself in yards and yards of black, her face peeking out like a dead cat's. Elena, see that Miss Nightingale is given several slices of fig cake. She has recently been starved."

Lord and Lady Minto, the Herberts, Charles, and Selina lounge about on richly upholstered divans and velvet armchairs in the Mintos' resplendent drawing room. I stand, looking out a set of leaded windows. The heavy skies and gusts of wind have turned into a violent storm; strikes of lightning, like the flicker of serpents' tongues, flash though the drawing room, followed by close rolls of thunder. In the hearth, a blazing fire, crackling between brightly polished brass dogs, sends up showers of sparks.

Awaiting my answer, various expressions of pained sympathy cross their faces, though Sidney frowns up at the ceiling, noting how poorly the fresco is done—plump, naked putti with blue sashes and golden crowns, all swirling pointlessly about.

Aware of Lady Minto's antipapist, anti-Catholic prejudices, I decide to reply honestly. Selina is correct; nothing pleases Lady

125

Minto beyond her tortured parterre and the oversized oil portrait of herself suspended above the mantel.

"I chose to go on spiritual retreat to better know God's will. I cannot speak for the few nuns I met, other than to praise them, particularly Madre de Sainte Colombe. The food was plain but healthful. My chief complaint was the cold—I found it hard to sleep. Being locked in a cell is a humbling exercise. I learned how far I must go to achieve any degree of selflessness to match that of the nuns."

Sidney Herbert tears his gaze from the aimless ceiling cherubs to look closely at me. "But do they laugh, Miss Nightingale? I cannot imagine life without gaiety."

"Why, yes, they do! On my walks around the convent grounds—I was permitted one walk per day—I would sometimes meet nuns and find them mirthful and quick to laugh."

"I have noticed that same quality among them!" Liz Herbert appears inspired by a thought. "Perhaps joy rises from self-forgetfulness."

"I lack such joy," I admit.

Lord Minto coughs into a large monogrammed handkerchief, a deep, phlegmy sound. His face reddens from the convulsive effort. "What about a game of whist for the gentlemen?" he manages to gasp out. "We mustn't run off our guests with too much talk of nuns and God."

"Absolutely," agrees Lady Minto, looking irked by the very idea of nuns' joy. "I have just had designs drawn up for a new suite of bedrooms, and should like to show them to the ladies. Miss Nightingale, I have no idea how you survived among those dry husks of women, *virgo intacta*, but you have, and you must never do that again. You're far too attractive and clever to hide yourself from us—unrepentant, worldly heathens that we are."

As the men follow Lord Minto into his library, the women wreath themselves around a marble-topped table and prepare to admire a commissioned set of architectural drawings. Above the mantel, Lady Minto's flattering portrait, bearing but the faintest resemblance to its subject, gazes down with an amused, derisive smile.

July 1848

Lea Hurst
Derbyshire

FRANCES NIGHTINGALE TURNS THE ENVELOPE over in her hands. Bearing the seal of the earl of Pembroke, the note inside comes from Wilton House, near Salisbury in the county of Wiltshire, nearly three hundred miles from Lea Hurst. Splitting the wax seal with her ivory opener, unfolding the single sheet of stationery, she admires the author's neat, French-trained, feminine hand.

Dear Mrs. Nightingale,

My husband and I should like the pleasure of your daughter's company during the third week of July at Wilton House. We were most impressed with her when we met in Rome through mutual friends, the Bracebridges, and should like to continue our conversations on hospitals, schools, and convalescent homes. I would be personally grateful, as well, for her skills in light nursing, as I have been unwell since returning from Rome. I assure you your daughter will be well looked after. If you and your husband are in favor, I will arrange for one of our carriages to go to Lea Hurst on a date you approve.

Most cordially,
Lady Elizabeth Herbert

Wilton House

"WHY REMOVE THEM, FLO?" Selina frowns down at one boot. "Though there is a nasty bit of muck on mine."

"You can't be serious!" Sidney Herbert looks at me, incredulous. "Liz intends this new floor mosaic to welcome all into the sanctum sanctorum of our little church. It is a replica of the Cosmati mosaic at Santa Maria Maggiore. Didn't she tell you?"

"She did."

He returns my muddied boots, laughing. "Next time, keep them on."

Like the interior of many country churches in England, Wiltshire has its straight rows of dark wood pews, its altar made from local stone, a few modest windows of stained glass. We emerge through a side door into the glare of midday, pick our way through a crowd of headstones in the parishioners' cemetery. As we walk, Selina and I listen to Sidney's brief history of his family's estate. The house, originally an abbey, came into the possession of the Herbert family in the sixteenth century, a gift from King Henry VIII to William Herbert, first earl of Pembroke. It is one of the great country houses in the region, and Sidney laughingly admits to not having the faintest idea of how many rooms it has, though he and his brother grew up there. He is taking us to see the estate's architectural marvel, a stone bridge crossing the River Nadder. The bridge has an elegant Palladian design, with peaked end pediments and an Ionic colonnade.

While Selina walks to the far end of the bridge, I stop at its center, gaze into the water. "It is a chalk stream, actually," Sidney says, standing so close our sleeves touch. "Positively thick in summertime with pike, grayling, brown trout." From a clump of meadowsweet, a white swan glides toward us. Others drift into sight from an oxbow bend in the river, sunlight shimmering on their feathers. Until I tilt my parasol and shake it free, a frantic bluebottle fly buzzes, caught in the fringe of my parasol.

"What is its history?" I ask.

"The ninth earl of Pembroke designed this bridge after Palladio's drawing of the Rialto Bridge in Venice." A tour guide, proud but slightly bored, talking of a bridge. Abruptly, he changes the subject.

"Florence. Tell me your honest opinion of Wilton House. Your unedited opinion."

"A monstrosity, overwhelming to anyone living inside it. I find my parents' homes equally oppressive. I attempted to run away from Lea Hurst when I was twelve, live among the villagers of Cromford, but they thought me mad and promptly delivered me back to my parents. Liz says you have a second home in London?"

"We do. In Belgrave."

A second swan, snowy feathered, golden-beaked, slips from a blind of brown sedge along the riverbank. I push a strand of hair back from my face.

"And your opinion of my wife's health?"

"Liz needs to walk. Fifteen minutes in the morning, fifteen in the evening."

"We wish to try for another child."

"She will be fine. Her miscarriage likely happened because of the long journey from Rome."

"That is what she thinks, too. Both of us are inspired by your zeal for reform, Florence."

"And I admire you for bettering the lives of your tenants."

"All credit to Liz. I merely trot along behind."

Selina returns, perspiring, flushed. "Is it true swans mate for life?"

"They do," Sidney replies. "A pair may live twenty to thirty years; when one dies, the other rarely takes a second mate. What news from yours, Mrs. B.? Your swan mate?"

"He's poking around Tintern Abbey, turning over monastery stones. In his letter, he wrote he would prefer seeing Wilton House when it was a monks' house. Charles gravitates to whatever is in the throes of religious disintegration."

We turn back. Rising fortresslike from hundreds of acres of green lawn, Wilton House is an enormous square of local stone, a high tower at each corner. Its interior contains a vast maze of courtyards.

It is quite grand. Quite ugly. Two people live inside that monstrosity, not even knowing how many rooms, how many ancestral portraits line the numerous staircases. Long unlit corridors, livried servants planted like funerary statues every ten paces. I must remember to ask if I could spend tomorrow at the local school, then visit the spot where the medieval leper hospital, St. Giles, is said to have been.

✍

"Didn't Shakespeare come here to Wilton, act in one of his own plays?"

We are dining in a great, high-ceilinged room, pitch-dark but for the table's lighted candelabrum. Elizabeth has already gone up to bed.

"I believe so, Mrs. Bracebridge. Stratford is not far—it would have been easy enough for Shakespeare to have traveled here with his players, and there is some proof. You've seen his likeness in the Front Hall? After dinner, I must take you both to the Upper

Cloisters. I have several historical rarities I keep there, and you might catch a glimpse of Wilton's most notorious ghost. You've already seen the best of the family's art collection—Rembrandt's portrait of his mother, various paintings by Reynolds, Rubens, van Dyck, Tintoretto, del Sarto. But there is one painting Florence especially must see. A Tintoretto, it is Liz's favorite and down in the Ante-Room."

"And the notorious ghost?" Selina asks.

"Philip Herbert, the seventh earl of Pembroke. A homicidal maniac pardoned by privilege of peerage. While he lived here, he kept some fifty-three mastiffs, thirty greyhounds, half a dozen bears, a lion, other captured beasts. The servants tell me they see his troubled spirit at night, roaming the corridors of the Upper Cloisters."

∽

Selina has gone upstairs to bed. I follow Sidney down to the Great Ante-Room, where we stand before the Tintoretto.

"He is said to have painted five versions of this same scene. Christ washing the disciples' feet."

I lean in to examine the quick, vivid strokes of paint, details of the scene itself—disciples lounging about, some reading books, one pulling off another's boot. Christ is kneeling, gesturing for Peter to put his naked foot into a golden basin of water.

"Do you believe in God?"

Rocking back on his heels a little, he laughs. "As much as any other dutiful Anglican. Liz complains I have a child's faith. It's true I prefer doing a bit of practical good in the world to getting tangled up in theological debate. What about you? Anyone who would clap herself into a convent for a fortnight must have one or two thoughts of God."

I am finding little inspiration in the false figure of Christ, humbled before Peter. "God is at the center of my life's purpose."

"And that purpose . . ."

"To nurse the sick and suffering." There. I have said it, and saying it, feel the hollowness of my words. Sidney takes my arm and, relating some memory from his childhood, escorts me upstairs, unknowingly saving us from an impulsive confession of my inadequacies and fears.

Dearest!

I come home tomorrow or the next, depending on the roads, with much to tell you. Florence has become a friend of the Herberts, though my "worm of suspicion," hatched in Rome, continues to grow. I speak of Sidney, of course. Liz adores Flo, and, seeing only good in everyone, is oblivious to any danger. Perhaps it is the cynicism of maturity that alerts me. He is a man of immense charm and good looks, attracting men, women, and children alike. He is easy in his ways, patrician, intelligent. An air of benevolence follows him everywhere; people are drawn to his light and warmth. I worry Florence draws too close. For his part, he is much taken with her. When she openly chafes at the restrictions of her sex and class, he sympathizes. If she rattles on ad infinitum about the glories of mathematics, the usefulness of statistics, he is all patient attention. Oh, Charles, I can only hope theirs will be a beneficial friendship and not an attraction.

I am eager to hear of your rattlings among the Cistercian ghosts and monks' bones of Tintern. As you are fond of saying, no corpse can argue, and ghosts give only passing alarm.

All love,

S.

Commonplace

MAMA IS TAKING PARTHE AND ME to the water cure at Karlsbad. The Protestant hospital I have read about, Kaiserwerth, is one hour from there. I must insist on going to Kaiserwerth
for a fortnight of study.

It has become oppressive here at Wilton House. Since it is his
birthplace and childhood home, Sidney is unaffected. Liz tells
me she, too, found the place overwhelming when she first arrived,
though she is learning to use the privilege of her marriage to uplift
the lives of the people of Wiltshire.

Today I sat a full two hours in the library with him. Among
other things, we talked of how best to use government funds to
improve the health of the poor, and though he is a Tory, it seems
we agree on a great many things. Running invisible beneath our
conversation was an electric current, a common pulse neither of
us spoke of.

*His habit of sweeping back his dark hair with one hand, the way
his eyes will rest on some far, fixed point whenever he falls deep into
thought, his tenderness with Liz, yes, I even manage to find delight in
that. Mama once declared me a sensual child, and at the time I did
not understand her meaning, but in his presence, gazing on him, I
begin to understand—and feel afraid.*

Wilton House itself does little to encourage a life of prayer and
selflessness. Thankfully, we leave tomorrow, Selina for London,
myself for Lea Hurst. I am determined to travel from Karlsbad to
Kaiserwerth and will defy Mama to do so.

∽

There have been riots in Karlsbad, we cannot visit the spa, and now Parthe claims she is too ill to travel. I am to go alone with Mama to the water spa at Malvern. All hope of Kaiserwerth—gone.

White Rind of Flesh

Great Malvern
Worcestershire
October 1848

THE DOCTOR LEANS DOWN TO MAMA, perched on a red leather divan. Seizing her soft, beringed hands, he stares through her outer body, the "white rind of flesh," as he declares it, into the inner, secret workings of her organs. Stares so intensely, Mama's face reddens to the roots of her hair and she giggles, a girlish flitter to her voice I have never heard before. It is her external beauty that is always commented on, exclaimed over, not her kidneys, or liver, large intestine, et cetera.

A man of middle years, prone to dressing up his speech with little frills of French phraseology, James Gully lets go of her hands to jot down his observations with a gold propelling pencil. I cannot hear Mama's answers. Embarrassed, she whispers them into her skirts.

"The working of the stomach?

"Is the appetite intact?

"The tongue. May I see it? Lean toward me, Mrs. Nightingale. Stick out your tongue. Very nice. No furring, no split. No fetid breath.

"Are the air tubes, the lungs, taking air in and out well?

"The movements of the bowels, are they obstinate? Sluggish? Flatus? Constipation?

"Do you suffer from hysterics? Fainting? Anxiety? Palpitations of the heart?

"Is your sleep dreamy or broken?"

His inquiry over, he pronounces Mama moderately healthy, outlines a cure for her dyspepsia, eyelid tremor, and mild constipation before turning his slow, penetrating gaze on me.

Aside from the chronic irritability typical of an unmarried woman nearing thirty, I am declared sound as a horse. Far quicker in his inspection of me, he takes so few notes, I am certain were I to peek at what is scrawled on his notepad, I would find a diagnosis consisting of two words: old maid.

Enfin, he draws a gold watch out from his vest pocket to check the time.

"Here at Malvern, I can promise you ladies an increased feeling of *bien-être*. A daily regimen of douches, cold-water foot baths, rides on our sturdy donkeys, hikes up the mountain, and we shall have you ruddy and cheerful in no time! No need for calomel, leeches, cupping, laudanum, or mercury—all phamacopoeia to make a sick man sicker. My aim is to make any man strong enough to fell an ox with one fist and able to roll up a pewter plate with the other. *Adieu*, ladies." As he bows in our direction, two women wearing starched white uniforms and white pleated caps come into his office. "Ah, here they are. Your bath attendants. *Bonne chance. À tout à l'heure!*"

"He is not a real doctor, Mama. He is a hypnotist."

"Don't be silly. I find him charming. Do you have our printed regimen?"

"Yes."

"Read it to me."

"'Up at five A.M.

"'Dry scrubbing followed by rubbing with the dripping sheet.

"'Packed in the wet sheet, covered by blankets'—apparently we are to foment or stew, whatever you might call it, for two hours.

"'Shallow bath, followed by "Neptune's girdle," a wet compress to the trunk to be worn all day.

"'Water. Seven to eight wineglasses of Malvern water throughout the day for you, Mama, and fifteen tumblersful for me.

"'Baths. Daily sitz bath followed by the ascending and descending douche.' Why do you suppose our bath attendants are so grim and pasty-looking? You'd expect they'd be jolly. Ruddy with health."

"Exercise, Flo? What does it say about exercise?"

"'Strenuous hikes of several hours or pleasant donkey rides, wearing as little clothing as possible.'"

"What?"

"'Clothing interferes.' A direct quote."

"Interferes?"

"With circulation. It says that, too."

"What is our diet to be? I'm starving, aren't you?"

"Diet? Here it is, on the back of the booklet.

"'Breakfast: dry biscuits and water.

"'Dinner: boiled mutton or fish.

"'Supper: brown bread, butter, milk, as much water as desired.'"

"Heavens. We are to be tortured. I hope the mutton is not stewed to rags. God knows I require a bit of cake. I cannot live without cake."

We lie on twin tables, oversized infants swaddled in wet sheets, bundled over with quilts and feather bedding, only our faces exposed. The light in the room is dim, the air humid.

"I must purchase a copy of Dr. Gully's book, Flo."

"He has a book?"

"*The Water-Cure in Chronic Disease*. Do you really believe he is a mesmerist?"

"A mesmerist and a hypnotist. I am told he is deep into homeopathy."

"And I'm certain he is a brilliant doctor."

"Questionable."

"He has treated Charles Dickens, Samuel Wilberforce, Thomas Carlyle, and Charles Darwin. The best minds come here to be cured."

"The cures are dubious. I saw Mr. Tennyson jog by on a donkey during my walk into the Malvern Hills this morning."

"You must write Monckton; he and Tennyson are great friends."

"When are we to be freed from these steepages, Mama? I feel mummified. Embalmed."

Because they have been listening, the expressionless bath attendants, each named Rose (Mrs. Nightingale calls them "Rose One" and "Rose Two"), step forward to unwind us from our wet sheets. They fling pails of cold water over our naked "rinds," douse us like garden shrubs before taking us to the steam, then the oil-lamp bath.

A Month of Drowning

Dear Monk,

It did me good to read your letter amid this atmosphere of water, water, water, chased by a dry biscuit or lump of mutton. Mother heard of Malvern through friends in London; we are here for an entire month of the latest cure.

Since you have asked, you shall hear our daily regimen:

Cold water in every form imaginable. Shallow baths, wet sheets, sitz baths, head baths, douches, Malvern water by the glassfuls. Strenuous walks in mountain air (I am given an alpenstock and a leathern flask containing . . . what else . . . water!)

A spartan diet, no spirits. Mama is dying for a slice of raisin cake and sugared tea. More and more drowning—the most punishing treatment of all is the douche, an icy torture that Dr. Gully, a verbose sort of quackster, seems to think I am in need of. Walking to the douche house, I am treated along the way to the sound of other victims' yells, squeals, and howls. Descending into a deep well, I stand beneath three pipes ten feet above me. Holding fast to a horizontal bar so as not to be blasted off my feet, I await the freezing cataract of water to pound over me from the overhead pipes. The whole torment lasts two minutes.

Mother spends a good deal of time with Dr. Gully. They go on walks; she blushes when he sits beside her at dinner. Last night, over a dish of bland mutton, I was obliged to remind him I had a father living!

I look forward to your biography of poor John Keats. May you deliver him from undeserved ignominy! Liz H. has invited me a second time to Wilton House to help after the baby's birth and to oversee progress on the tenants' new hospital.

I saw Alfred Tennyson as he was leaving Malvern. His skin, he told me, had become so tender, he had to walk backward when the wind was northerly or easterly. He had been persuaded to give up his "vile tobacco" after Gully insisted it coarsened his imagination and made him write bad poetry!

Yours,
Flo

Envy and Despair

Whitsun Week

May 1849

"Y ou envy me? I have never been so melancholy in my life."
"After three months in Rome? A fortnight with the Herberts? A second visit to Wilton House, and now, London's most prized bachelor here to ask for the sixth or seventh time if you will marry him?"

The sisters stand close beside each other at Parthe's bedroom window, looking down at the procession of carriages. Mama's guests, arriving.

"Put that way . . ."

"I am the one who should be melancholy. Mama's plain little duck, twaddling behind her with no life of my own. Look, isn't that Monk? Your fiancé?"

"He is *not* my fiancé."

"Well, he should be. He's here to ask you to marry him. This time you must say yes. We are all so fond of Monckton, and you have kept him waiting ages. Years. Mama says it may be too late."

It will never happen. I turn from the window.

"You see? All cool indifference. You have no heart, Flo. You never have. Well, if you won't, I will go downstairs and greet him myself."

Go. What do I care? I would sooner think on a thousand other things. God. Nursing. The purity of numbers. Sidney's large, beautifully dark eyes.

Love's Hidden Code

IHELPED LIZ CARE FOR HER NEWBORN daughter, Mary. I did her errands, taught the children at the local school. Even so, my thoughts strayed, though not from any encouragement on his part. Only once, one night, did he say something that nearly gave me hope. Hope of what? All month he had stayed in London, but on this particular night he was home. Liz had retired early, and we were dining alone, though I scarcely touched my food. At last, he broke the lengthening silence.

"Do you like anagrams, Florence?"

"Parthe and I played at them as children."

"Wilton has an intriguing example. May I show you?"

I followed him down a long flight of marble steps to the great Front Hall. At its center, a life-size sculpture of William Shakespeare stood on a fluted pedestal. He brought me close to a marble scroll held in the statue's hand, asked could I read what was written there.

Life's but a walking SHADOW
A poor PLAYER
That struts & frets his hour
Upon the STAGE
And then is heard no more.

"This fellow's exact twin lives in Westminster Abbey, though his scroll bears a verse from *The Tempest* instead of *Macbeth*. Our statue is said to commemorate the time Shakespeare and his players visited Wilton House and performed for James the First, a guest of Mary Sidney's. The king had come here to escape the plague in London."

He went on, telling me more of his ancestor, Mary, countess of Pembroke, known to be adept in the writing of codes. She had been part of the Wilton Circle of Poets.

"Clearly a clever woman. Was this verse intended as a sort of code?"

"I like to think so. There is an anagram inside the verse formed from the words *shadow, player,* and *stage.* It may have been a secret message of love between Mary and a young poet whose name has been lost to history. You grasp things quickly, Florence. My mother, Catherine Woronzow, was a brilliant, beautiful woman. So much about you reminds me of her. You have the same quicksilver mind."

As he spoke, I traced the words on the scroll with my finger, feeling his warm breath as he came near and murmured, "Had we met even two years ago, our lives would be different. My life, surely. Why did you and I not meet sooner?"

I crossed the room to view, with feigned interest, a dull painting. A landscape. I felt my face burning with pleasure. From there, anything could have happened. Nothing did.

After that night, I made certain never to be alone with him. He left for London the next morning, and for the remainder of my visit, I tended the baby, a placid, cross-eyed creature, read Catholic meditations aloud to Liz, and slept, so as not to think. Many nights, I walked to the river and stood on the Palladian bridge, waiting for the first stars to appear.

On a morning of cold, pelting spring rain, I embraced Liz, who suspected nothing ill of me, and left for Lea Hurst. As the carriage wheels rattled and spun, throwing off thick gouts of mud, I struggled with my guilt, my inward betrayal of Liz. Fretted over the last letter from my mother, which informed me I would soon be seeing Monk.

❧

Home on the Sunday before Whitsun. My twenty-ninth birthday came and went with little fanfare, just as I had asked.

And now my sister has traipsed downstairs to greet Monckton Milnes, arrived for a week of prayers and festivities, and more privately, urgently, to press for my final answer.

Refusal

To avoid him. That was the whole of my plan.

But where I am concerned, Monckton Milnes is a man with no patience left. After the Whitsunday service at St. Margaret's, after the vicar read from chapter 2 of Acts, then delivered a homily on the Descent of the Holy Spirit in tongues of flame, as everyone filed from the small church in East Wellow, he found me and asked if I would join him on a walk. I nodded, remembering my written speech, my three-point argument against marriage, concealed in a drawer of my desk.

On the gravel path, we exchange pleasantries with others coming from church, until he takes me by the elbow and steers me down a sweep of lawn past the yew hedges and cherry trees. Once inside the cedar grove, I glimpse Madonna lilies, a shock of white in the shadows.

He paces, hands clasped behind his back, head bullishly tucked into his chest. Since Monk arrived, he has looked battered, haggard. His newly published biography of John Keats, the first book to come out in praise of the late poet, has met with savage criticism. I sit on the granite bench, braced for what I expect is coming. He sits beside me.

It seems, he, too, has a speech.

"My dearest Florence. It has been seven years since you refused my first proposal of marriage. Since then, you remain at the center of my heart, yet I find myself worn down. You draw me near, put me off, draw me near, put me off. I must have a final answer. Yes or no. For the last time, will you consent to be my wife?"

He stares at the mossy ground with a set, stoical expression. I recall my argument against marriage. I remember every word.

"Dearest friend, I do have an answer. I have an intellectual nature, which requires satisfaction, and yes, I would find it in you. I have a passionate nature, which requires satisfaction, and yes, I would find it in you. But I have a moral, active nature, which requires satisfaction as well, and would *not* find it in you. That is the reason I cannot marry you."

A priggish speech. One of which I am not proud. He lifts his head with the slack, resigned look of a man who has lost his battle.

"Monk." I reach for his hand, but he withdraws it, an action surprisingly hurtful. After all, he has been a close friend. It is not his company I refuse, but the prison—the gaol of marriage I object to. Instead, he plucks a handkerchief from his breast pocket, flaps it open, blows his nose. Pushing it back down in his pocket, he stands and, without looking at me, mutters, "Neither one of us is suited for love, Florence. God knows, we may be incapable."

Without another word, we walk out of the grove into the harsh sunshine. By the time we reach the top of the stone steps and cross the lawn overlooking Mama's rose garden, we are as far apart as any two people can be.

Oh, Excellent Choice!

"CALLED AWAY? I CANNOT BELIEVE IT. He was to give a talk on Mr. Keats this evening. And Parliament is on holiday, isn't it?"

I say nothing.

"Florence. You must tell me what has happened."

"Nothing has happened. I refused him, that's all."

"Is this true?"

"It is, and I will not be dissuaded."

"Mama?" My sister, her nose ever keen for trouble, has found us. "What is it? Flo, what have you done?"

"Your sister refused Mr. Milnes. He has left for London."

"Is there no end to your thoughtless cruelties?"

"It's because she wants to be a nurse." Mrs. Nightingale's voice trembles.

"Of course," Parthe bursts out. "That. A nurse. To wash bodies and be exposed to every sickness there is. To see and hear things no decent woman should see or hear—to prefer depravity over marriage to dear, kind Mr. Milnes. Excellent choice, Florence. I congratulate you."

She sets a comforting arm around her mother's shoulders. "Let me take you to your room to rest, Mama. You have a full week of guests, but of course Flo does not think of that. She never considers the effects of her selfish actions."

"Your father can't know. We'll give him Mr. Milnes's excuse. Oh, my head. It feels as if it is splitting in two."

"Stop it, both of you. My decision is final. And Parthe, you have my permission to marry Mr. Milnes yourself."

"Your permission? How dare you!" Parthe, furious, wrenches the silver bracelets I had lent her that morning off her slender wrist, flings them to the floor. "No thank you. I have no need of your discarded men or bracelets. Come, Mama, leave Florence to her holier-than-thou self. She thinks herself a saint, a martyr, while we, who must put up with her, know better."

After they have left, I stoop to retrieve the bracelets, a gift from Monk.

Since that terrible Whitsunday, I have kept to my room. By refusing marriage, I have sacrificed his friendship. But would a true friend have forced me to make such a choice? Even God's silence feels more of a rebuke, a rejection, than ever.

∽

Still in her dressing gown, Mama cracks open the door. "Florence? I have a letter from the Bracebridges. They invite you to join them in November on a journey of some months down the Nile."

Frances Nightingale does not add that she had written to Selina out of desperation.

My dear Selina,

Something must be done about Flo. She has turned down Monckton Milnes for a final time and shut herself in her room. I am desperate. Even as we pack for Lea Hurst, her actions affect everyone. A pall hangs over the entire household. William fears we will lose her entirely.

I pray you have some suggestion of help.

Yours,

Frances

PART FOUR

The Nile

November 1849–March 1850

Iron bedsteads
Carpets
Rat-traps
Washing tubs
Guns
Staples, especially tea and English cheese
Piano
Sheep, turkeys, chickens and mules

—Sir John Gardner Wilkinson,
A Handbook for Travellers in Egypt

A few common dresses for the river
Flannel and Brown Holland underclothes
Brown Holland dressing gown
Bonnets and shawls
Veils
Gloves
Umbrella
A green eye guard to protect against the sun

—M. L. M. Carey, *Four Months in a Dahabëéh*
or Narrative of a Winter's Cruise on the Nile

Hammam

Alexandria
November 1849

SHIELDING OURSELVES FROM THE OVERHEAD sun with dove-gray parasols, Selina, the Bracebridge's new German servant, Trautwein, and myself follow our "protector," a young Arab in long, white robes, bearing a palm stick in his right hand.

"Why do you suppose he carries that? To beat off thieves? Slow down, Florence, you walk at such a pace," Selina says, panting.

"I doubt we shall be robbed. It is broad day, and since we left our hotel twenty minutes ago, I've seen far more Europeans wandering about the streets than Egyptians. No, I think Ali's staff is purely for style."

"Well, if we are to be accosted, I would hope he knows how to use it. How much farther to the hammam do you suppose? It's been such a long day already. I could not budge from my bed this morning, until a pack of beastly fleas woke me. According to Charles, they are especially bad in Egypt."

Following Ali, we thread our way down a narrow passageway cooled by shadows cast from close-set mud dwellings on either side. At last, he brings us into an orchard of blossoming lemon, orange, and almond trees. Past the orchard, we find ourselves on a dirt footpath lined with palm and banana trees, sweet-smelling purple petunias, thickly massed on white-painted trellises.

Ali stops before an unremarkable dun-colored building. "Hammam." With an indifferent bow, he leaves. Flushed and perspiring, Selina pushes open the heavy door. Trautwein slaps after with her lumpy bag of knitting. I am convinced the woman plies whalebone needles in her sleep. Charles hired her on the spot in Marseille; already, on our first day in Egypt, I am trying not to be irritated.

"Trautwein, wait in the vestibule. I'll see you are given water and something to eat while Mrs. Bracebridge and I visit the baths." "Trout," as I privately call her, shows no interest in the exotic country she finds herself in. Knit, knit, knit is what she does—that and chew with her mouth wide open. She refused the hammam when Selina invited her, preferring the hotel's washstand with its cracked pitcher and basin.

Two female attendants come into the tiled vestibule, lead us down a marble hallway to a large octagonal room that is sweatingly hot. Sunlight pierces stars through dozens of tiny windows cut in the high, domed ceiling. Taken into a private chamber, I am undressed by the attendant and wrapped in a plain linen towel. She gestures for me to lie down on the white marble floor. Kneeling, she unwraps the towel and begins to massage each of my limbs with long, practiced strokes, her hands scented with rose oil. Closing my eyes, I give in to blissful waves of pleasure. Using a brush of bound palm fibers, she scrubs my bare, oiled skin until the grime of a weeklong sailing journey, crammed into the *Merlin*'s foul quarters, is stripped away. Next, she helps me to stand and, using a clay pitcher, pours streams of rose-scented water over my body. Patting me dry, she wraps me in another towel and escorts me back to the sunny, steamy octagon-shaped room. All without a word. Stretching out on a sun-warmed marble bench, I close my eyes, hoping for a new, better life to begin.

After the visit to the hammam, during which Trout put more length on the ugly black thing she clicks and clacks away on, I tell

Ali, who has returned for us, that I would like to see the inside of the nearest mosque. Accustomed to eccentric requests from English tourists, he explains that I must first return to the hotel to change clothing. Foreigners are forbidden entry to mosques, so I must disguise myself. He will bring the clothing I need and ask the British consul, Mr. Gilbert, to join us.

Parthe,

> *Today Mrs. Bracebridge and I went to a Turkish hammam, where we were scrubbed back to our birth skins. Afterward, disguised as a local Arab woman, I went inside a mosque. I wore a blue silk sheet (one's head pokes through a hole in the middle), a white strip of muslin fitting over the nose like a horse's nose bag, followed by a second, stiff band that passes between one's eyes, then over and behind one's head, much like a horse's halter, followed by a white veil. A sort of black silk balloon is then pinned to the top of one's head, with two loops at the ends through which one sticks one's wrists—this holds the whole contraption together. How does one breathe? you ask. Through one's eyes!*
>
> *Well camouflaged, I staggered behind my young Arab protector, Ali, and the self-important figure of Mr. Gilbert, the British consul. I ducked into the mosque, packed to the gills for afternoon prayer, remembering Mr. Gilbert's admonition to hide my hands. I observed how the men were granted full freedom to lie about, talking, playing at games, even sleeping, before prayers began, while the women huddled together, not talking, barely moving, like so many mummies, only their eyes peeking above their veils. I admit to feeling a little disgusted by a society that treats its women so. Before leaving, I climbed the spiral staircase to the minaret and listened as the call to prayer*

rang out over Alexandria. Leaving the mosque and stumbling along in my odd getup back to Hôtel d'Europe, I changed clothes in time for evensong in a tiny English church close by. Now I am tired, dear sister, and will write more tomorrow.

Yours,
Flo

Commonplace

THIS MORNING I VISITED A MEDICAL CLINIC run by the Sisters of St. Vincent de Paul. Nineteen French nuns treat hundreds of Arabs who come and stand politely in long lines each day. They have invited me to return tomorrow to help dispense and compound medicines, bleed and dress wounds. The miserable poverty in this city is like nothing I have seen, not even in the worst of our European cities. Many who come to see these nuns suffer from diarrhea, dysentery, and opthamalia, a chronic inflammation of the eye said to be most painful. While we wait for the ferry that will take us to Cairo, I hope to work with these good sisters.

I have passed a whole day not thinking of him. If it is true that distance dissolves ties, may Egypt annihilate my guilty, covetous dreams.

As for Monk, had we married, I am convinced he would have expected me to host his many breakfasts and dinners. I would have become that thing I most dread, an ornament to a man. Who has not heard such stories, common as weeds? So few women escape diminishment.

Parthe's Petticoat Flag

December 1849

Dearest Family,

No doubt this finds all of you sitting around the breakfast table without the clairvoyance I should wish you to have. Since you cannot see me, I will attempt a description of our journey.

Beginning in autumn, winds blow up the Nile north to south, so yesterday, we set off to make the most of the good winds we did have. Our captain, a terse misanthrope, explained that should the winds carry us past certain tombs, we will stop to see them on the way back. Autumn is a short season here, the summer's heat ended, winter's cold not yet set in.

We moved into our barque yesterday, our dahabiya, and cast off our lines, loosened the sails, and set off upstream against the current, toward Abu Simbel. Paolo, our interpreter, repeats what the captain told us, that we sail when winds are fair, and what we miss on the way upriver, we will see on the way down.

Time is not measured in timetables, almanacs, lists, calendars, charts, or clocks. The Nile is the one single road through Egypt, and our floating home is subject to winds, currents, all the whims and furies of nature. Soon I will measure the hours and days by what meals I've eaten, temples and tombs visited, birds spotted (owl, osprey, white ibis, and moorhen so far) and by the unfailing rise and set of sun and moon. It is a languid existence, disorienting to a creature like myself, who prefers planning, listing, counting, reasoning. I am that most pathetic of English creatures, dependent upon clocks and calendars, certainties and facts. Here, on the Nile, no measurement exists beyond the wind's direction and the water's current. All is in God's hands, not ours.

Tell Parthenope I have named our ship after her. Using a strip from my petticoat, I spelled her name from Greek letters cut and taped along its length. I did endless stitching, used up all my white tape, added a Latin red cross and four swallows cut from blue bunting. Our "petticoat flag" was hoisted this morning at the yardarm. A Union Jack flies at the stern, and Mr. Bracebridge's colors are halfway up the rigging.

Our rented dahabiya (it belongs to a local official, Hasan Bey, and normally serves as the boat for his harem!) has a cabin for the B's, and one for myself, each furnished with a mattress of beaten cotton. Trout, a massive German flounder, snores on a divan in the green-painted sitting room. I had read that in getting a boat ready for travel, it must be submerged in the river to rid it of rats, but we had no time, so, for us, rat traps will have to do. Fleas are constant companions. We are all discreetly scratching. Even as I write, the fleas jump onto my paper! Our things are organized and stowed, our little library of books lined up on its shelf; the divans are out, our Turkish slippers beside them. Everything is on its proper hook, our food hung high to keep it from rats. There is bread in a basket, meat in a safe, oranges in a box, and three great clay jars of water. How tidy we are in our nutshell!

There are eight sailors to eight sets of oars. These same men climb the riggings, furling and unfurling two white cotton sails. Silent by day, by night they sing and beat, drumlike, on water jars. Selina has sewn each of them a pair of flannel drawers and makes them wear them, for modesty, beneath their long, loose blue shirts.

We are sailing to Abu Simbel, going beyond the first cataract to our end destination, a place on the very edge of Africa.

A hopeless description, but torpor afflicts all of us, drifting along the Nile. A lassitude quite impossible to shake off. Pazienza!

All love from your "Wild Ass of the Wilderness"—so the B's have taken to calling me. They claim I am as obdurate as an Egyptian jackass, as prone to misadventure!

Flo

Commonplace

OUR DAHABIYA IS A STURDY LITTLE LEAF journeying down the river of Eternity. Wind fills the triangular white cotton sail, deck timbers creak, the crew sings as they pull us upstream, toward Africa. It is a mysterious feeling, as if I have entered a watery passageway into the underworld and drift through a valley, not of death, but down a river where, along the shorelines (and the Nile changes color capriciously, from green to yellow to bluish gray), all those one has ever known in life appear as wavering ghosts, spirits with great imploring eyes and outstretched arms.

Were I able to rouse myself, I would no doubt find Mr. B. reading and puffing on his pipe, Selina sketching the white minarets of Cairo, and Trout, her broad back turned to every wonder of the world, knitting yet another grim row of squares. From the shoreline, hidden deep within the spiky green fronds of a palm forest, comes the desolate howl of golden jackals.

Abu Simbel

January 1850

B Y MIDMORNING, THE *PARTHENOPE* IS SECURED, tied between two great temples. Delighted to find ourselves the sole visitors, the Bracebridges and I prepare, with Paolo's help, to hike to the first and largest of the two temples. Charles leads the way, sporting a felted pith helmet wound round with a turban of white muslin. He is followed by Selina, a green eyeshade attached to her black bonnet, and myself, wearing a pair of green-tinted spectacles with gauze sides to protect against the glare.

"No parrots, no gold dust, eh? No boats filled with ostrich feathers and elephants' teeth, as von Minutoli's travel dispatches would have us believe—we see no such marvels—but look ahead, ladies, can anything be grander than those two temples cut cheek by jowl over a thousand years ago into a mountain of sandstone? Good God, eh?" Charles stops, lifts his helmet, mops his forehead, drinks from his water flask before plunging ahead, eager to be first inside the Great Temple. Paolo and I follow; Selina falls behind, fretting over the state of one of her boots, its strap broken.

As the others go inside the Great Temple, I break off, walk to the second temple. Inside, the scale and eerie quiet within this place, dedicated to cow-headed Hathor, goddess of nursing, is profound. Passing between evenly spaced columns of stone, each crowned with a head of Hathor, I plunge deeper into the dim, cool interior, study images of Ramses II carved into the walls.

Here he is seated beside Isetnofret, his second wife, mother of his favorite sons, a woman given equal size and power to her husband. Stopping before another image of Ramses II, I notice he is crowned by symbols for good and evil alike, and am struck by a thought: *What theory of the world goes further than the idea in this temple? That evil is not good's opposite, but its* collaborator—*evil as the left hand of God as much as the good is His right. A profound, unsettling philosophy.*

"Madam?" Paolo, our guide, has come in search of me.

I follow him into a hot glare of sunlight, slipping and scrambling up a sand dune that has, over eons, blown and settled against the opening of the first temple. On hands and knees, I wriggle into a three-foot space beneath the great doorway and slide feetfirst, as if down a twenty-foot chute, to land on the temple floor, where Charles gallantly brings me to my feet. In its scale, this first temple is far grander, yet I am less moved. When we return the next day, Selina with her sketchbook and pencils, Charles with a canvas sack of candles, I study, more deliberately, the rows of engraved columns, each formed in Osiris's image. Osiris, god of the underworld. By the light of one of Charles's candles, I admire the inner sanctuary of the four creator gods—Ptah, Ra, Amun, Khnum; beside me, Charles intones their names from his pocket guidebook. "Rather like musical notes, eh? Ptah, Ra, Amun, Khnum."

"Charles," Selina admonishes. "You would make a joke of eternity."

I wander off to examine other engravings on the walls. Here is Osiris, performing acts of heroism; here is Ramses II, deep in prayer. There is a feeling of sacredness inside these temples more tangible and occult than in any church I have yet entered. Climbing out of the temple, sliding down one of the great drifts of sand, trailing behind the others, I stumble over the skeleton of a camel, sun-bleached, ghastly, and recall reading about Napoléon's camel corps during his Egyptian campaign, how his French soldiers, corpsmen, suffered from "camel sickness" as they swayed atop their Bactrian camels over a sea of rolling desert, much as sailors suffer ocean sickness.

At a tactful distance, Paolo keeps watch.

Holy Isle

A THOUSAND MILES FROM ALEXANDRIA, having reached Abu Simbel, we turn back. Our laconic captain says he will stop at the island of Philae so we may explore the Temple of Isis.

I have adopted several chameleons as pets. I find it amusing to watch their colors change, see how deftly they catch the fleas that constantly plague us.

It is late in the season. Temperatures remain high, the river's level low. Charles claims that on Philae we may come across a nilometer, an ancient instrument that measures the changing depths of the river.

Since visiting Abu Simbel and being forcibly struck by the idea inscribed in Hathor's temple—that evil is as necessary to life as good—I find myself wondering how the god of the underworld would judge the balance of my deeds up to now.

It is near midnight when we sail up to the island of Philae. The *Parthenope* drops its lines as a spectacular full moon lights the walls of the temples of Isis and Osiris. I have been reading about Jesus and His mother, the uncanny parallels to Isis and Horus, her son. With everyone asleep but the crew and no one to hinder me, I wade ashore and climb the rocky path to the temple. Stepping between a pair of enormous stone columns, I enter an immense forecourt flooded with moonlight. In that instant, by the moon's ghostly, supernal light, I am certain I glimpse *Him*. Christ's *shadow*.

Dearest Family,

I write to you from the Holy Isle of Philae, where we have already been for four days. It is another world here. It is Eternity. We arrived the twenty-second of January, and when all were asleep, I waded ashore and, alone, hiked up to the temple.

The story of Osiris is so like our Savior's, and I felt I was in the place where He once stood in Jerusalem. Coming into the moonlit courtyard, I glimpsed a tall, shadowy figure standing between the stately temple colonnades. Do not Christian ideas begin here, with the story of Osiris and Isis?

Do you recall that story? How Osiris marries his sister, Isis; then Osiris's brother, Seth, marries Isis's sister. Osiris and Isis rule along the Nile, while Seth and his wife govern the outer wastelands. Jealous of his brother, Seth kills Osiris. Isis finds his body and hides it in the Nile Delta. Seth, finding it, cuts it into fourteen pieces. Gathering up all the pieces but one (lost— another story!), Isis puts the body back together, wraps it in linen. Changing into a bird, she hovers above Osiris and, in an act of divine conception, conceives their son, Horus. Wherever the fourteen pieces of Osiris's body fell, cults formed. In hope of an afterlife, Egyptians paid to have their corpses wrapped in linen. On this island, Isis is still worshipped, and on nearby Biga, where a piece of Osiris is said to have fallen, there is a cult that worships him.

The story of Isis and her divinely conceived child, Horus. The story of Mary and her divinely conceived child, Jesus. Does not all human life spring from one source—from holy, eternal mater?

Affec
Florence

✍

Why should one God be any less plausible than another? Why do we put greater faith in those gods who suffer? I trace with my fingers, counting lotus blossoms running in a sandstone frieze along the wall, each blossom one year. By the dark measure of my fingertips, Osiris was not yet thirty at his death, Jesus but a few years older when he died.

In four months, I will be thirty.

The B's consult their guidebooks, make preparations for another exploration of Isis's temple. Trautwein has taken to her divan with an earache. I wade ashore a last time, hike up to the temple. Crossing the massive courtyard, I climb to the roof, descend into the earthen chamber. Lifting the baptismal cross from around my neck, a glint of gold in the half-light, I lay it in its little scooped-out grave, kneel until my limbs ache. Childhood fears, failures, wrong loves, all buried now.

Temple of Seti I

THE CREW OF THE PARTHENOPE PULLS ON all eight oars, skimming along the Nile. They row us toward Luxor, through a storm churning the river to brown, heaving yellow foam, turning the sky to swirls of ocher mist. Coming out from the worst of the storm, we pass a fringe of electric yellow-green growth along the riverbank, a tightly bunched flock of sheep stumbling down a hill of pinkish sand toward the river. Women in rags walk behind goatherds, stoop to collect dung in baskets. Water buffalo with great lyre-shaped horns stand up to their water-blackened flanks in the river. Children splash in the shallows, their mothers alert to the deadly stealth of crocodiles. Palm trees droop with heavy clusters of amber dates. Beneath us, the chameleon Nile—silt yellow, mineral green, hard pewter, mouse dun.

Trautwein clicks her needles, her earache better. My remedy of a warm compress with drops of laudanum has brought relief. Poor Trout. She hates this hostile landscape. By keeping her head down, knitting, she imagines she has not left her homeland, is less frightened.

By midday, the *Parthenope* is tied up near Luxor. Grayish donkeys, a dozen or so, stampede down grassy dunes; some swim out to meet our battered little dinghy. On shore, I am helped onto one donkey's back by an old man smacking its bony rump with a palm stick. Jolting along with Charles, Selina, and our guide, we come to the first tomb, dismount, and go inside. Lit by local guides holding resin torches, it is an unspectacular site, so we ride

to a newly opened second tomb, cut into a sandstone cliff. Crawling in on hands and knees, we immediately back out, fleeing the
ugliness, the fluttering bats, dung beetles, and cockroaches, grateful, on emerging, to find a feast of bread and sweet, splitting dates
laid out for us on a table of rock.

Commonplace

WE ARRIVE AT LUXOR, THE FORMER CITY of Thebes. We are in the Valley of the Kings. Karnak, et cetera. I feel poorly. Sore throat, fever. Staying on board. Old, familiar demons possess my head. The arid whine of mosquitoes.

Sycamore

I STAND ON THE RIVERBANK NEAR QURNA, the mortuary temple of Pharaoh Seti I. Near the temple pylons, the *Parthenope* is tied to an ancient sycamore. The tree's figs are food for the dead, who, in the form of birds, rustle among its mottled branches. While the Bracebridges have gone off to explore the Luxor side of the river, I keep to the shade of this small, lesser-known temple, move with the sun as it shifts between colonnades. My view to the west: bright green cornfields, a palm garden. To the east, across the Nile and above the colonnades of Luxor Temple: a plantation of tall, spindly date palms.

I walk into the temple as a cloud of white-plumaged birds bursts from the limbs of the sycamore.

In the temple's darkness, I hear God.

Thirteen years. Waiting.

Commonplace

February–March 1850

THE *PARTHENOPE* IS UNTIED FROM the low-spreading sycamore. The river is choppy; wind stirs low eddies of dust along the passing shore. It picks up force, becalms the dahabiya, so the crew must go ashore and, with long twists of rope, tow the boat downstream. Sand, fine-grained, ocher, obscures everything. On board, eerie winds shriek and whistle through the pitching boat. The red sand stings our eyes, cakes our hair, finds its way inside clothing, chafes our skin. Our mattresses of beaten cotton are coated with it; a half-cooked dinner tastes of grit in our mouths. As the boat rocks in the terrible wind, Trautwein huddles beneath the sand-reddened quilt on her divan, the tips of her Turkish slippers sticking out.

28 February 1850
Five days later, inside the gales of wind, the hissing of sand, I hear Him again.

7 March 1850
Wind shrieks, howls through slats in the wooden shutters of my cabin.

Do you hesitate between the God of the whole earth and your little reputation?

Madre's words now His.

9 March 1850

Unsteady in body and soul.

To be alone with Him, I manage to send Trout ashore to buy bread, dates, tea.

Help all who suffer.

By the time we reach the city of Memphis the dreaming sickness stops. It will never overtake me again.

17 March 1850

Trout has broken a tooth, Paolo has taken a fall and hurt his hip, and Charles is unwell. Our storm-battered little dahabiya—a hospital.

Palm Sunday

Cairo

Attending my last prayer service in the mosque, I discern no difference in the world's religions. At some point, do not all people acknowledge one God?

I will miss the steady plashing of oars in the Nile, drifting through the changing colors and currents of the river. Parthe's pennant is taken down, packed away with my things. Who will walk the boards of the former *Parthenope* once we are gone? The veiled women of the Pasha's harem? Every dahabiya, plagued by fleas and rats, should have its party of cats and chameleons on board.

Egypt. A rebirth. Letting God have His Way.

The annihilation of self.

Tomorrow we sail for Alexandria, then Athens and home.

PART FIVE

Going Mad

Thirty now, the same age at which Christ began His mission. No more childish things, no more vain things, no more love, no more marriage. Now, Lord, let me think only of Thy will.

—Florence Nightingale
12 May 1850

I sought Him but did not find Him,
I called to Him, but he did not answer me.

—Song of Solomon 3:1

Two Pets in One

Lea Hurst
August 1850

"**B**RAVE BEASTIE, TRAVELED ALL THE WAY from the Parthenon! Patience, I'll soon find you a bit of meat."

In the pocket of her dusty travel dress, Athena stirs a little. In another pocket, hidden in a cedar box with brass hinges—her second captive, a cicada. The journey from Athens to London's Euston Station, to Amber Gate and home, has been too long for all of them.

Miss Edgarton's *Floral Fortune-Teller: A Game for the Season of Flowers*, drops from Parthe's hands, hitting the carpet. She runs as fast as her petticoats will allow, flinging her arms around what she had at first thought a specter—Flo, away too long to ever possibly be forgiven. She covers her sister with caresses, cries of welcome and reproach.

"The time away has suited you." Their dinner finished, Frances Nightingale smiles, passes around a box of Egyptian dates—one of her daughter's many gifts. Strewn across the mahogany table are shawls from Cairo's silk merchants, jewelry from that same city's goldsmiths, dozens of daguerreotypes with sepia images of camels, pyramids, palm trees, markets. Draped around Parthenope's shoulders is the "petticoat flag," her name sewn on it in Greek letters, the very pennant that had fluttered up the Nile from Cairo to Abu Simbel and back again, a journey so exotic, Parthe can scarcely imagine it. Next to Florence's water glass sits a little cedar box. Perched on her shoulder, a small speckled owl plucks shreds of lamb from her fingertips.

"Savage beast." William Nightingale holds up one forefinger, bandaged with a napkin.

"Sorry, Papa."

"Well named after the goddess of war."

"War and wisdom. She'll like you in time."

"Tell us how you found Athena." Frances Nightingale selects another of the sweet, moist dates. "I've sent Kitty to find a nicer home for the other creature."

"Thank you, Mama. Plato needs a bit of twig, plus a damp towel to drink from."

"Horrid thing." Parthe wrinkles her nose in distaste. "I don't know how you can bear to have it near you. But Athena is a darling little puffball! Tell us how you saved her."

"I was leaving the Parthenon, a bit ahead of the Bracebridges, when I saw some street urchins huddled around something at the bottom of some steps. Whatever had their attention, judging by their excited jabbing with sticks, was clearly being tormented. I went over and found a baby owl on its back, terrified. Mr. Bracebridge, who is fluent in Greek, hurried down the steps to question the boys. The owl, they told him, had fallen from a nest nearby. I scooped up the tiny creature—she weighed nothing, a handful of feathers—while Mr. Bracebridge, giving the boys six *lepta* to divide between them, told them to run off. I carried her home in my shawl, and Selina found a wooden box for her bed."

"And you've trained her?"

"To bow, to curtsy, and, as you see, take food from my fingers."

"What is that dear little overcoat she wears?" asks Mrs. Nightingale.

"Selina sewed her a little travel sack. Her head sticks out so she can look all around. She is content in it, though she prefers to ride on my shoulder or on top of my head."

"She looks to be twenty centimeters." Mr. Nightingale unwinds his napkin to inspect the red spot where the owl pecked his finger. "*Athene noctua* means 'little owl.' I wonder how long such a creature lives?"

"I'm not sure how long they live in captivity, Papa. In nature, Athena would live ten or so years."

"See what Kitty has found," Mrs. Nightingale says. "A mustard pot!"

Florence taps the red-eyed cicada out of its box into a sterling and glass mustard pot. Closes the lid. Cicadas, she explains, have no lips or tongue, so Plato "drinks" by sucking moisture with its mouthpart. With an expression of revulsion, Parthe passes her sister a water-dampened handkerchief to drop into the pot.

"I could never make a pet of something so hideous. Oh, look, Athena's eyes are closed. Is she asleep? I'm much fonder of her than that other thing."

Mr. Nightingale, eager to impart knowledge where it is needed, takes on a pedantic tone.

"The Greeks were fond of cicadas. They saw them as symbols of death and rebirth and even dedicated poems of praise to them."

"I wish I had stayed longer in Greece, Papa. There was still so much to see there."

Parthenope pushes back her chair, leaves the room.

"What did I say? What is the matter with her?"

Mrs. Nightingale sighs. "She was convinced you were never coming home."

"That's absurd. I'm here, aren't I?" She points to the mustard pot. "I've even brought friends."

William Nightingale clears his throat. "Shall we retire to the drawing room? Your mother and I would like a word with you."

Not twenty-four hours and already a crisis.

"Certainly, Papa."

Frances Nightingale attempts false cheer. "Bring Plato along, dear. I wouldn't want the servants to discover a foreign insect hiding in a mustard pot. Thank you for your gifts, Flo. We cherish them."

The Nile, the tombs and temples, my rebirth in Him. How distant it all seems—did it even happen?

As they settle near the hearth, Florence, sitting in her sister's chair, reaches down to pick up the book Parthe had dropped earlier: *The Floral Fortune-Teller: A Game for the Season of Flowers*. Leafs through it. The book is filled with poems and phrases by well-known writers, each paired with an illustrated species of flower. The game is to assemble a bouquet of five different flowers, then read one's fortune according to the flowers one has chosen. Destiny in a buttercup, fortune in a geranium. Very Parthe-ish. She shuts the book as a servant comes in to stir the embers and adjust the oil lamps. The mantel clock chimes half past eight; in the foyer, the tall clock echoes the hour. The old sensations of captivity, boredom, suffocation, close in.

Mrs. Nightingale, her false cheer evaporated, turns to her daughter. "Parthe suffered in your absence. For a time, she tried to be like you, going into the village to care for those who were ill. But she hasn't your temperament and came home unwell herself. She kept on her person those few letters you managed to send."

Her mother's criticism is not lost on Florence. Mr. Nightingale speaks.

"We grew so concerned about Parthenope, we wrote to James Clark, the queen's physician."

"I know of him, Papa. He is a friend of Monckton Milnes

and was John Keats's physician in Rome. What was Dr. Clark's opinion?"

"He diagnosed your sister with debilitating depression, then wrote out a list of diversions—amusements, special foods, short visits to friends, relatives, et cetera—for us to try. The 'prescription' worked for a time; then she fell back into her same state."

"We worried for you, too, dear, being so very far away. Your letters arrived weeks after you'd written them, and when a letter did come, Parthe tore it open at once."

"Now that you are home with us, your mother hopes Parthenope will be well again."

Home for a moment. I am called to Kaiserwerth to learn nursing. I am certain it is part of God's plan for me. Stay? Families are nothing if not tyranny. Hysteria. Clinging on.

"Florence. Are you not glad to be home?"

"I am pleased to see you and Papa looking well."

"You must stay until Parthenope is herself again."

"How long might that be, Papa?"

"She already fears your leaving again. She is most unsettled in her mind. These past months have frightened your mother and me."

"What can I do?"

"Remain with us until she is better."

"How long?"

"Six months? It is hard to say."

Six months? I will die here.

"Flo."

"Yes, Mama?"

"One caution. On no condition must you speak about that hospital in Germany, Kaiserwerth. You must not say anything about nurses or nursing or your going away. She cannot bear it. Speak of immediate surroundings, of light, pleasant things. Your sister has literally pined away for you. At times, I feared for her life."

"Fanny, that's a bit dramatic."

"No, William, it isn't. Dr. Clark has seen patients much like Parthenope perish of heartbreak."

Florence stands abruptly. "Enough. I will stay until you think she is well."

Startled by the sudden movement, Athena flaps soundlessly across the drawing room, settles on a set of oversized geography books held between a bronze bookend of Theseus and another of Mercury. As for the cicada, in three days' time, it will become Athena's dinner, after Mr. Nightingale, lifting Plato from his mustard pot to better compare him to an illustration in his world compendium of insects, neglects to close the silver lid when he puts it back.

On being told, Florence shrugs, saying her two pets have turned into one.

Commonplace

FOUR MONTHS AND STILL I AM MET with daily hysterics. Whatever I say vexes her; whatever I do makes her cross. Mama insists it will be far worse for Parthe should I leave, yet each day I am made to feel like the assassin, not the savior, of my sister.

A letter from Liz Herbert with news of a second child, a boy. She mentions Sidney's being away too long in London, invites me to Wilton House. Staring at his name, penned in his wife's flowing, graceful hand, I force myself to feel nothing.

A letter, too, from Pastor Fliedner, asking when will I be coming to Kaiserwerth to study nursing. My application has been approved. I would be there this minute! Why am I here, in this house? A seething creature, poisoned by rage, with an oversized brain.

Portraits

"MY NECK ACHES. How much longer?"

"Nearly done. Sorry, Flo."

"I must go into to the village, sit with Mrs. Fernsby. She hasn't long."

"Fiddlesticks! What is it you *like* so much about death?"

The sound of ripping paper.

"Why are you tearing up your sketch?"

"I can't draw when we are quarreling."

"We're not quarreling. You're overexcited."

"And why am I 'overexcited'? Because you'd rather be anywhere with anyone, doing anything than be with me."

"I'm sorry, I—"

"You'd rather visit the poor, the sick, the disgusting and dying than do nice things and go pleasant places with me."

"You mean gig to other people's homes, babble and tattle on about nothing, then leave a calling card so they can return the favor?"

"What is wrong with visiting one's neighbors, having conversation and tea?"

"Everything, Parthe. Everything is wrong with it. It's a twaddling life for imbeciles."

"Oh? I'm a twaddling imbecile? You're mean, Florence. A mean person. I don't wonder Mr. Milnes married Annabelle Crewe. From what I hear, they are perfectly devoted to each other."

That hurts. I miss Monk and haven't seen or heard a word from him since that terrible Whitsunday.

Parthenope's face is hot, splotched-looking. Flinging herself facedown on the silk divan, she sobs, shoulders heaving. *An act. Childish, transparent.*

"Nothing I do pleases you, Parthe. I cannot say a word without vexing you, yet if I am quiet, I am condemned for that, too. I have no idea what you want from me. What are you doing?"

For the past week, Pop has made dozens of sketches of me, Athena perched on my shoulder. Now she is sitting up, furiously ripping those same drawings to pieces.

"Why must you leave? Why do you not love me? That is all I want. For you to stay with me."

"That is what I have been doing, Parthe."

"Mama agrees you are cold, unfeeling."

"Does she? Well, you are both wrong. I feel a great deal, just not for the same things you do."

"You are entirely selfish. Disloyal. To me, especially."

From the carpet by my feet, a torn bit of my face stares up. A single baleful eye.

"I am sorry you are unhappy, but can any of us help who we are? Stop ripping up your drawings and look at me. Listen to me. I do love you, but since Egypt, I am called to be other than who you wish me to be. It is that simple."

She rushes over to embrace me, her chin smudged with charcoal. "I do so love you, Flo, but no, you do not love me back."

"I do. And if you would support me, even a little, our love as sisters could grow."

"I try, I do, but every day a new wound opens. Letters from Wilton House. Kaiserwerth."

"You have made a medical metaphor." I smile, trying for calm.

"I have, haven't I? Oh, look what Athena has done!"

Perched on the mantel, beside a foul scrap of excrement, she regards us with huge, blameless eyes.

With the toe of one boot, I nudge at Pop's torn sketches, scattered over the carpet.

"You've demolished me."

"Kitty will pick those up. I'll draw more."

"Do me a favor, Pop?"

"What?"

"Stop drawing me every minute. It's embarrassing. Can you not draw something or someone else?"

"But, Flo. Since you've come home, sketching is my best way of loving you."

Hopeless. I may as well be in prison. Or dead. She will never let go.

I dig down, find Athena's carrying pouch in my skirt pocket. "Help me dress her; we'll take her with us on our walk."

Thirst

Embley
May 1851

"Papa, do you know what I see whenever I pass by the big windows in the drawing room?"

He returns his quill to its stand. My father is writing a memoir. An intelligent man with no need to earn an income has ample time, it seems, to record the minutiae of his life.

"Your mother's rose garden?"

"I imagine the room full of hospital beds with patients sitting up, looking out the windows."

"You would turn our family's drawing room into a hospital ward?"

"Just as I would turn cathedrals into hospitals."

He frowns. Florence's tendency to dramatization, her passionate exaggerations, cannot come from his side, the Shores. It must come from the Smith side, his wife's politically volatile family.

"Papa. My Kaiserwerth application is accepted. Pastor Fliedner invites me to train with his deaconesses. He suggests I stay three months."

William rubs his eyes with his fists.

"Do your eyes pain you?"

"They have hurt all week. My far sight blurs from time to time."

"A compress of comfrey root and chamomile will help." *How I crave understanding. Permission. The freedom to leave.*

"You are kind, Florence. I will try a compress before asking the doctor to come."

He says nothing about Kaiserwerth. Not one word.

Papa's eyes are soon better, but I revert to my old dreaming sickness. Shut away in my bedroom, I invent thrilling lives for myself, perform heroic deeds. I cure the sick, invent new medicines, design and build hospitals. . . . *As bad as gin drinking. My thirst increases the more I slake it. Dreaming saps my strength, until I have but one frightening impulse, one temptation, left.*

In May, on my thirty-first birthday, bidding my family good night before going upstairs, words, bitter, long suppressed, burst from me.

"I will say it though none of you will hear. When I go up to my room each night, I have but one prayer. That my bed will be my grave."

Strict Order

Lea Hurst

June 1851

FOR DAYS NOW, HEAVY SHEETS OF RAIN, a biblical deluge, have fallen continuously. The air is humid, oppressive, the skies dark and thunderous-looking. By afternoon, lightning flickers, followed by the slow tread of thunder, like the approach of an invisible army. Every mud-sloshed road in Derbyshire runs with rills, streams, runnels of water. Lakes of rainwater shimmer over fields and pastures. Tying on my bonnet, I slog, day after day, to the village school.

My regimen is strict. Up before dawn, light the bedside lamp, study. Dress, go down to breakfast at eight. Walk thirty minutes to the local school, teach the children for two hours. Return home, act pleasant. Join Parthe and Mama in their tiresome, frivolous pursuits until dinnertime. Read, go to bed.

Anything to slow this ceaseless irritation, sleeplessness, and disturbed dreaming. But with each day, the regimen hollows out, works less well, until I am half-terrified, half-resigned to what may become of me.

Commonplace

OVER DINNER, PARTHE IS PEEVISH, demanding to know why I must always "blow a trumpet." Her exact words. I have no idea what she means but answer that all real struggle must make a noise, and that to accomplish anything in this house there has to be a loud, if not an obnoxious, struggle.

I have begun collecting lead pieces, hiding them in a box beneath my bed.

Rid of Me

DESPITE THE STEADY RAIN and blustery winds, Mrs. Nightingale and Parthenope brave the half-drowned roads to visit relatives. I beg off, complaining I am unwell, and ask if Parthe will take Athena. Look after her.

What honest relief in their faces, to be rid of me.

Upstairs, I sit down to write.

Deprived of meaningful activity in the world, imprisoned within the bonds of family, denied the slightest departure from "proper womanhood . . ."

I crumple up the paper. Dig my pen into a fresh sheet, press a single terrifying truth on it.

The following morning, I do not study, I do not go down to breakfast, I do not visit Papa in his library. I do not even go to the local school. I will do no more of these or any other things.

Near Tragedy

FROM THE LANDING, WILLIAM NIGHTINGALE calls upstairs. She'd not come down to dinner the previous night, complaining of a headache. She has not appeared at breakfast. Hearing no response, he takes the stairs. The door is unlocked, her bed is neat, unslept in. He stoops near the desk to retrieve a piece of writing paper, uncrumples and reads it.

Raising his eyes from the half-finished sentence, he stares out her window to a misty view of the stone terrace, the broad terrace steps with their stone columns, the green meadow, and, beyond the meadow, the woodlands that slope down to the banks of the rain-swollen Derwent.

Where is she?

At that moment he spots a dark, still shape at the farthest edge of the meadow. Hurtling downstairs, flinging open the front door, shouting her name, he runs.

In her cold, lifeless-seeming hand, a small vial of white powder. Pulling her to sitting, he strikes both cheeks hard. Strikes them red. Shouts her name. Her eyes flutter open, close.

She had not, thank God, taken the arsenic. She had simply laid down in the freezing, drenched meadow and begged for the rain to annihilate her.

Slipping the vial into his pocket, he helps her to her feet and, as he does, finds the dozens of lead pieces in her pockets. Weights. To drown herself with.

On the terrace, she whispers something.

"What is it, dear? I can't hear you."

"I wish to die, Papa."

"I know."

Removing her wet clothing by the library fire, he finds a second note folded in the breast pocket of her dress, the words rain-smeared, barely legible.

Unafraid of death. Already dead.

His hands shake as he watches the awful note burn in the flames. He nearly lost his "young squire," his youngest, whose intellectual powers impress anyone who meets her, a young woman whose one desire in life is to help the less fortunate. Could it be he and Frances have been wrong—that she does have some great, God-given purpose in life? She helped the affliction in his eyes, eased his digestive complaints when no one else could. He looks down at this odd, remarkable creature they created, asleep on the couch. He must do it. Give her what she wants, give in to the pleas he has, up to now, ignored. To hell with objections, fears, jealousies, tantrums. To hell with Frances. She must go to Kaiserwerth. If not, he will lose her. This morning he nearly did.

෴

"I can't imagine what's gotten into him." Mrs. Nightingale sighs, rereading her husband's letter. "He demands I cut our visit short, return home, and take Florence to Karlsbad. He gives his full permission for her to go to Kaiserwerth. You and I will visit the water spa."

"Obviously Flo did something dramatic. That's how she gets what she wants. I'm happy to go to Karlsbad, Mama. I hear the waters there are especially good."

PART SIX

The Institution of Kaiserwerth

July–September 1851

Düsseldorf

THE SERVANT, MARIE, STAYS with Parthenope at the spa's hotel while Mrs. Nightingale travels with Florence to Düsseldorf. She wants to see for herself where her daughter has chosen to waste the next three months of her life. But she had slept poorly; her head bangs like a drum. A terrible quarrel had erupted between her daughters at bedtime ("I should think when people have an entire day to themselves, they might give up a few hours in the evening to be with their family"—Parthe's complaint, met by Flo's cutting reply—"I have given up the whole of my life to be with you! Because of you, I have no life at all!"), ending with Parthe hurling a book at her sister, striking her in the chest, and Florence fainting dead away.

Touching the sore place on her chest where the hard edge of Parthe's book had struck it, Florence rests her forehead against the window of the carriage, eager for her first glimpse of Kaiserwerth. All she has ever seen are pencil drawings.

"Look, Mama. That must be the roof of the hospital."

But Frances is asleep, head lolling against the seat, mouth slightly open. Florence turns back to the window as a low outbuilding comes into view. She sees a few adult patients standing with attendants in the shady grounds, a group of children supervised by a deaconess, playing near the banks of the Rhine.

❧

Pastor Fliedner, the pink dome of his head stopping short of Mrs. Nightingale's shoulder, vigorously punches two fists into his ample hips, spreads his short legs wide. With an exultant blast of air, he looks over his Christian creation with pride.

"All our Protestant women come from an order of deaconesses, nurses whose members serve Christ. All are unmarried. Here at Kaiserwerth, we have established a hospital, an infant school, and an industrial school. Straight ahead you can see our newest addition, the Female Penitentiary, a halfway house for women released from imprisonment. We feed, clothe, and house these women, train them for reputable employment. Many are mothers, and we do our best to keep their children with them. Florence has a sister, is that right?"

"An older sister, yes."

"Is she interested in nursing and education as well?"

"I'm afraid not. My daughters are night and day."

"So often the case. Mrs. Fliedner and I are grateful to you and Mr. Nightingale for allowing Florence to remain with us. Judging from her letter of application and essay, she seems a fine young woman possessed of a superabundance of the virtues we look for in our deaconesses." Rising on his toes, he rubs his hands together, made buoyant by his tour, his vision come to fruition.

"What have I left out, Mrs. Nightingale? You have seen the infant school, the orphan asylum, the deaconess's dormitory. I have shown you the forty or so acres where we grow vegetables, herbs, and fruit trees, pasture our cows and horses. You have seen the new Female Penitentiary as well as our largest building, the one-hundred-bed Training Hospital. I began Kaiserwerth fifteen years ago in one building, an abandoned summer garden house. I envisioned an institution that would embody and practice the principles of Christian service to the poor. We strive to work in a spirit of Evangelical love. Now, it is late in the day and you must be anxious to begin your journey back to Karlsbad. Mrs. Fliedner is disappointed not to meet you, but she is attending a difficult child-birth case in town. I'll return you to the dormitory so you and your daughter may say your good-byes."

Hands clasped behind his back, coattails flapping, Pastor Flied-ner strides up the steep lane to a two-story dormitory, its plain entrance flanked by a pair of climbing roses in desperate need of water.

Before they can go in, a young woman steps from the door-way. Changed from her brown silk travel dress, velvet bonnet, and leather gloves, she wears the uniform of a deaconess, a dark blue dress and apron, white cotton collar and white linen scarf. The uniform, Pastor Fliedner explains to Frances, is meant to signal respectability and high moral character. Above the uniform, Flor-ence's reddish gold hair is covered by a snug-fitting plain white cap. Such serenity radiates from her daughter, Frances questions how little she knows this odd child of hers. To leave her in such a dreary, dispiriting place, with this puffed-up, garrulous pastor, may, as William insists, be exactly what Florence needs.

Letters Posted Here and There

August 1851

Dearest Mama,

One month and never happier. I've just come from compounding medicines at the apothecary station to write and reassure you I am exceedingly well.

As you know, I have never done my own hair in my life; now, each morning I do precisely that. I comb and part my hair, stick it back over my ears, pin it into a bun—a plain style made plainer by the small white cap that ties under my chin. Tell Parthe I do not think she would approve of my new look, but oh, I do take pride in self-sufficiency! Tell her, too, the food here is coarse, plenty of vegetables and broth, brown bread, very little meat but for an occasional mutton chop, and on Sundays a dessert that says it is apple Charlotte.

I have been given work in all areas—I teach English lessons in the school, take part in twice-daily church services, and, of course, work in the hospital.

With the orphan children, we celebrate birthdays, go on walks and little excursions. Pastor Fliedner's good (I should say "saintly") influence shows everywhere at Kaiserwerth, most especially in the prayerful atmosphere. On Sundays, during the Bible lesson, he asks the orphans to listen for the voice of God within them.

As for nursing, I clean and dress wounds, practice bandaging, compound various medicines. Yesterday, I learned to do a cupping and apply leeches of the Hirudo medicinalis type. The leeches are slimy, bloated, loathsome creatures, gathered by a local collector, a fellow named Figs, who wades bare-legged into ponds, waits for the leeches to attach themselves to his feet and calves, then walks out again!

Beginning next week, I am to assist at operations. Already I keep watch over patients at night, sit with those who are dying. I have become quite good at making hot, wet poultices with mustard or linseed, also soap and oil. I make fomentations and stupes (hot, wet, medicated pieces of muslin laid against the skin). Here the miasma theory is strongly adhered to, as it is in England. Breathing in foul or bad "night" air from decaying matter is to be avoided at all costs. I could go on with all I have learned in just four weeks, but I risk mortally boring you!!

Mama, know I am renewed in body and spirit, and that I should be sorry to leave such a life.

Write and tell me how you are, if Parthe's health has improved, if you have had any news from Papa. I've had only one letter, too short.

Yours,
Flo

September 1851

Selina,

You know how I have thirsted for "right work," and though I go to bed "dead beat" every night, I have never been happier than here at Kaiserwerth. I passed my first training and have put in a request to be assigned to seriously ill patients, especially the dying. Last night, an older gentleman, Karius, died quietly as I read aloud to him. Sitting on the windowsill beside his bed, looking out over the lighted town, it occurred to me that death is so much more impressive when it comes in the midst of life.

Parthe writes from various spas. In each of her letters, she complains of the heat, the food, the dull conversation, of how pretentious the people are. If Parthe and Mama could see how happy I am, training *as a nurse, if they could accept me as I am—why, then, all of us would rejoice in our love for one another.*

As for Athena, she is in Parthe's good care, well spoilt and plump.

Florence

September 1851

Dearest Flo,

This will be brief, as Charles is suffering an attack of gout, and I am run off my feet, tending to him. You are the idol of your sister's imagination. She cannot picture life without you, yet your life's purpose pulls you ever further from her. God has called you—if only she could accept that! Were you to return to your old existence, as she wishes, you would find life more insupportable than ever, now that you have had a taste of your "heart's choice."

Know there are those who love you, who champion your ideals and ideas, who hold faith in God's plan for you.

It is beastly here in London. Every afternoon, great towering clouds gather overhead, then fray to wisps, dashing any hope of rain. My petunias are dust!

Charles and I rejoice in your happiness, dear.

Utmost affection,
Selina

Meurer's Leg

I was sick and you visited me . . .

—*Matthew 25:36*

I KEEP METICULOUS NOTES, perfect charts, graphs, tallies of numbers. Before sleep, no matter the hour, I write down each day's observations, details of wounds, illnesses, deaths, recoveries. Last night I wrote of the importance of sitting up with patients during the night. Tonight, I describe assisting at my first amputation:

Thursday, 31 July 1851

9:00–11:00 A.M. Two doctors arrived, room prepared for Mr. Meurer's amputation, the leg taken off as high up as possible. Chloroform acted well. Dressing difficult. It was 10:30 A.M. before I left the room to tell Mother (Caroline Fliedner) that it was over. A beautiful operation. Patient suffered much in the afternoon. Cold water compresses every five minutes . . .

7:00–8:00 P.M. Sitting with patient. Prayed with him—he is Catholic. What made the operation difficult was the adhering of flesh to the skin from disease, preventing the reserving skin enough to fold over the wound, dressed with collodion strips. Taking up of the arteries was beautiful. Sawing of the bone momentary. Collodion strips removed, replaced by Maltese cross bandage.

Thursday, 7 August 1851

Sudden relapse. Meurer delirious, bleeds from nose and temples, falls into stupor. Bladder (cold pack) placed on head. Pulse 130. Cold water compresses on back of the neck, temples, hands, chest. 3:00–10:00 P.M. Sister Sophie and I put leeches on his temples. Meurer occasionally audible.

Friday, 8 August 1851

6:00–8:00 A.M. Bleeding at temples continues. Held dry compresses, pressing upward, with flat of hands

7:00 A.M. Extreme unction administered by priest. Patient unconscious.

9:00 A.M. Doctor declares typhus . . . every half an hour thirty drops of ether on the head; every two hours ice bladder removed. Anxiety Meurer's chief symptom—Chamomile compresses to the stump every hour . . . stump healing nicely. Acids every hour internally—& as much water as he can drink, mixed with raspberry vinegar. By evening the tongue and teeth are black.

Saturday, 9 August 1851

Meurer still alive

9:00 A.M. Doctor saw him & did not strip stump.

10:00 A.M. He was hardly breathing, then, in minutes, without struggle, died.

1:00 P.M. Body removed with all possible precautions—chloride of lime and vitriolic acid fumigating the room—taken to the chamber of the dead, where it was sprinkled with chloride of lime; no one allowed in.

Sunday, 10 August 1851

1:00–2:00 P.M. Two of Mr. Meurer's sisters came, not knowing of his amputation, wanting to see him. They had to be told of the amputation, then that he was ill & they could not see him & lastly that he was dead. Sister Amelia told them all this & did it beautifully. The doctor would not let them see his body. They went away brokenhearted.

What Manner of Man?

2 September 1851

Dearest Florence,

I hope these months at Kaiserwerth have proved a happy time for you and given rest to your spirit. Though I have always thought there were better things, happier things for you at home, though our opinions have differed as to what is the right path for you, believe me, we will do our best, Papa, Parthe, and myself, to have faith in you. Take our faith and love with you as you work out the road you are to walk, which leads you so very far from us all. You yourself cannot have been more thankful to Kaiserwerth than we have been, as balm in a thirsty land and a halt to your struggle with *life. We trust and believe you will return stronger & calmer for having had this rest to your spirit.*

Goodbye, my love. I cannot write long on such matters. It pains me. I will do my best to let you follow the manner of man *you are, though be merciful and do not lay upon me more than I am able to bear.*

Mama

Kaiserwerth
10 September 1851

Mother,

From now on, you must look upon me as your vagabond son. *For me, there is no turning back. No dangling about drawing rooms, no womanish needlework, no sitting around the sewing table, one reading to the other to "pass the time," no tinkling out pretty airs on the pianoforte, no exclaiming, pencil poised above paper, over bits of architecture. Do not give me the latest novel to read—give me the latest book of statistical tables! In numbers are God's laws revealed. Mine is not a punitive God, but one whose universe is scientific and, above all,* Benign! *Ours is the task, to measure, analyze, and live in harmony with His laws, to relieve suffering & cure disease through discovery and action. These will do more for humanity than any amount of kneeling in prayer. We must search out and adhere to the* science *in God's laws.*

As soon as I return home, I intend to look for work. Pastor Fliedner tells me of an order of nuns in Dublin that does exemplary nursing.

You must know me as you named me in your last letter—as your son—though without his inheritance.

M. Flo

PART SEVEN

Birkhall

Dr. Clark's Meteorological Pillar

Aberdeen, Scotland
September 1852

"How is she, Doctor? How is my sister?"

The tall case clock in the hall chimes as I stand in the doorway of his study, wearing my mud-spattered traveling cloak. Oblivious to my arrival, Sir James Clark, the queen's physician and now Parthe's, darts from one meteorological instrument to another, muttering to himself.

"Yes, yes, as I expected. Splendid numbers. Just so."

His steel gray hair springs in a frizzled aura from around the top and sides of his head, as if sparked by the weather patterns he is studying.

The study blazes with a second-long white shock of light, followed by the rolling peal and crack of thunder. At the sound, he strikes his hands together like an excited child, then glances up and sees me in the doorway.

"Ah! Miss Nightingale! You have braved the storm! Come, meet my newest acquisition. A sling psychrometer. Lovely, isn't she? I've named her Edith. You whirl or sling her handle through the air—like so—then measure the wet wrapped thermometer's humidity against the unwrapped one to find the relative humidity."

"Do you name all your meteorological instruments?"

"Yes, naturally."

He darts to the opposite end of the table, working his way back to where I stand, naming each one. "This is Clarissa, my brass Ausburg

equinoctial compass sundial. Here we have Frances, my cup ane-
mometer, she measures wind speeds—*ánemos* is Greek for wind,
you know. Hortense the hygrometer—Hortie measures moisture
content in the air. Here are Willy and Nilly, a pair of brass pocket
barometers, and Portia, a gentleman's portable dial thermometer.
My oldest instrument, Violetta, is Copeland's eighteenth-century
pluviometer, more simply, copper funnel rain gauge. Jove! I am boring you. I bore everyone. The subject of weather is not for the faint
of heart. My own interest began as a young man in the Royal Navy
at the height of the Napoleonic Wars."

"You have given most of them women's names."

"Hah! Ha ha! Not aware of that." He plucks a brown pocket
diary from inside his plaid waistcoat. "Must make a note of that.
Writing a new book, you see."

Jotting something down, presumably my comment about his
instruments having women's names, he pokes the diary back into
his waistcoat, straightens to his full height, smiles down at me.
Deep creases run parallel to the silver fringe of whiskers along his
cheeks. His overshot chin is compensated for by large gray, twin-
kling eyes. It is easy to see why the queen remains loyal to her private physician, despite rumors of his lethal incompetence. "I would
not trust Clark to attend a sick cat," George Villiers, the fourth earl
of Clarendon was quoted as saying in *The Gazette*. Like the queen,
my own mother is passionately, irrationally, devoted to Clark.

"Dobson will take your cloak and bring you a pot of tea, a nibble
of cheese toast, perhaps? You have come from . . ."

"Belfast. I traveled first to Dublin to study with the nuns at St.
Vincent's, but found the hospital closed for repairs. I ended up in
Belfast, where I kept busy touring orphanages, asylums, schools,
and hospitals, when I received a letter from my father with your
sister Charlotte's letter enclosed."

"Ah, good of Lottie to write, as I'd asked."

"How is she? Parthenope?"

"Asleep. Unless the storm has awakened her. Any storm, when accompanied by lightning, overexcites the blood. Not ideal for someone in her delicate condition."

He pulls up a chair beside the cold hearth, opposite his own, a worn blue leather monstrosity hedged in by slipping stacks of journals and half-opened books. To one side, a portable easel holds a pencil drawing of an elaborate weather instrument. I walk over, examine it.

"Ah. My meteorological pillar. I've commissioned her to be copied after an extraordinary pillar I saw in Salzburg, a weather station measuring temperature, barometric pressure, and humidity, an eight-foot-tall hybrid—from the Latin *hybrida*, meaning "mongrel"—of art and science. She is being made for me in London. Frightfully expensive, but Euphemia will be the crowning gem of my entire collection of meteorological instruments. She will be installed out of doors, on the front terrace. My dear, you are shivering. Is it too arctic in here? I'll have Dobson do up a fire for you. I abhor heat, you know, part of my theory about weather and its effects upon health. Bodies thrive best in cold. Drina—the queen—adores the cold, though the prince suffers from it, or so he complains. A hypochondriac of the first order. Chilblains, constipation, boils, ague, catarrh, the entire deck of cards. I doubt the man has enjoyed a single day free of complaint, and if he did have such a day, he wouldn't know what to do with it."

Dr. Clark rushes over to his cluttered table of instruments, returns with a book handsomely bound in black morocco leather with gilt lettering: *The Influence of Climate in the Prevention and Cure of Chronic Diseases, More Particularly of the Chest and Digestive Organs.*

"My second book on the powers of climate and mineral waters in the treatment of disease. Have you seen it? My gift to you. It's been extremely well received."

"Thank you, I shall read it," I say, though my more honest gratitude is reserved for Dobson, who has come in and is putting down a tray of hot tea and toast.

"Dobs, do build up a good fire. Miss Nightingale is unused to our frigid temperatures."

"Dobs," made into a shapeless lump by the number of sweaters and shawls piled on herself—she sports two caps as well—begins setting up a fire.

As I stir milk into a cup of strong black tea, Dr. Clark steeples his long, bony fingers, presses their tips to his forehead, as if lost in thought. Then reaching across a side table, he locates a pipe and pouch of tobacco.

"Permission?" He raises the pipe.

"My father smokes. I enjoy the scent."

The crowded study soon fills with the woodsy, amber fragrance of tobacco. In his blue leather chair, Dr. Clark tilts back his head, blows a series of perfectly round smoke rings.

It is clear I must prompt him.

"What can you tell me about my sister's condition?"

"Parthenope has been with us a month. I had Lottie write your father and recommend she be returned home immediately. Your parents are where now? Lea Hurst or Embley?"

"Lea Hurst. We return to Embley in November."

"Good grouse hunting in Derbyshire, though not as fine as here in Deeside. I bagged ten brace last weekend, so I expect you may find a bit of roast grouse on your dinner plate tonight. How long will you be staying?"

He seems to have forgotten my point in coming to Birkhall.

"I plan to leave tomorrow. Can you tell me more, Dr. Clark? About Parthenope's condition? My parents are most concerned about her."

"Of course. Poor creature."

Fiddling with his pipe, tamping moist shreds of tobacco into the pipe's bowl with a tiny silver instrument, he makes a long fuss of relighting it as the tall clock in the hall bongs its sad hours, seven now—have I been here this long?

I am weary from the journey from Belfast. Worn-out, too, from years of waiting for just such a misfortune—for Parthenope to break. I recall the dolls we played with as children, the rows of beds for our patients, the few we "buried" in the back garden, then resurrected. Parthe had been the sweetest child imaginable. We had been close. Inseparable. Rarely apart.

"She is dangerously unwell. I fear if she is not returned to her family, your sister's condition will further worsen, until she approaches a state of imbecility."

Imbecility?

"Her fixation is as obstinate a case of monomania as I have seen. It lifts, only to be replaced by shorter-lived fixations. Dresses, for instance."

"Dresses?"

"In a single week, she ordered dozens to be made and sent here to Birkhall from Aberdeen. Summer dresses, ball gowns, useless, extravagant things. Now she has fixed on pears."

"Pears?"

"She eats three a day. That is all she eats."

"Oh! What was that?" Something just skittered across my feet. Too light and agile for a dog or cat.

"Ha ha. Hahahaha! I expect you have met Rollie. We have the most marvelous species of red squirrel here in Deeside. *Sciurus vulgaris.* The queen you know, lives five miles from here, so I am often invited to Balmoral for dinner, or she comes here, riding her fat little Shetland while the prince consort is off in the woods, hunting stags, or out on the moor, shooting grouse or pheasants. A weak-chinned fellow, he finds strength in killing things. Ah, here is little Rollie. You must have startled him. I keep a bowl of hazelnuts for him. He's better behaved than his brothers and sisters."

"Brothers and sisters?"

"Squirrels have families, just as we do. It makes my sister Charlotte irate, but I always leave the front door ajar during the day so they can come in and out. Charming sight, a scurry of red squirrels bounding down hallways, streaking up and down the furniture. Rollie is my pet, aren't you, boy?"

As Dr. Clark feeds bits of nut to Rollie, I begin to tell him about Athena, how I found her on the steps of the Parthenon. He interrupts me.

"You must take her home at once. Your sister. With one caution."

"What is that?"

"You must leave home immediately afterward. If you stay in the same house with her, her condition will deteriorate beyond anyone's being able to help her."

"But what if she demands I stay with her? Her whole trouble began with my leaving!"

"A conundrum. If you stay, she breaks down. If you leave, she breaks down. I admit it's impossible. But based on similar cases and in my best medical opinion, to stay would be worse. With you gone, she may summon the mental strength to focus on other things. With you present, the wound festers, brain irritability increases, her obsession takes deeper root."

"What wound? What obsession? I don't understand."

"A poisonous jealousy. Debilitating envy. Parthenope is like a spurned lover where you are concerned. It is a pity there are only the two of you—another sister, or better, a brother, would have helped dilute that bond."

Have I not been my father's "son" all my life?

"About the pears, Dr. Clark . . ."

"Three unbroken crates in the cellar. You may take them with you."

"*Des poires?* Who speaks of pears?" An airy, feminine laugh.

I turn to see Parthe near the door of the study, spinning in a dreamy circle, wearing a summer dress of muslin the color of double cream. Her hair is loose, her legs and feet bare. The effect, summer in autumn, is chilling.

"Flo, is that you? Pray, what took so long?" She comes close, snaps open a painted fan, peeps flirtatiously over its top. "With so many patients, pitiful creatures with bandages to dress . . . and undress . . . that you have managed to find a single moment to spare for me . . ."

"Miss Nightingale. Calm yourself. Won't you join us for tea?"

"No, *danke.* I will ask Dobson for one pear, though. Peeled and rolled in white sugar. I'll give the peel to Rollie. Is he here? Rollll-ee . . ."

"He's gone off."

"Oh, *tant pis.* Waddly old rodent anyway. Nothing like Flo's *chouette.* My sister brought an owl home from Greece, you know."

"Yes, she'd begun telling me about it."

"Athena prefers me to her. Adores me, in fact." Pirouetting around the room, Parthe comes to a standstill before Dr. Clark's table. From the clutter of meteorological instruments, she plucks up the pluviometer and, pressing it to one eye, scans the room.

I had expected to find resentment, anger, a tantrum, anything but this giddy detachment from reason, this strange, shrill gaiety. And isn't she cold in her summer dress, legs and feet bare?

Over dinner, Parthenope's mood changes. Staring down at her plate, she stabs the grouse meat as if to kill it, snatches up a large piece of bread, and stuffs it into her mouth, tears streaming down her face.

By midmorning, we have left Birkhall, I with my few things, Parthenope with her summer dresses from Aberdeen, the stoic maid, Marie, and three crates of ripening Beurre Bosc pears brought up from the cellar.

The journey is without incident. Aside from a fit of hysterics when Dr. Clark and his sister Charlotte say good-bye and Parthe, nearly catatonic, must be bodily placed into the carriage by the coachman, and a second time, when porters are needed to pack her, sobbing, into a railway carriage in Edinburgh, she is strangely meek, does whatever I ask.

Back at Lea Hurst in October, I speak privately to my parents. I am leaving in January, I tell them, to train with the Sisters of Charity at a hospital in Paris. While preparing for the trip, ignoring my mother's predictable tears and tiresome objections, I receive a surprise letter from Lady Charlotte Canning of the Ladies' Committee, inviting me to accept a position in London as superintendent of the Institution for the Care of Sick Gentlewomen in Distressed Circumstances. My name, the letter goes on to say, was suggested by one of the committee members, Elizabeth Herbert. "A friend of yours, I believe," wrote Lady Canning. Before leaving for Paris, I reply with a detailed list of questions.

Spite

MALICIOUSNESS. SPITE. ILL WILL. *My sister's way of loving me. Having to say good-bye, having to look on her pallid face, cheeks splotched, tears sprouting out of her eyes, her blond hair in piggish little ringlets, oh, how I hated her at that moment! Recoiled from her wet kiss.*

Even now, I hate her. A jail can be one's own family, one's chief jailer a sister whose idea of love is tyranny, hysteria, threats.

I have sometimes wondered if her madness isn't feigned. It works, madness, terrifying my parents, making them exert control over me.

But if those threats prove real? If she does go mad? Destroys herself? Blames me?

So be it.

The coldness I feel, writing this. The absence of any affection. The bitterness. If the choice is her sanity or mine, if my loyalty is to be to my family or to God, I make my decision.

I am on my way to France. Gone.

La Maison de La Providence Hospital

Paris
March 1853

Dearest Mama,

I have become two persons in one! The first attends balls, concerts, salons, and parties—four balls this week alone! The second, in a Sisters of Charity uniform, scrubs floors and walls, changes bedding and bandages, dresses wounds, sits with patients, observes surgeries. Between these two opposing creatures, a hastily snatched hour of sleep . . .

I do not mention a third Florence, corresponding with Lady Canning, listing the many provisions needed to run an institution. Liz Herbert's endorsement carries weight, so Lady Canning raises no objection. She asks only that I come soon to London to meet with the committee members in person. Also, she writes, their current building on Chandos Street is old. Will I help them locate a better site?

Envy

April 1853

Miss F. Nightingale
Brown's Hotel
London

My dear Florence,

Shall I pick you up in my brougham tomorrow about twelve o'clock so that you may meet with our Ladies' Committee? Sidney may or may not accompany—lately he is worn to a shadow by his duties as secretary at war for Lord Aberdeen. He asks about you often and praises you so lavishly, I would be jealous did I not believe in the purity of his admiration, so akin to my own.

Affectionately,
Liz Herbert

Oh, but I am jealous, Elizabeth Herbert thinks. *Eaten up with it. I may be his wife, mother of his children, our tie one of kindness and affection, but she occupies some lofty, untouchable place in him. She is his ideal, elusive, alluring, with a soul hard and polished as armor.* She folds the note, seals it, prays for absolution. Relief.

Institution for Decayed Gentlewomen

June 1853

LADY CANNING (WHOSE FIRST REMARK, on meeting me, is to exclaim how "startlingly young" I look), along with other members of the committee, approves of me. They approve, too, of the building I select on Upper Harley Street. I have also let a modest set of rooms on St. James's Square, in nearby Pall Mall, for visiting friends and family, as well as to give myself an escape on Sundays. With massive Harley Street renovations still underway I return to Paris to complete my final weeks of training, and as often as I can, I write to Parthe. Dr. Clark would be interested to know how strangely eager my sister has become to ingratiate herself. She insists on decorating my little apartment even as she offers the tart opinion that I am "far too good" for the menial work I have taken on. To put my "genius" to use ordering cheap candles, pounding rhubarb, and tallying bills for milk, coal, and flour, is, she says, a waste of my talent. Her wish to help is straightforward, if surprising. As for Aunt Patty, Papa's other sister, I am told she boasts to everyone she knows about my new place of employment, calling it "the Institution for Decayed Gentlewomen."

After the usual tears and a new tactic, a refusal to eat, Mama, like Parthe, turns shockingly helpful. She writes that she intends to regularly send parcels of flowers, fruits, vegetables. Fresh game, too—pheasant, grouse, and partridge.

Writing to thank her, I ask if she can spare any books for reading. Art prints, too, to cheer our bare walls.

Retreat to the Athenaeum

DISTRUSTING THIS "TRUCE" BETWEEN the warring females of his household, William Nightingale takes up half residence at the Athenaeum Club on Pall Mall. Retreats to the club's library to work on his memoir. Even he is surprised by its ever-growing number of pages. Could he be a natural author? He knows, too, that he must work out some way to pacify the female factions of his family. Scribbling down possible solutions, he finally decides on one, setting in motion the first act of what he hopes will not turn into a family tragedy. He has decided to grant Florence an annual allowance of five hundred pounds, the sum suggested by his sister Mai, adamant on the subject of Florence's "genius." Mai has long championed her niece's ambition to achieve distinction beyond the domestic circle, or "noose," as she calls it.

Haunted by the memory of finding Florence nearly dead, William has his lawyer draw up the necessary financial papers. He knows by this decision, God help him, he may well be sacrificing one daughter for the other.

Free As Any Man

August 1853

WHAT BETTER PLACE TO BEGIN my destiny than in this home for broken-down gentlewomen? I have refused the salary offered by the committee, telling them I can live well enough on my new allowance.

On an overcast, humid Saturday, Mama and Parthe visit from Embley. While they pretend to admire my little bolt-hole on St. James's Square, and direct the carriage driver to bring in boxes of books, art prints, and baskets of food, I see, to my joy, that Parthe has brought Athena. After an hour of awkward silence, hand-wringing, heavy sighing, and faint praise, my mother and sister plant damp kisses on both my cheeks and, sobbing, leave.

For the first time in my life, I am free as any man.

I look at my little beastie, perched on the windowsill.

"Athena, what say you to our new and useful life?"

PART EIGHT

Institution for the Care of Sick Gentlewomen in Distressed Circumstances

Wanted: a young lady who has had advantages, for a situation as governess. To sleep in a room with three beds, for herself, four children, and a maid. To give the children their baths, dress them, and be ready for breakfast at a quarter to eight. School from nine to twelve and half past two to four, with two hours of music lessons in addition. To spend the evenings doing needlework for her mistress. To have the baby on her knee while teaching, and to put all the children to bed. Ten pounds a year salary and to pay her own washing.

—The Times of London

1 Upper Harley Street

London
September 1853

"HERE WE ARE, PAPA. My own establishment. At the moment, we have twenty-seven beds and seven patients. I will take in governesses, daughters of military men, clergymen, professional men, the navy, and the like. Yesterday, the Ladies' Committee urged that I house only women affiliated with the Church of England, and certainly no Catholics, but I wished them a good morning and said I would not superintend an institution that was not nonsectarian. I will house anyone I please—Catholics, Jews, Muslims. Any woman who comes to my door shall be welcomed."

Speaking, I struggle to open the front door, until a workman pulls it open from inside with such force that I nearly fall across the threshold. My father follows me into the dust-filled foyer, holding a box of books.

"As you see, there is a good deal still to be done. I have just had a dumbwaiter installed, since I do not want the nurses to be mere sets of legs dashing up and down stairs all day long. I've taken two rooms for myself, one on this floor for an office, another on the second floor."

"Where shall I put your mother's books? Good Heavens, what is that shouting?"

"An altercation between the workmen. A daily occurrence, I'm afraid. The foreman is hot-tempered and a drunkard. I would replace him, but when he is sober, his skills are invaluable. Good morning, Miss Draper. How are you feeling?"

"Fair, Miss Nightingale. But Miss Gill is feverish."

"I will check on her, but here, take these books, see if any appeal to you. *Bleak House, The Christian Year,* volumes of poetry. A little start to our reading library."

After checking on Dorothea Gill, I find Papa downstairs in the kitchen, peering out a begrimed back window. His view is of a garden gone to weed, a pile of refuse, an unused, broken-down stable.

"The woman I gave Mama's books to, Ivy Draper, worked as a governess for Lady Teignmouth. For her trouble, she received less than ten pounds a year. She came to us very ill, without any family or income. Her neighbor, Miss Gill, is emaciated, skin and bone. Papa, what these women of gentle birth and education have endured in their lives is unimaginable."

"You recall Miss Christie?"

"Yes, of course."

"Do you think had I been more generous, she might have stayed on?"

"And not married Mr. Leipzig? You could not have altered her fate, Papa."

"Right. And I was pleased to take over your education."

"And on no salary at all! Come up to the third floor; I want to show off the water pipes I've had installed. A new boiler at the top of the house carries hot water to each of the floors. I've even had bells and valves put in so the nurses ring for assistance without having to trudge up and down the stairs."

"Ingenious, Florence. You've thought up these improvements on your own?"

Before I can reply, a series of muffled explosions goes off downstairs. As soon as the workmen determine the cause to be a gas leak, I order the necessary repairs, then take Papa a hastily made cup of tea from the kitchen. He drinks it, and before leaving, says he is impressed by what I have done in such a short time. After he has gone, I realize I hadn't told him that with his first check, I purchased eight commode pails with mahogany seats and two dresses for myself—uniforms, really—one of black silk, another of dark gray linen. For now, I must shut myself in my little office, ignore the workmen's shouting and hammering, jot down household reminders.

Household Notes

— Hire a new housemaid; settle which of the two will clean the candlesticks and grates, which will sweep passages between rooms.

— Manage Mrs. Clarke's tendency to take to her bed whenever some perceived unpleasantness offends her.

— Remind the housemaids that no artificial flowers are to be worn in caps or bonnets. Reinforce the importance of punctuality!

— Order six bedcovers refashioned from Chandos Street curtains.

— Use money from Papa's second check to replace all household linens, as the vermin wander tame in all directions. Tablecloths, kitchen cloths, towels, sheets, quilts. Quilts especially are ragged and insect-eaten.

— Replace furniture covers, as their present color is indistinguishable from dirt.

— Cut six bedside carpets from Chandos St. carpets (cleaned).

— Purchase kitchen utensils. I have found no preserving pan, no saucepan for steaming potatoes, no dustpan, no brushes or brooms.

The Plight of Gentlewomen

THEIR NUMBERS HAVE RISEN from seven to twenty-five. The women suffer from general disability, scrofula, internal inflammation, rheumatism, and ankylosis, a stiffening of bones that join unnaturally together. Miss Goodridge has a cancer of the breast. Dr. Henry Bence Jones will remove it next week at St. George's, and has asked that I administer the chloroform. I miss assisting at surgeries, and am especially adept at the tying up of arteries. Were I a man, I should have made an excellent surgeon.

All of my patients face lives of impoverishment. Most are ex-governesses. At the least kindness, they express the most touching gratitude. I have sent poor Margaret Hobbs, at my personal expense, on holiday to Eastbourne. If I have any difficulty with the women, it is in getting them to leave. The Ladies' Committee has agreed to a two-month limit on each residency, but there is not a trick in the whole legerdemain of hysteria that has not been played to persuade me to prolong their stay. Alice Tynbee, for one, waits outside my room every night, offering to rub my feet before I retire.

Reading the 1851 census, I learn that 365,000 Englishwomen sought employment as governesses with only 24,470 open positions. Those obtaining work are considered fortunate, yet the tasks put to them are burdensome and their health is quickly broken down by long hours and slave's wages. I compare my sister, flittering about, half mad in her gilded cage, to these gentlewomen who through no fault of their own are forced into work that destroys them. Many can find no legitimate employment at all. Those who marry are thought to be luckiest, yet how many suffer hidden abuse or die in childbirth, leaving healthy husbands to marry a second, third, or even fourth time? Is it hard to understand why these women scheme to stay beyond their two-month limit, leave off their flannels at night to bring on a chest cough, or show no appetite during the day, then secretly forage at night? What is to become of them when they leave? How are they to survive?

Miss Lowndes

January 1854

BREAKFAST. ATHENA PECKS AWAY at a good Stilton while I
yawn until my jaw cracks. This morning I woke more tired
than when I had gone to bed. If I am lucky, I might scratch up some
rest later today.

"Beg pardon, ma'am, Miss Lowndes is not in her room."

"Reverend Garnier's governess?"

"Yes, ma'am. She is gone."

"Why did you not tell me sooner, Mrs. Clarke? Is anyone
looking for her? Have you searched the house?"

"Top to bottom. Addie found the back door wide open, cold
air pouring in."

"Why didn't you say so at once? If Miss Lowndes has run off,
who knows what harm may come to her?"

As if in reaction to my reprimand, Athena flaps across the
breakfast room and settles on the mantel, where the fireplace once
again spews coal smoke. For most of the winter, a heavy, obstinate
fog has clung to the city of London, backing up fireplaces, filling
drawing rooms and bedrooms with black smoke.

"Quickly, find my woolen cloak and bonnet while I look for my
gloves. I must find her."

"Not going out on your own, ma'am?"

"Of course I am! Don't I buy food at Covent Garden on my
own? Pursuing a madwoman should interest passersby with

nothing better to do. I'll have help. Ah, here are my gloves, rascals, stuck inside my bonnet."

As I wait for my cloak, Addie, the newest house servant, pushes herself backward out the door of the dining room, holding a tray piled precariously with breakfast cups and dishes. Abandoned at birth, raised in a workhouse, Addie can't be a day over twelve. When a cup falls from the tray and crashes to the floor, shattered, she stares down at the breakage with wide, terrified eyes.

"Don't fret, Addie. It's only crockery. Next time, fewer dishes on the tray, more trips to the kitchen."

Mrs. Clarke returns with my cloak.

"See about opening the windows, Mrs. Clarke? Though we'll only be letting smoke out and fog in."

"I will, ma'am. Pray you come on Miss Lowndes straightaway."

"I intend to. Then it's off to St. Luke's with her." St. Luke's is London's worst lunatic asylum. A badly run institution for paupers, but I can think of nowhere else.

Feeling my way through the damp murk that has clung to the city's streets all winter, I call out for Miss Lowndes. When a man emerges from the fog, I ask for his help, and within a quarter of an hour, he has assembled a small mob of men eager to pounce on an escaped lunatic. They scour the streets and back alleys, hunting for a scraggly-haired woman in a flannel wrapper and pair of oversized men's slippers. I now suspect Reverend Garnier brought his former governess to me yesterday well sedated with laudanum, for at the start she appeared meek and passive. Within an hour of his leaving, she was raving, hurling objects about, demanding to be taken to India to locate her husband, a soldier in the King's Light Dragoons. I sat by her bedside last night, spooning out laudanum, rising every two hours from my own bed to see if she was still asleep. When I checked early this morning, she was dead to the world. Or so I thought.

"Over here! The back garden!"

Like baying hounds, four or five men have surrounded a woman in an overgrown garden, cowering against a brick wall. Her wrapper half off, she is shoving fistfuls of dirt into her mouth. Asking the men to step back, I approach and quickly cover her.

"Miss Lowndes? Cornelia? We must get you home to a nice hot breakfast and tea, yes? Take my arm, that's it, stand up. We'll walk together, dear; it isn't far."

The men trail after, no doubt expecting a reward. I'll make sure Mrs. Clarke gives them something. Back in her room, I give Miss Lowndes a large dose of laudanum, sit with her until she falls into a drugged sleep, then quickly write a note to be delivered to St. Luke's, asking that a Miss Cornelia Lowndes be picked up immediately. It will be nearly noon before a carriage arrives with two nurses to collect the governess's few things and take her, unprotesting, to the asylum. Once they have left, I dash off a letter to the Reverend Garnier, apprising him of what has happened.

As I am finishing up paying bills, the last a monthly charge from Fortnum & Mason, Mrs. Clarke appears in the doorway.

"What, Mrs. C.?"

"Best see for yourself."

In the smaller pantry off the kitchen, Addie is sprawled on the brick floor, stockinged legs splayed, a half-empty bottle of gin sticking up between them. Gin, the scourge of London's workhouses. What to do but send her back? She cannot stay, not with twenty-seven patients needing care and a household to manage. Handing the bottle over to Mrs. Clarke (who, unbeknownst to me, will drain off what's left), I help the child to her feet and quietly dismiss her from service.

"What else? What else can go wrong today, Mrs. Clarke? We are down to one nurse and no housemaids. Surely there is better news somewhere."

"There is. Miss Birdthistle is cured and going off to her new employment tomorrow."

Emily Birdthistle had come to Harley Street two months before, claiming she could not get up from bed and could take no nourishment but port wine and cream. Five weeks later, she walks miles, wolfs down plates of eggs, sausage, vegetables.

"That we have managed to cure Miss Birdthistle without a drop of medicine is good news indeed. Now I must lie down for a few minutes."

As I say that, the outside bell rings sharply, followed by a vigorous thumping of the brass door knocker.

"Who could that be? The Reverend Garnier can't have received my letter; I haven't posted it. Has Miss Lowndes already escaped from St. Luke's? I'll see who it is, Mrs. Clarke. Make certain Addie has safe passage back to her workhouse—let her sleep off the gin, pay her extra, and give her plenty of food to take with her."

Wishing this day over, I crack open the door.

Handsome, sanguine, perfectly cheerful.

"Florence! Hope you don't mind my popping by, but I was on a walk and suddenly wished to see for myself what all the buz-fuz is about. Your establishment is the talk of London. Liz boasts you receive high marks from every quarter; some, she claims, call you the 'miracle worker' of Harley Street. Might I come in? Can't imagine how I found you—how can anyone find anything in this devil of a fog? Will we see blue skies again? That is what everyone wants to know. Do you remember a blue sky, Florence? I do not."

Mute, heart thumping, I take his hat, his stylish greatcoat

with its braid trim, peek in the hall mirror to brush away any garden dirt from my earlier tussle with Miss Lowndes. I merely look tired. Very tired.

"I'm afraid I've turned into one of my own 'distressed' patients. As of yesterday, I've lost two of three nurses, both housemaids, rounded up a lunatic, and at the moment, I have no idea where Mrs. Clarke has gone off to. Forgive me, it's been an impossible day."

"Then you must tell me about it once I have a quick look around. We can't have you distressed."

"Mrs. Clarke, put Mr. Herbert's things away while I show him the first floor; then you may bring our tea into the drawing room."

Seen through his eyes, or what I imagine his eyes see, the place looks dreary, patched, drab, my proud economies translated into a shabbiness of cheap repair, threadbare carpets, mismatched curtains. But if I am embarrassed, Sidney is all generous approval, peppering me with eager questions.

Even the tea is pathetic—we are out of milk and cake, down to a few teaspoons of sugar—though he seems not to mind. I answer each of his questions, and when he finally asks about my "trying" day, I describe Miss Lowndes's running off, Addie's gin drinking, the black smoke even now crawling out of fireplaces into patients' rooms.

"Had you come yesterday, you would have seen me dismissing one of the house servants on account of her passion for dirt and laziness. You would have seen me letting Nurse Bellamy go, a nurse in name and wages only, due to her passion for opium. And you must forgive—"

"Minor annoyances, Flo. What you have done for these women and in such a short span is remarkable! According to Liz, the committee members are falling over themselves in praise of your administrative skills and the money you've saved them. I'm told the patients adore you, that you pay out of your own pocket for fees they cannot afford, and at your own expense, have sent some on holiday. In only a few months, you have worked miracles. Liz asks me to convey the committee's hope that you will stay on past your year's contract."

"I would if I could establish a training program for volunteer nurses. Lady Canning tells me there is neither the room nor the budget for that."

"Perhaps something can be worked out. Meanwhile, would you consider a personal favor? Liz tells me you have been finding a bit of time to visit hospitals in London. You observe how they are managed, then write up detailed reports. Might I see those reports? I am most interested in your opinion of St. Bartholomew's."

"St. Bartholomew's is a disgrace. Whatever rumors you hear are true. Kaiserwerth was ill-managed and unclean, but the spirit of the place was as Christian as any I have seen. That spirit is utterly lacking at St. Bartholomew's."

"I am sorry to hear that. Still, I should like to see your studies of hospital systems. As you may recall, I intend to reform our local hospital at Wilton."

"Should I send the reports to your office?"

"Yes. Liz will give you the address. I would also like you to dine with us one evening in our Belgrave home. You'll be positively astonished to see how fast the children have grown. But perhaps you are too busy?"

"Impossibly busy. All twenty-seven beds are filled, and between administrative work, medical duties, and attempting to hire trained nurses and new housemaids, I am run off my feet. Dinner will be a delightful respite."

"Wonderful, Florence. And you do look well. As well as I've ever seen you."

I put a hand to my untidy hair, resist the temptation to look for stains on my dress.

"I don't mean your appearance. You look tired, doubtless from the upsets you describe. But you are vital. Happy in your work. That is what I mean."

He leans close, his eyes bright with what I assume is simple admiration. We regard each other in an increasingly strained silence.

"I'm afraid I must pop back to work. Aberdeen has me scheduled to the hilt; our meetings on the Crimea run late into the night. But I am delighted to have found you in a milieu that so suits you. Have you any idea what you will do once your contract is up?"

"Unless I begin a nursing program here, I will have to trust in what comes next. My father's sister, Aunt Mai, is a bit of a seer. The family Sibyl. She insists something very great awaits me. But what that something is, on that point, she is maddeningly vague."

"Well, since no one may have told you, I will. Outside of news of the war, you are on the tip of everyone's tongue here in London. Should you choose not to renew your contract, you will find yourself instantly in demand by other medical establishments. I, for one, have—"

"Ma'am? Excuse me, the new nurse is here."

"Thank you, Mrs. Clarke. I'll be there shortly." I smile at him. "Pray my luck turns today."

"I'm certain it will. I'll see myself out."

"No, please. Let me get your things."

Hurrying ahead, thinking to ask whether I should send my

diagrams along with the hospital reports, I turn and find him gazing at me with such intensity of feeling, I lose all breath.

For having been surprised by Sidney's look of passionate affection, I should curse God. Instead, a blaze of joy overrides my conscience.

It was in that moment his name came to me. The name I would secretly call him, even knowing how wrong it was.

Master.

1 Upper Harley Street

January 1854

Dearest Liz,

I enclose reports, statistical studies, visual diagrams of several London hospitals, including St. Bartholomew's. They are for both of you to look at before I come to dinner next week.

Do not breathe a word to Lady Canning or the other members of the Ladies' Committee, but Dr. William Bowman, the eminent ophthalmologist, has asked if I might consider becoming superintendent of nurses at King's College Hospital. The offer is a dead serious one.

Have you been well? How are Mary and little George? Do we dare hope for clear skies again? This endless fog and the ever more distressing news of war threaten to dissolve my brain into one great fizzle of gloom.

Affectionately,
Florence

Final Report to the Ladies' Committee

August 1854

The year having now expired for which I undertook the office of superintendent of this institution, the Ladies' Committee will naturally expect that I should give some notice to them of my views as to our success. I would wish, therefore, to express that my work is now done, & that the institution has been brought into as good a state as its capabilities admit.

I have not affected anything toward the object of training nurses— my primary idea in devoting my life to hospital work, for owing to the small number of applications, the committee have not been able to select, in all cases, proper objects for medical & surgical treatment—and accordingly the result has not been satisfactory to me. In every other respect—viz, good order, good nursing, moral influence & economy— the result has been to me most satisfactory.

I therefore wish, at the close of the year for which I promised my services, to intimate that—having, as I believe, done the work as far as it can be done—it is probable that I may retire, if, in pursuance of my design & the allegiance which I hold to it, I meet with a sphere more analogous to the formation of a nursing school. I give a notice of three months, to be extended, if possible, to six.

Sincerely,
Florence Nightingale

Middlesex Hospital

September 1854

As the sun struggles but fails to shine through London's dark, filthy air, I walk those streets and neighborhoods where cholera has added its stamp of suffering to the more common afflictions of starvation, poverty, violence. Having left my rooms on St. James's Square and headed to the Duke of York Street, then Jermyn Street, Church Place, Picadilly, Sackville, and Vigo Streets, I walk down Brewer and Little Pulteney Streets, turn left on Wardour, then on to Broad Street, and finally pass through a set of open gates into the cobblestoned courtyard of Middlesex Hospital. I have left the running of Harley Street to my nurses and Mrs. Clarke. Here, at Middlesex, the majority of my patients are cholera victims. They are not governesses or gentlewomen, but prostitutes, many mere children.

"Ellen? How badly does it pain you?" I have removed the cheaply made dress, the muddy slippers, torn stockings. Her small body, emaciated, hot with fever, is mottled with bruises, virulent blossoms of yellow, violet, tan—an evil garden on her pasty skin. With her clothing removed, the stench is foul, but I have taught myself to be impervious to the worst odors. Smells of diarrhea, blood, vomit, infection, even the faint, distinct smell that precedes death, none of these affects me. Nothing about the human body disgusts or repels me. What I do feel is an outraged tenderness for this ill-used girl.

"How old are you, Ellen?"

"Don't know."

"And you live . . ."

"Wardour Street. Near Soho."

"I see. Hold quiet now." *The skin cold, moist. The tongue white, loaded. Pulse rapid and feeble. High fever. Bowels loose, watery, unrestrained, spasms of pain in abdomen. Complains of muscle aches, difficulty swallowing.* "I am going to wash you, dear, and place a stupe of turpentine over your abdomen for the pain."

Wringing out a piece of flannel from a tin basin of water, I wash her body, lay a lint cloth of turpentine and belladonna over her abdomen. From its swelling, she is four, perhaps even five, months pregnant.

Ellen says little. Near the end, she only murmurs, "Thank you, ma'am, God bless you, ma'am," before her soul loosens and breaks free of her beaten down, abused body.

Hundreds die in a single day. I nurse countless Ellens, their names slipping off like beads on a rosary—Meg, Polly, Nell, Sophy. In hope of saving even one, I undress and bathe them all, apply poultices, fomentations, stupes soaked in turpentine, opium, belladonna. Offer kind words, tenderness of touch, prayers if asked, until each body is carried off and replaced, moments later, by another.

I hold no judgment against these young women, these girls. Children. I reserve my judgment, my fury for a society that abandons its women and children to such desperate measures and destructive fates. Men's callousness toward the poor is writ large in these ruined souls, in the befouled wards of Middlesex, these overcrowded corridors of hell where, one after another, they die.

Nameless

BY THE DOZENS—POOR CREATURES, each staggering off her night's "work." One pretty child wanders in alone, deathly ill. I hold her in my arms, and when she whispers, I bend closer to hear. "Pray God, you may never be in the despair I am in at this time." Looking into her eyes, I reply with all the love I can summon, "Dear child, are you not now more merciful than the God you are going to? Yet God is far more merciful than any human creature ever was or can be. You are safe in Him."

She leaves this horror called earth before I can know her name.

Lea Hurst

September–October 1854

NOT UNTIL DR. JOHN SNOW tracks down the single source—a contaminated water pump on Broad Street—does the epidemic slow, then die down. Mama writes, begging me to come home and rest. Reluctantly, I return to Lea Hurst.

In one year, I have borne witness to all my family hoped to shield me from seeing, what they have no wish to see or admit for themselves. Home but a few days, I already long to return to London, take the position offered me at King's College Hospital. That is, until a far more audacious, fantastical thought occurs, due to my father's compulsion, over each morning's breakfast, to read to us the daily war reports from the Crimea.

To Mama's displeasure, he reads aloud graphic eyewitness accounts sent from the Crimea by telegraph and printed in the *Times*. The most popular eyewitness pieces written from the field are by William Howard Russell. ("A luckless Dublin hothead," Mama says, indicating her disapproval.) His accusations of British commander Lord Raglan's incompetency, his lurid descriptions of the thousands of British soldiers dying not of wounds but of dysentery, cholera, frostbite, and starvation—neglect—shock and anger the reading public. Throughout England, appalling numbers and gruesome stories are passed around the breakfast table like so many platters of toast and sausage, eggs, mushrooms, bowls of stewed figs and tomatoes. As the sensationalist reporting of wartime correspondents like Russell reaches a frenzied pitch, subscriptions to the *Times* triple. On one particular morning in late September, as Papa reads the latest vehement dispatch from Mr. Russell, I feel as if physically struck. Assaulted by conscience. Russell's impassioned appeal, his urgent plea to the women of England, comes like a clarion call from God:

> *If I could, I would clothe skeletons with flesh, breathe life into the occupants of the charnel house, restore the legions that have been lost, but I cannot tell lies to make life pleasant. Are there no devoted women among us able and willing to go forth and minister to the sick and suffering soldiers of the East in the hospitals of Scutari? Are none of the daughters of England, at this extreme hour of need, ready for such a work of mercy?*

I listen to Papa, electrified by one thought. Why not go myself to the Crimea? What higher calling than to care for the brave, wounded soldiers of the British army? On the fourteenth of October, I compose a brief, formal letter to the secretary at war, the one person I know who can make such a miracle happen. I request that with three or four other nurses, I be permitted to sail immediately for the Crimea. As though we were strangers and had never met, I sign the letter "Miss Florence Nightingale." Afterward, I write a second letter to Elizabeth Herbert requesting release from my duties on Harley Street.

At that same hour, Sidney Herbert is away at Bournmouthe. Reading Russell's newest piece in the *Times*, he can think of only one woman in England capable of answering the popular journalist's call, of calming public outrage over his accusation of military incompetence. In his capacity as secretary at war, he writes to Florence on the fifteenth of October, asking if she might consider taking a small party of nurses to Scutari Hospital in Constantinople. No one is better suited to the task, he says; no one is better prepared to apply her administrative and nursing skills to what is a dire situation. Sealing the letter, it occurs to him that by sending this educated, upper-class young Englishwoman as a nurse to the Crimea, he will be shielding the reputation of the military from increasingly vitriolic attacks by correspondents like Russell. Such a story, compassionate and appealing, of Miss Nightingale and her nurses sacrificing themselves, tending to the wounded soldiers of Britain, would be a distraction for the English people, a sentimental story of feminine mercy for the newspapers to wallow in. That he might be protecting his own heart as well as deflecting negative attention from the British military, does not occur to him.

Our two letters cross in the mail.

Yes, I write back. I can be prepared to sail for Constantinople in ten days, as soon as I have interviewed and hired nurses. Sprinkling sand over the fresh ink, sealing the folded note, I notice Athena, her enormous yellow eyes fixed on me. With the quill tip of my pen, I tap her curved beak. "Who knows, little beastie? Your mistress may soon be caught up in a great war."

49 Belgrave Villa Square

London

M Y SISTER, LIZ, AND SELINA spend hours in the drawing room, questioning the steady stream of respondents to my ad in the *Times*: *Nurses wanted for an expedition to the Crimea.* Most are widows, ex-governesses, women seeking a husband or hoping to escape a husband, women attracted to fourteen shillings a week. Few have any real interest or experience in nursing; most are quickly weeded out. Parthe declares all the applicants unfit; Selina lines them against a wall and fires questions at them, with nearly every answer cut off by her shout of "Dismissed!"

We sit across from one another in your study, hashing out details. How many supplies will be needed, what should my range of duties be, how broad my authority? So much to consider. For a few short hours, we are merged in a common purpose. Since that brief moment at Wilton House, since your impassioned gaze on Harley Street, I have never felt happier than I do now.

Roster of Nurses

Bowmett, M. A.	St. John's House
Barrie, Georgiana (Sister Mary Gonzaga)	Bermondsey Convent
Barnes, S.	"hospital nurse"
Blake, C. Elizabeth	
Coyle, M. A.	St. John's House
Chabrillae, J. G. (Justine)	"hospital nurse"
Mrs. Clarke	F. N.'s housekeeper
Mrs. Elizabeth Drake	St. John's House
Davy, J.	
Erskin, Miss Harriet	Miss Sellon's
Fagg, Emma	St. John's House
Faulkner, A.	
Grundy, E.	Middlesex Hospital
Higgins, Mrs. Ann	St. John's House
Huddon, Maria (Sister de Chantal)	Bermondsey Convent
Hawkins, E.	Night nurse at Guy's
Jones, Margaret (Sister Stanislaus)	Bermondsey Convent

Jones, S.	
Forbes, Eliza Isabella	
Kelly, Sarah (Sister Anastasia)	Bermondsey Convent
Lawfield, Mrs. Rebecca	St. John's House
Langston, Mrs. Emma (Mother Eldress)	Miss Sellon's
Goodman, Margaret (Sister Goodman)	Miss Sellon's
Moore, Mary Clare (Reverend Mother)	Bermondsey Convent
MacClean, Marie Therese	Norwood
O'Dwyer, Elinor	Norwood
Pillars, Ethelreda	
Purnell, Frances	Norwood
Mrs. Parker	
Mrs. Roberts	St. Thomas's Hospital
Sharpe, Miss Clara	Miss Sellon's
Smith, Elizabeth	St. Thomas's Hospital
Terrot, S. A. (Sarah)	Miss Sellon's
Turnbull E. B. (Elizabeth)	Miss Sellon's
Wheeler, Elizabeth	
Williams, Margaret	Guy's
Williams, M.	
Wilson, Mrs.	

One Great, Reckless Gamble

REFOLDING THE LIST OF NAMES into my carpetbag, closing my eyes, I sink back into the hired carriage. I have finished meeting with a gabbling flock of magpies, thirty-eight women crammed cheek by jowl in the Herberts' drawing room. They quieted when I began to speak, telling them what they must take ("as few personal items as possible and an endless will to work"), warning of the difficulties ahead ("a foreign land, great numbers of sick, wounded, and dying soldiers, supply delays, though our government, specifically Mr. Herbert, our secretary at war, assures me that there will be more than enough supplies, a *bounty*, the word he used"). Thanking them for joining my cause, I then took questions. The first, posed by Miss Hawkins, a night nurse at Guy's, sparked others, until after more than an hour, I ended the meeting and asked that everyone return home and be prepared to depart in four days' time. "What is the route?" someone persisted in asking. From Paris to Boulogne, then on to Marseille. On the twenty-first of October, from the port of Marseille, we will board the P&O mail packet, *Vectis*, a paddle steamer. Crossing the Mediterranean, the Sea of Crete, the Aegean, the Dardanelles, the Sea of Marmara, sailing through the Bosporus Strait into the port at Constantinople. How long will the voyage take? Between twelve and fourteen days. I remembered to add that for those nurses not in any religious order, uniforms are being made and will be distributed the day we depart from London. The uniforms are dresses, "wrappers" of gray tweed, each accompanied by a gray worsted jacket, white cap, and short woolen cloak. Because of disproportionate numbers, fewer than forty women to thousands of soldiers, I have designed the uniforms to be unattractive. Over her religious habit or uniform, each nurse will wear a banner made from Holland cloth with the words *Scutari Hospital* stitched in scarlet thread.

So many details. Nuns from Bermondsey Convent wear black, with a white linen gimp and coif; nuns from the Norwood orphanage wear white. Both St. John's House nuns and the women from Miss Sellon's Anglican order, the Sellonite Sisters of Mercy, dress in habits of black serge. In total, ten Catholic nuns, eight Anglican sisters, and twenty secular nurses—most with little to no experience in nursing.

One great, reckless gamble.

Lining the bottom of my carpetbag are contracts written up by Liz Herbert and signed by each of the nurses. Counting Mrs. Clarke from Harley Street and the Bracebridges, who insisted they would not dream of missing out on such a heroic adventure, the party boarding the *Vectis* will consist of forty-one women and a married gentleman.

Beastie

SPLITTING APART THE CARRIAGE CURTAINS, I search the heavily wooded landscape for a glimpse of Lea Hurst's rooftops, bristling with redbrick chimneys. I am making this unplanned trip for a terrible reason. While Parthe was in London, someone at Lea Hurst accidentally left Athena in the attic, then forgot her. Papa eventually found her and carried her lifeless body downstairs, blood draining from her beak. In answer to his letter, I insisted she be taken to a taxidermist. I have come home to say good-bye.

Athena is in his study, mounted on a simple arrangement of dry branches and moss. Stroking her preserved little body, I press my lips to the top of her feathered head.

"Odd, beastie, how much I loved you."

Port of Marseille

21 October 1854

WAITING WITH THE OTHERS on the stone quay, I read from Thomas à Kempis's *The Imitation of Christ*, a gift from Liz Herbert. Tucked into its back pages is his etched image, cut from the *Times*, along with a note, penned on official stationery in his rapid hand:

18 October 1854

To Miss Florence Nightingale, Superintendent of the Female Nursing Establishment in the English General Military Hospitals in Turkey:

I wish you and your stalwart companions, fellow nurses, and the Bracebridges, safe passage to Constantinople. When you arrive at Scutari, may your real work commence and your graceful presence bring both succor and strength to our brave heroes—the British soldiers.

God Bless and Keep You.

Yours,
Sidney Herbert
Secretary at War

Doughty Mrs. Clarke charges up the ramp, followed by Charles and Selina. The nurses follow, some already doubting their decision. Several openly complain to one another about the uniforms I designed; one refuses to wear the "hideous" cap. Waiting until all are on board, I gaze up at the gulls wheeling overhead, breathe in the sea's sulfurous, salty odor, close my book on a favorite passage.

> *Jesus has always many who love His heavenly kingdom but few who bear His cross. He has many who desire consolation but few who care for trial. He finds many to share His table but few to take part in His fasting. All desire to be happy with Him; few wish to suffer anything for Him.*

The paddle steamer slips from its moorings; using my field glasses, a last-minute purchase in Marseille, I watch the harbor flatten to a distant smudge. A waning glimpse of Europe. The possibility of dying in a foreign land has more than once occurred to me.

"Miss Nightingale." Mrs. Clarke breaks into my melancholy. "Sister Stanislaus is below, asking for a seasickness cure."

Taking a bottle of pills compounded from arsenic and white hellebore, I begin my descent into the abyss, the nightmare, of war.

PART NINE

Crimea

November 1854–December 1854

We are steeped up to our necks in blood.
                              —Florence Nightingale

Scutari Hospital

4 November 1854

Hard berths, sour, seething with roaches. The Vectis, *notorious for pitching and rolling in high seas, nearly wrecked in the Mediterranean, the galley and stewards' cabins washing overboard, cannon dumped in the sea. All, beginning with Sister Stanislaus, are sick, myself more than any. None can eat, with Sister de Chantal joking we have left half our combined weight at sea. Nine miserable, retching days until the mail packet finally creeps into the fogged-in harbor of Constantinople.*

She stands on deck, lost in thought, cold rain streaming off her black umbrella, waiting with the others to be lowered down into caïques, small open boats that will carry them across the Bosporus Strait to Scutari. In her pocket, a half-finished letter to her family.

We reached Constantinople this morn in a thick, heavy rain, through which the Sophia, the Suleiman, the Seven Towers, the Walls, and the Golden Horn looked like a washed-out daguerreotype. We have not yet heard what the Military Hospital has done for us, nor received our orders.

Bad news from Balaclava. In the newspapers you will hear of the awful wreck of our cavalry, four hundred wounded, arriving at this moment . . . two ships damaged, Arethusa *and* Albion. *Lord Raglan insists he shall take Sebastopol. The army has built another hospital at the Dardanelles.*

Starting now for Scutari. We are to be housed in the Barrack Hospital this very afternoon, the newly wounded to be placed under our care. They are landing them now. . . .

Charles Bracebridge will be the first onshore, offering shelter with his large, broken umbrella. One by one, they disembark, until the entire party is huddled in a shivering knot on the rocky shore, waiting for oxcarts to haul them up the steep hillside to the Barrack Hospital. Although it is impressive, grand from a distance, the hospital's true horrors are concealed within its massive, fortresslike sides, an imposing tower at each corner.

In London, in the book-lined study of his Belgrave villa, she had been reassured by Sidney Herbert, just as the army's chief purveyor had assured him, of an abundance of medical supplies awaiting her at the hospital. Yet she feels heavy dread as the oxcart sways up the rutted, muddy path, and is glad she had thought, at the last minute, to purchase some supplies in Marseille. Wooden crates, packed with those supplies, jolt along in the last of the carts, along with leather trunks containing the nurses' belongings. She can hear a few of them grumbling about the rain, their cloaks and bonnets soaked; she hardly blames them. When they reach their hospital quarters, a fire, dry clothes, and hot tea will soothe everyone's exhausted nerves. A good night's rest, breakfast, and they can begin the work they have traveled halfway across the world to do.

But there will be no welcoming fire, no hot tea or breakfast, only broken windows, freezing air, half-flooded rooms, and a Russian officer dead and decomposing, the muddied tips of his black boots sticking out from behind the coal stove in a makeshift kitchen.

∽

Scutari Hospital, formerly a Turkish military barracks, is a white-washed monstrosity. Standing outside its forbidding entrance, with Charles gone in search of someone to greet them, she sees an immense inner courtyard, former parade ground for Turkish soldiers, littered with sodden piles of refuse, islands of garbage adrift in darkening pools of rainwater. Behind her, oxcarts wait with their English cargo—thirty-eight nurses, wooden boxes, leather trunks. The drivers wait, too, drenched and unmoving, as stoic as their thin, malnourished oxen.

Charles emerges from inside the hospital with a tall, sandy-haired army surgeon and two sullen orderlies following behind him. When Charles introduces her, the surgeon nods curtly, points up to a corner tower.

"You will stay there. Northwest tower, second floor. I've been told the third and fourth floors are empty, should you need them. These useless fellows,"—he throws a nod to the orderlies, lounged against a wall, their bloodied aprons hanging off their waists—"will carry your things. Now if you'll excuse me, I have four hundred wounded just landed from Balaclava to attend to."

"Sir, I should like . . ." She wanted to ask if she might view the wards.

Ignoring her or possibly not hearing, the surgeon turns on his heel, disappears back into the hospital. The orderlies push sulkily off the wall. Yawning, one turns his head to the side, hawks a stringy gob of spit into the mud.

"Well. This is a rum greeting, I say." Charles draws out his watch, peers at it, thumbs it back into his pocket. "We could all do with a spot of tea now, couldn't we? I'll help the black and whites down first, then the others." He has taken to calling the nuns "black and whites." "I move 'em about like chess pieces," he joked. "Now where is the ever-resourceful Mrs. Bracebridge?"

"Here, Charles." Selina has come up behind him, animated, alert with purpose. "I have found the way to the northwest tower, the shortest way, out of the rain. These good lads will help us, won't you, boys?" She asks each of the orderlies about himself as Charles and Florence help the nurses down from the oxcarts, pay the drivers, make certain all of the boxes and trunks are accounted for before being carried into the hospital by two of the drivers, eager for extra pay.

Black Ribbon

ON THE TOWER'S SECOND FLOOR are six filthy rooms for thirty-eight people. Trudging up a half-rotted spiral of stairs to the tower's third floor, Charles soon makes his way back down to report it infested with bats and rodents. Uninhabitable. Confined to the second floor, she delegates Charles and Selina to a small space off the common sitting room. The Norwood Anglicans, the whites, will share a room, the Catholics and Sellonites, the blacks, can share another. For herself, a glorified closet smelling of linseed oil. Secular nurses can stay in the room that serves as a kitchen. Suddenly, from this last room comes a piercing volley of screams, and Charles, agile for his bulk, gets there first. He emerges a minute later, his face drained of color.

"An officer, Russian, quite dead. Miss Terrot came upon him behind the stove. The odor is very bad. Flo, don't go in."

She goes in. Sprawled on his back, the Russian wears a dark green uniform emblazoned with gold cording, epaulets, ribbons, medals of honor. His black hat with its silver insignia, a Russian double eagle, sits upside down on the wooden floor, a pair of black gloves and a slender sheaf of letters tied with black ribbon stuffed inside. His broad, handsome face, mottled, looks haughty even in death. A clean shot to the heart, very little blood, the pistol still in his hand.

"Where are the orderlies? Charles, have them remove this man. Someone will need to determine his identity, decide what to do with him. He's the enemy, after all. How did he come to be in an enemy hospital? The lay nurses will sleep in the common room for tonight. Tomorrow, this entire kitchen, particularly behind the stove, will need to be scrubbed down."

Unflappable, cheerful, quick to act, Sister George (formerly Georgiana Barrie, now Sister Gonzaga, and asking to be called Sister George) has found sticks of wood to burn and brewed a pot of tea even as the orderlies, muttering curses, lug the corpse from the kitchen. In the common room, the lay nurses sit resting against a wall, passing a single cup of weak, lukewarm tea back and forth, too tired to remove their wet clothing, too cold to complain about a situation far worse than any of them could have imagined. Outside, rain falls steadily, leaking in around the warped, cracked windows, plashing mud all along the hospital's outside walls, drenching the backs of the oxen, the hunched-over drivers. Oxcarts, emptied, creak and jolt down to the harbor. Half sleet now, rain falls into the white-capped navy blue Sea of Marmara and the Golden Horn, falls, too, over hundreds of unburied men and dead horses, their bloated, grotesque shapes scattered, sown like handfuls of darkened grain over the bleak, windswept plains of Balaclava.

In her curtained closet, she unpacks. Opens the mahogany medicine box first, checking that the glass-stoppered bottles of powdered rhubarb, carbonate of potassium, quinine, carbonate of magnesia, carbonate of soda, ipecacuanha wine, paregoric elixir, citric acid, essence of ginger, carbonate of zinc, tonic pills, and cough pills, as well as the small brass scales for measuring, have not broken. She has misplaced Kempis's *Imitation of Christ*, along with the note from Sidney and his small blurred portrait cut from the *Times*. For luck, she wears the green bracelet with the snake's head clasp, its locket preserving intertwined strands of Mama's, Papa's, and Parthe's hair.

In the dark common room, she makes her way around the sleeping forms of the nurses, wrapped in their cloaks, over to the windows. The rain and sleet have stopped, the clouds mere wisps. A brassy half-moon sits above the black sea, its glittering stillness untouched by war. She wonders about the Russian officer, if he had a wife, now a widow. Were his letters, so neatly bound with black ribbon, from her? From a lover? What brought about his disgrace, his despair, his suicide? If he was married, will his widow be sent what remains of her husband—his clothing, war ribbons, medals—a career of murder, dignified by military decoration? Musing on these things, she is startled by a drawn-out wail coming from the high minaret of a mosque very close to the tower. A muezzin's call to prayer.

"Good night, Miss Nightingale," one of the Sellonite sisters whispers from the floor. Sarah Terrot, the one who had found the dead Russian.

"Miss Terrot? You're awake? You've had a bad shock today."

"Yes, ma'am. I'm fine now. Glad to be here with you."

"Thank you, but you must rest. Tomorrow will require all your strength."

Exhausted, she lies on the sagging military cot, thoughts racing until she drops into an aching sleep. The muezzin's predawn call to prayer wakens her, and she thinks to pray to the God of many faces, many names, Allah's among them, when she hears one of the women in the common room helplessly, miserably retching.

Bread and Tin

ON HIS FIRST FORAY around Scutari's Barrack Hospital, Charles scavenges a few tin basins, scrub brushes, two loaves of greenish black bread, gritty with sand. He even finds "butter"—a lump of rancid lard, wrapped in a strong-smelling bag of camel's hair. Mrs. Clarke, who has gotten the stove going, boils water for tea, black tea smuggled from Harley Street's pantry. She tries not to see how clouded and dingy the drinking water is, bits of organic matter floating in it. All thirty-eight nurses must share the half dozen tin cups she scavenged from a roach-infested cupboard the night before. There is no milk, only a small packet of sugar, quickly used up. The nurses stand or sit on the floor, crowded together in the common room, passing six cups, sharing torn-off pieces of bread. Cold, dejected, hungry, they look to Florence, who comes in to stand among them.

"Good morning. We have arrived safely and together; that is the important thing. In a few moments, I am going to look for the inspector general, the chief medical officer in charge of this hospital, and introduce myself. Part of my written agreement with London's War Office is not to begin our work until he, at the behest of the doctors and surgeons here at Scutari, requests our help."

"Surely they will welcome it?" That from Mrs. Elvira Roberts, speaking with the authority of a long career at St. Thomas's.

"One would assume so, Mrs. Roberts," Mary Clare Moore, Bermondsey's Reverend Mother, says gently. "Yet assumptions can prove wrong."

"Mother Moore is correct. As you know, we are the first female nurses to ever work within the British army's hospital system. The French military have their Sisters of Charity, but our British military has had no medical help from women. We are the experiment. As such, it is imperative we proceed with utmost diplomacy. Because we are women, we may not be as welcome as you might expect. We will have to prove ourselves. How? First by obeying the orders of the medical officers and doctors. Second, by our efficiency, decency, and skill. We must take great pains not to offend."

"Bosh. We need to do what we came here for. Save soldiers' lives." That from Miss Barnes, whom Florence suspects of having an alcohol problem. She had swigged eau de cologne all the way from Marseille, claiming it helped her seasickness. Even now, on land, she appears tipsy.

"And so we shall, Miss Barnes. But how we begin our work is critical to how well we will be received by doctors and surgeons completely unaccustomed to women nurses working alongside them. All England knows our mission; the people of England will be eager to learn more of it. We must set the highest example. Now, some practical things. Mrs. Clarke has found a number of small copper basins in the kitchen storeroom. Each of you will be given one for your washing as well as to drink water from. We will try our best to find more tin cups, plates, and cutlery. You may take turns drying your wet or damp clothes before the stove; Mrs. Clarke tells me she has set up a system for that purpose. Space is extremely cramped; I should like our Sellonite sisters to try to find a room or rooms on one of the floors directly above us that can be cleaned and made habitable. Mr. Bracebridge, will you help them? While I am off speaking with the inspector general, I should like everyone to finish unpacking, clean up your rooms, open and organize our crates of supplies. Miss Erskine, will you

make a list of every item in the crates? Thank you. Mrs. Bracebridge? Is Mrs. Bracebridge here?"

Charles speaks up. "She is resting. She was taken ill early this
morning."

"Nothing too serious, I hope. One final thing. Mr. Bracebridge
was informed this morning there are over two thousand wounded
and sick here at Barrack Hospital, with several hundred more
housed at the smaller General Hospital, a kilometer or so from
Scutari. Hundreds of others are expected on ships coming from the
Crimea over the next several days. I dare assume"—she looks at
Mother Moore—"we will be called to our work very soon."

Petticoat Impérieuse

*B*LASTED ADVENTURESS, JOHN HALL THINKS irritably, grinding out the stub of a cigar on the heel of his boot. *Petticoat impérieuse. War is man's business, and because some low, vulgar Irishman, damned liar, sails his arse over here and telegraphs back to the* Times *whatever wild inaccuracies, exaggerations, and insults he can invent to increase his readership and get fifty thousand readers up in arms—because of him and liars like him, here comes this garden tea party, this lace brigade of church bells led by some upper-class twit determined to complicate my life and make me miserable. I'll keep such a tight lid on her and her kind, they'll soon grow sick of blood, puke, and death and be begging for the first ship home. Thanks to the damned War Office, the government wanting to save its own skin, I have to deal with them. Too many women already—one in six brings the wife, so we have them, plus their squealing brats, plus the usual threepenny uprights, soldiers' dolly mops, slammed together in cellars underneath the hospital, some two hundred worthless, troublesome cunts. Now aren't we lucky? Here come the nuns and nurses, led by some high-nosed flibbertigibbet named Nightingale. Dim bird.*

He had awakened that morning with a sharp pain in his liver, a pain that has wormed its way up to his head, threatening to blow up his overheated brain.

ᕲ

If she'd knocked, he hadn't heard it. She stands in the doorway, a wan, willowy thing in an ugly black dress, not bad-looking, though

269

her otherwise fine gray eyes lack softness. Something cold in those eyes. And the smile, unwomanly, humorless, puts him on guard.

"Dr. Hall? I am not disturbing you?"

"Not in the least." (*Of course you are, silly peahen.*) Extends her hand straight out, as a man would. He takes it, barely—his message clear in the lukewarm touch.

"Florence Nightingale, sir. I arrived yesterday evening with a party of thirty-eight nurses. I was told you had been apprised of our coming here at the behest of the War Office."

"I was informed." He had skimmed the letter, thrown it away.

She waits for him to ask if their accommodations are sufficient, if there is anything they need. She already has a list in her pocket, supplies needed, repairs to be made.

But there is only awkward silence, stretching on. She will need to be direct.

"How soon may we begin work, Dr. Hall? My nurses can start today. Can you tell me what your doctors and surgeons most need and how we might render our immediate assistance?"

By turning straight around and paddling home. And take all those blasted women in the cellars with you, along with their snot-nosed, mewling brats. Leave the glory, the business of war, to men. Keep the whores close by, though.

He decides to take a formal approach. Intimidate her.

"Miss Nightwood is it? Nightingale? I am a career medical officer, thirty-five years in the service of Her Majesty's army. I have served throughout the British Empire, from Jamaica to South Africa to India. As a career army officer in charge of these hospitals, my authority goes unquestioned. What I say, as plainly as I can, is that we have no need of you or your nurses. We have adequate supplies and the necessary number of doctors, surgeons, assistants, and orderlies. Certain unfactual reports have appeared in the *Times*, false stories, accusations of incompetence and corruption put forth by a few irresponsible journalists, scandalmongers, who have stirred up a tempest of public protest. Now we have people at home demanding better treatment of our nation's soldiers. I assure you they are treated well. We need no help. So, Miss Nightwood, I'm afraid your long, arduous journey has been in vain."

"I see. Then the reports we read in the *Times* are at variance with the truth? I am at once sorry and glad to hear that. As for myself and my nurses, we only arrived late yesterday. It is impossible to leave immediately. We will make ourselves quietly useful until we are informed what to do, where to go next. I trust, should the situation change, you will call on us to help in whatever way we can. We are women, Dr. Hall, but we are fully capable nurses, proud to serve this hospital, the British army, and our nation."

Turning his back on her, John Hall stares out the window at the ever-growing refuse heap, stinking detritus of war that had once been a Turkish parade ground.

She leaves without a word. Her first battle. Fine. Though she doubts any English soldier, wounded and suffering, would refuse care from a woman nurse. She will wait out this man's hostility, follow military rules, requirements, and restrictions to the letter until the needs of the injured and sick overwhelm his petty, choleric resistance. In the meantime, she is going nowhere. Certainly not back to London.

Striding through a dark warren of corridors, finding her way back to the northwest tower, propelled by a gathering fury, she feels the ground moving, a residual sensation, perhaps, from nine days on board the rolling, pitching *Vectis*. She slows, stoops to examine the floor. Whole planks of wet, rotting wood are giving way underneath the thin stone flooring. The hospital, it would seem, is rotting away beneath her feet.

Scissors and Thread

ALL SOUND HAS DRAINED FROM THE SITTING ROOM but for the bite of scissors through flannel, the tearing of linen into strips, an occasional cough from one of the nurses. All movement confined to the subtlety of wrists turning, practiced fingers plying needles, tying knots, folding and stacking bandages. One of the Norwood nuns, in her white wool habit, sits near a broken window for better light, darning a pair of stockings. Three nurses stand around a long table; others sit on broken-down chairs; several sit, tailor-fashion, on the floor. Pinning, stitching, cutting, tearing, counting out shirt buttons in a heavy, resentful silence.

After the first meeting with John Hall, she had had to come back to this same room, inform the women they could not go into the wards until their services were formally requested. Confined since then to their quarters, they had scrubbed, cleaned, washed, rearranged furniture, and now, after one week, they work silently, too dispirited, too full of complaint to gossip or feign pleasantness. Even Sister George, normally jovial, is a study in gloom.

Returning from her second meeting with Dr. Hall—this time she had been "summoned"—she finds the floors reswept, the walls freshly scrubbed and whitewashed, each nurse sewing her own mattress, thin sacking to be stuffed with straw, the mattresses placed on low platforms, a protection from insects and rats. Someone has taken a rag to the windows, improving the view of the navy-dark sea, the white, needlelike towers of the mosque. As their quarters are scrubbed, tidied, organized, the muttered complaints and grumblings increase—they hadn't come all this way to scrub, do laundry, and sew like so many housemaids, seamstresses, and washerwomen. She had not, complained Emma Fagg, one of the St. John's nurses, crossed an ocean to twiddle her thumbs.

Pausing in the doorway, she takes note of the stacks of newly made flannel shirts, the rows of bandages, rolled strips of linen, the dozens of stump pillows for amputees, the atmosphere of resentful industry in the room.

"Good day, ladies!" She steps into the room with such uncharacteristic cheer, the nurses look up in surprise. While they still respect her as their superintendent, they are fast becoming a sullen, disgruntled lot.

"I've brought fresh loaves of bread and welcome news. I've just come from seeing Inspector General Hall. He tells me some eight hundred men are to be received into the wards today, coming off ships from the Crimea. Seven hundred more wounded are expected tomorrow." She pauses. "The doctors and surgeons say they are overwhelmed by these new numbers and ask for our help." She pauses again. "Immediately."

The room's earlier, aggrieved silence turns to exclamations, questions, the commotion of thirty-eight women standing up, putting away their things, seeking out shawls, bonnets, shoes, an excited rushing about. Those who are not nuns hurry to change into their uniforms.

In twenty minutes, they are prepared, gathered around her, though it seems there is a problem with the uniforms she had had hastily made in London. They are all one size, and though they fit some of the women, those who are either taller or shorter than average look ridiculous. On the taller nurses, the gray tweed dresses are so short, their stockinged legs and boots poke out. On the shorter women, the dresses drag along the ground. Impatient,

Florence recommends "home tailoring"—the simple taking up or letting down of hems whenever the women can find time to do so. In the midst of this sartorial crisis, the Sellonite sisters file down from the third floor, fully disciplined and ready to work. When all are assembled, looking to her for direction, she falters. *I've made a terrible mistake. Where is my confidence?* A short silence and she finds her voice.

"Two rules, ironclad. No proselytizing, not Catholic or Protestant. No socializing with soldiers, no idle chatter among yourselves. As female nurses, it is imperative you conduct yourselves with dignity. Sister George, would you and another of your sisters bring along rolls of bandages and some of the stump pillows? I expect they are needed. Some of you, bring half of the new shirts. Mrs. Clarke, I will need your assessment of dietary needs. I also need two nurses to take these blocks of chalk and number each of the beds. We will pair numbers with patients' names and histories. The Bracebridges will not accompany us; they have gone to the Grand Bazaar, to Constantinople, to purchase supplies. Is everyone ready? God bless you all, and remember, "'Things won are done, joy's soul lies in the doing.'"

"*Troilus and Cressida.*" Reverend Mother Moore, an avid reader of Shakespeare, names the quote.

"Yes. We go from Shakespeare's Trojan War to a war all our own. Mother Moore, will you lead us in prayer?" She has learned that one third of the British army is Irish Catholic, so the Bermondsey nuns should be a welcome presence. She bows her head, appearing to pray, anxious about details she might have overlooked.

"On second thought," she announces when the prayer ends, "leave everything here, shirts, bandages, pillows, even the chalk. Better we gauge the situation, return for what is needed."

A silent procession of religious and lay nurses leaves the

northwest tower. Subdued, nervous, they descend the stairs and file into the first corridor before stepping through an open-air passageway, the stomach-churning stench reaching them long before they enter the first ward. As Miss Terrot will record in her journal: *Today, we walked straight into a slaughterhouse. We descended this day into Hell itself.*

Slaughterhouse

"Miss, I am going under."

She slips the normally resolute Mrs. Clarke a small brown bottle of smelling salts. "We are well and truly in the bowels of Hell, Mrs. C., but you must not appear affected. For the sake of these men, it is your duty to stay calm."

She will have to struggle for the calm she urged on Mrs. Clarke as Andrew McGrigor, the sandy-haired surgeon, going bald at the crown, leads them on a long, ghoulish tour of Scutari's wards. She keeps to his side, asking numbers, statistics, how she should requisition supplies. His answers are grim, clipped, as she sees firsthand that Barrack Hospital is a far cry from her genteel patients at Harley Street, even the cholera-stricken prostitutes at Middlesex.

"As of yesterday, we have over seventeen hundred patients, one hundred and twenty with cholera. In the General Hospital, there are six hundred and fifty soldiers, wounded. Six hundred more arrive today from Balaclava. We have no beds, only straw and India mats. Beneath the stone floors, much of the wood is rotten. The men prefer their vermin-infested blankets to the stiff canvas ones the Turks provide. They lie in their own waste and blood. You will need to watch your step, as the sewers back up constantly. There are eight latrines for thousands of men and hardly anyone to empty them. Floors can be four or five inches deep in raw sewage. When it rains, you will be slogging through feces and drowned rats. The water in the fountains is bad; I advise you not to drink it. Drink wine or porter. Supplies? Next to none. A request to the purveyor general chokes its way through a byzantine maze—a request for chloroform, for example, is sent to London, where it is passed through various departments. If by some miracle, it is approved, then the chloroform must be located, possibly even manufactured, before it can be shipped here. Half our supplies are lost at sea, the other half pilfered; they disappear into Turkish customs houses or show up for sale in Constantinople's Grand Bazaar. Yesterday, I was given word that the *Prince*, carrying a great many of the supplies I had personally asked for—medicines, blankets, new boots, winter jackets—sank in a hurricane off the coast of the Crimea. Shipwrecks are common; theft occurs daily. Purchasing supplies at the Bazaar? Not so simple. Every item must first be requested in writing, approved of, signed off on by the purveyor, a miserable clot by the name of Wreford. Tight as a clamshell. Drives his bookkeeper mad, totting up figures, boasting how little he spends. Seeks advancement through parsimony. Because of him, men die."

Walking as fast as he has been talking, McGrigor halts abruptly beside a man sprawled on a bed of dirty straw, scarlet uniform jacket bunched under his head, one arm crudely splinted.

"This officer's aide had two horses shot out from under him at Inkerman. We've splinted his arm. If he has no fever tomorrow, he'll be sent straight back into battle. Simple cases like his are rare. Three limbs to a man the average. We lose as many to dysentery, diarrhea, and scurvy as we do to typhus, typhoid, cholera. Look at this poor devil, gone off during the night. When I find one, I'll send an orderly to clear him, make room for the next."

She follows the surgeon down dark corridors, her nurses filing behind. In every ward, windows are shuttered to keep out the winter cold. In the center of each ward, coal stoves belch out more smoke than heat. Everywhere men cry out, desperate for water or medicine. As if deaf, McGrigor strides doggedly on. Rats rustle and squeak by the hundreds through the wards, dart down corridors. Fearless, they feast on the dead, the almost dead. The thick, wet reek of sewage, blood, vomit, and unwashed bodies is unendurable.

Outside, in the fresh, bracing air, Florence turns to her nurses, pale and silent as ghosts. Some weep. One is being discreetly sick. Bolstered by her smelling salts, Mrs. Clarke merely looks grim. *A mistake? To bring them here? No. Isn't her mission theirs? They had asked, volunteered, to come.*

"Miss Nightingale, come down to the dock with me. I should like you to see where we receive the wounded. Ships cross the Black Sea from the Crimea every day, a journey of some three hundred miles. Conditions on board are abysmal; the wounded and sick receive no medicine, no treatment. Many die before reaching land, and if they live, there are but five surgeons like myself for thousands of men."

"These conditions are deplorable, Dr. McGrigor. Far worse than the reports we read in our newspapers back home. My nurses are impatient to work. I have kept them busy these past four days sewing a great many flannel shirts and cleaning their quarters. We have had soap, basins, Turkish towels, and other supplies bought for us in Constantinople. We are ready, Dr. McGrigor. Tell us how we may help."

"I must say, Miss Nightingale, I never thought to see ladies like yourselves in this putrid hole. It's a bloody charnel house. How may you help? What can you and your nurses do? Begin by washing as many of the men as you can. Clean their wounds. If their wounds are dressed, redress them. We have twenty chamber pots for a thousand men, fourteen slipper baths. The men are crawling with vermin, and lice here are of a giant size. No sooner has a fellow died than they desert him for the nearest breathing man."

"Look down toward the dock, Miss Nightingale. You'll see young men being carried off the ship by the hundreds. Behind that ship is another, behind that one, another. Endless." He glances down at her. "This may be too much for you to see or hear."

"Not in the least. You will find me as coolheaded and capable as any man. I appreciate that you have shown us all that you have."

She stands beside the weary surgeon. The wounded are passing close by now, soldiers slung onto the straining backs of Turks, writhing, mouths gaping, moaning, eyes slewed in agony. The dead are being stacked in carts like planks of lumber, limbs at broken angles. Behind her, a few nurses murmur among themselves. Most, handkerchiefs pressed over their noses, don't speak at all. The Bermondsey nuns are whispering the rosary. Reverend Mother Moore, on her knees, has turned her face to the sky.

"Hell of a thing," the surgeon says. "War. Most of these poor chaps had no idea what would happen to them. Told it was for the glory and honor of England, bribed by a shilling and a pint of beer, hauled off, flogged for the least offense, marched into the field and slaughtered. For what? For the queen. For land and sea. For pride of empire. For that and that alone, a generation dies."

He turns away, a look of disillusion and disgust on his face. "Let's go back. I've work to do."

Will the Purveyor Not Purvey?

IN THE COMMON SITTING ROOM, the mood is somber as the Bracebridges come to grips with the inadequacy of their personal contribution, supplies procured in Constantinople. Still, everyone is grateful for the sugar and tea, the loaves of soft bread. Stacked near the door, a pathetic sight, are twenty-five tin basins, a dozen rough-cut bars of soap, some Turkish towels, one sponge. Nearby are wooden crates filled with several dozen newly sewn flannel shirts, rolls of linen bandages, a few stump pillows and arm slings.

For thousands of men.

Waiting for orderlies to carry all of this down to the wards, she orders ten of the Sellonite sisters to move to the smaller General Hospital. Patients there are mostly sick with low fever, dysentery, and diarrhea, so there should be enough short-term supplies for the sisters. She writes out a requisition for Mr. Wreford, listing basic nursing supplies and digestible foods like arrowroot and sago for puddings, medicinal teas, and negus, a spiced port wine to be warmed and mixed with water. Despite McGrigor's disgust with the purveyor, she remains hopeful. Surely Mr. Wreford will address dire shortages. Why in heaven's name wouldn't a purveyor purvey?

Amputation

Latin: *putare*, to prune

Dear Sidney,

When we arrived here, there was neither basin, towel, nor soap in the wards. Thirty could be bathed in slipper baths each night, but this does no more than include a washing once in eighty days for 2,300 men! The consequence is fever, cholera, gangrene, bugs, lice, fleas & erysipelas. And a single sponge for hundreds of wounds! The fault, as I see it, is not with the medical officers, but in the insufficient numbers of minor officers in the Purveying Department, led by a parsimonious and negligent Mr. Wreford. His delay in obtaining the most basic supplies is inexcusable, as is the existence of one single interpreter who . . .

She leaves the letter, resenting the image of Sidney in London, out of all danger, putting his signature to bloodless pieces of paperwork. Sleep impossible, she returns to the wards—her Kingdom of Hell—and is soon observing her first amputation at Scutari. The patient, a strapping black-haired, black-eyed soldier from Belfast, has a gangrenous right leg that needs removing above the knee. In lieu of a surgery table, he lies on a length of dirty canvas laid over straw. A tallow candle and a Turkish lamp provide the only light. The surgeon appears from nowhere, a small, wiry man, his canvas apron splattered with blood. He carries a surgical box. Made of mahogany, it has neat brass hinges and a small lock. Inside, fastened against a lining of maroon velvet, is a bone-cutting saw with a

serrated edge, a bone brush, amputation knives, a Petit's screw tourniquet, hooks to pull arteries from limb stumps, a tenaculum, and
a bottle of catgut for suturing. Paying her no attention, he directs
an assistant, a "dresser," to wash out the wound so he can probe it
with his finger, feel for bits of bone, cloth, a bullet. A second assistant jams a fat plug of cloth into the Irishman's mouth, then kneels
behind him, holding down his shoulders with both hands. The
first "dresser" tightens the tourniquet above where the leg is to be
removed, holds the gangrenous leg steady. Deciding on the circular
rather than flap method of amputation, the surgeon slices through
skin and muscle, rolling them up before cutting down to the thigh-
bone. Clamping the knife between his teeth, he runs the bone-
cutting saw back and forth, pulls out the larger blood vessels with
his tenaculum hook. Tying off the main artery with a reef knot, he
ties off the smaller arteries as one of the dressers loosens the tourniquet and rasps smooth the sharp edges of bone with a file while
the other assistant brushes away bone dust. Unrolling the skin and
muscle, the surgeon takes catgut and sutures the wound closed.
The leg, purplish red, bubbled-looking, is dropped into a large box
of sawdust. The operation, she will later estimate in her journal,
took under fifteen minutes, accompanied by the man's agonized
screams and groans, half-muffled by the rag in his mouth. She will
note, too, that earlier that day, Dr. McGrigor had expressed vehement opposition to the use of chloroform; "The smart of a knife,
Miss Nightingale, is a powerful stimulant. Better to hear a man
bawl lustily than see him sink into the grave." Chloroform, he told
her, is not forbidden at Scutari, but few use it.

Clattering his freshly bloodied instruments into the velvet-
lined case, the nameless surgeon—she will never see him again—
moves wearily to the next man. The massive black-haired soldier
from Belfast will live twenty-four more hours before his corpse is

carted out to the Dead House, the severed leg tossed into a deep pit, to join a stiffening mangle of hundreds of blackening arms, legs, feet, sometimes one foot, still in its leather boot, crudely sawed off.

For now, she sits beside him, pressing wet compresses on the wound to sweeten it, resting the raw end of the limb on an oil-cloth-covered stump pillow. He is unconscious, his pulse thready. Men on either side, less than eighteen inches away and across the narrow "aisle," have heard every gruesome sound. Walking back to her quarters at dawn, she decides that portable screens must be found or made. The shock of listening is too great, discouraging survival when it is their turn. This is nothing she has read or been told, simply a thing she knows. From now on, she will see to it that for every amputation surgery, a screen must first be placed between the patient and any soldiers who lie close by.

Overwhelmed

Dear Pastor Fliedner,

Here at Scutari, the whole British army floods into the hospital. The task is gigantic. Alas, how will it end? We are in the hands of God. Pray for us. There are five thousand sick and wounded. My one comfort is that God sees, God knows, and God loves us all. Remember me to my Protestant sisters at Kaiserwerth.

Florence

Pushing up from her improvised writing table, leaving her plate untouched—stone-hard bread, leatherlike beef, cold tea—she walks into the common room. The others have gone to sleep, but if she lies down and closes her eyes, she hears the screams of the Belfast lad, his last cry for his mother, a whispered, agonal *"Ma."*

Every afternoon at one o'clock, the newly dead, stitched into filthy blankets, are lugged on stretchers to the Dead House near the British cemetery, a promontory that reaches over the Sea of Marmara. A macabre procession. Watching it out a window, she decides that to honor these never-ending dead, she will walk the wards at night, offer each living soldier a word of kindness, a drink of water, a prayer if he asks. If she cannot sleep, she can walk.

In the meantime, Wreford remains as scarce as his supplies. Searching, she found his office, an unmarked, windowless hole-in-the-wall, but whenever she stops by, there is no one there. She leaves written requisitions, but it feels as though she is dropping scraps of paper off the edge of the world.

Three Gentlemen from London

THREE GENTLEMEN HAVE ARRIVED from London, charged with reporting hospital conditions back to the government. John MacDonald, business manager of the *Times*; the Reverend Sydney Godolphin Osborne, Scutari's new chaplain; and Augustus Stafford, MP. What, they have been instructed to ask, does Miss Nightingale most need? What may they purchase for her, using money donated by the public to the *Times* fund? Rubbing his eyes, yawning, Charles Bracebridge comes out of his room and joins the three visitors at a table in the sitting room. Prone to heavy sighs and plosive huffs of indignation, fond of quoting Virgil (*Flectere si nequeo superos, Acheronta movebo*—"If I cannot move Heaven, I will raise Hell"), flamboyant with curses, and newly overtaken by the habit of counting and tallying, as if numbers could soothe him, Charles, excusing Miss Nightingale's absence—*a bird, alighting everywhere yet nowhere to be found*—appoints himself informal leader of the other three men.

Mrs. Clarke, who has become coarse and obstinate since leaving Harley Street and England, bangs down four tin cups of tea without offering milk or sugar. *Be glad there're no bits of shite floating in the water*, she feels like saying.

Charles explains the desperate shortage of supplies as the three visitors pass Miss Nightingale's list around—*flannel, calico, medicinal wine, soaps, three hundred scrubbing brushes, tin washing basins, combs, tea, port, sago and arrowroot, two hundred Turkish towels, wooden spoons, knives, forks, tin cups, saucepans, sheets, kettles for Mrs. Clarke to cook broth, tea, rice milk, negus, and, for the nurses, fresh fruit, vegetables, soft bread.*

"Negus," the new chaplain grimaces. "Foul stuff."

Doing God's Work

Dear Mrs. Nightingale,

Selina has passed along your gifts to Florence. Your daughter has begun her nursing work in earnest. It will not surprise you to know that in two weeks' time, working twenty hours a day (she does not sleep), your daughter has gained the love and confidence of all. Doctors who refused her at first now do her will, though a few older ones, calling her "the Bird," are not averse to handing on to her their most onerous tasks—which she does without complaint. And the deathbeds! She must see five or more expire each day and sits with each one devotedly. Around any and all contagion, she is fearless.

There are dismal complications here at Scutari due to shortages of supplies, the cruel indifference of the military to its infantry, and, if I may say, a bit too much tippling among the orderlies, who are careless in their duties and complain of interrupted dinners whenever a new influx of wounded is brought in. The nurses are an uneven lot. I expect we will require more as some are dismissed and others pick up and go home.

I have taken charge of the laundry crisis. After the one boiler, used to wash the shirts of thousands of men, broke down, I leased a small building near the hospital, and purchased several new ones. Small miracle, I've managed to recruit washerwomen from among the several hundred wives, widows, and other "ladies." The ambassador's wife, Lady Stratford de Redcliffe (do you know of her?), has had a drying machine built to add to our arsenal.

Florence's strategy is a good one—a clean shirt twice a week for every soldier, clean bedding, edible food (rations are so foul, the sick cannot digest them), opened windows to defeat the dread miasma, scrubbed floors and walls. She fights a war of her own, the enemy not the "Rooshuns," but the bureaucratic quagmires and hostile resistance from those in authority. Hers is not a war of opposing guns and cannon, but one spent battling a morass of useless rules and the sins of stubborn pride and ignorance.

Aside from a few tottering artifacts, the doctors are more and more in favor of her. They observe her tirelessness, the calm intelligence with which she meets every crisis.

When I asked Mrs. Bracebridge what power is it that gives Florence her superhuman energy, she replied, "She is at last doing what God called her to do."

I trust you are well. If you do not hear from your daughter, it is only that she is drowned in red tape and war blood—in equal measure.

Ever your humble, etc.,
Charles

Ojibwe Moccasins

Hidden between the pages of *The Imitation of Christ*—his image, cut from the *Times*. On her cot, she is pressing his face to her lips like an icon when Selina comes in, holding a package.

"Flo?"

She conceals the clipping in her hand.

"Liz has sent you something. My word, you look shot. I'll put it here. I'm off to find Charles; goodness knows where he has gotten off to."

The package is neatly labeled and secured with hemp string. She carries it back to her cot. Inside a bottle of White Rose perfume from Floris, a copy of Elizabeth Gaskell's latest novel, *North and South,* an exquisite lace cap to cover her hair, and a most curious gift: a pair of deerskin moccasins with red-felted throats, intricately beaded in a floral design. In the enclosed note, Liz writes that the moccasins, purchased at a trading post in Minnesota, were made by White Cloud, a woman from the Mille Lacs Band of Ojibwe. A friend of Liz's, returning from America, had brought them back as a gift. They came with a teaching, the first of the Ojibwe's seven sacred values: *Aakwade'ewin,* meaning "bravery" or "courage." Have bravery and courage in doing things right, even though it may hurt you physically and mentally. *These swim on me,* Liz writes. *I hope they fit you.*

She nudges her sore, blistered feet, first one, then the other, into the moccasins, their puckered seams neatly stitched with sinew.

They mold, like the softest of gloves, to her aching feet. *Have bravery and courage.* She will wear them tonight. Charles accompanied her on rounds two nights before and calculated she had walked over ten kilometers, an inhuman undertaking.

Charles Proves Useful

"Two hundred fifty-one, fifty-two, fifty-three—where the blasted deuce was I? Two hundred fifty-three, fifty-four . . ."

Not a doctor, a journalist, or a businessman, Charles is a sturdy, relatively fit man, capable of useful errands. He can even fix things. The laundry system, for one. Now he counts off paces in corridors, six hundred in the last. Jots the numbers down in his pocket notebook; from these, he calculates how many beds can be put down on either side of a corridor. The hallways and four adjoining wards need to be readied for the latest shipment of wounded from Balaclava, arriving any day.

The St. John's sisters are stuffing canvas sacks for mattresses, complaining about having been taken away from their true calling—nursing. But she had found all four of them scampering about the wards the other night, laughing with the soldiers, two of them wearing bangles, earrings, bits of lace. In order to save their reputations, she pulled them out of the wards and put them to work sewing. Mutiny brews as they stab needles in and out of sacking. Nightingale is heartless. Authoritarian. Tyrannical. Two of them will be asking to go home.

"I should rename myself brigadier general of the British army," she complains to Charles. "I have more fuss with thirty-eight nurses than with two thousand soldiers."

"Your nurses are either malcontents or saints," he says. "Not a damned thing in between."

Androgyne

Dear Parthenope,

Recently, Flo had taken to cold creaming her hair—tonight I found her shearing it off. When I asked, she said, "No time for long hair," then gave it to me to stuff in a mattress! I must say she looks neither man nor woman. More a kind of androgyne.

Will you send some useful clothing? She is down to a single straw bonnet with a hole in it, a single petticoat, a few grubby black dresses. A Maltese lace collar and a new lace cap would also be welcome, though I have never seen your sister as indifferent to appearance as she is now. Her every thought and action goes into aiding the wounded, comforting the dying, and having to stand up to a fortress of army resistance. The battle is not personal; it is more that the left hand does not know what the right is doing. Communications between the separate military compartments is nil. Florence insists that nothing less than total reform of England's military hospital system is needed, though her first concern is with the wounded. Some of the nurses have begun to complain of her impatience, her unfeelingness, yet I have never seen her be less than deeply tender with the soldiers. She sits with the most hopeless cases, showing infinite patience. Perhaps there is no reserve left in her to deal with petty complaints from her nurses.

Be assured your sister is in her "milieu," doing what God asks of her. The doctors and surgeons marvel at what they call the Nightingale "power," though the older ones pass their most onerous tasks on to her. She does them all, though with a certain energy derived from pent-up rage.

Yesterday, she had me find paper and pen with which to take down letters to relatives from the dying soldiers. The infantrymen are mostly Irish and illiterate—some speak only Gaelic! It has become an important part of our work to write letters for these men, to send their personal belongings and pay home to their families—decent things that have never been done before now.

Charles keeps busy organizing a laundry system. He has always been comfortable around women, so picture my dear husband sporting a white turban, a mob of soldiers' wives and widows churning around him as he persuades them to see the washing of filthy sheets, crawling with vermin, as patriotic work—which I suppose it is.

Affectionately,
Selina

Fanoos

THE MOCCASINS MAKE NO SOUND; the deerskin feels as soft and warm as butter on her feet. Holding her *fanoos*, a Turkish concertina lantern removed from the purveyor's storerooms, she moves unhurriedly, glancing down at each man to see if he is asleep, in need of a sip of water or a word of comfort. If he is dying, she sits with him. After, using her forefinger and thumb to close the still-warm eyelids, she makes note of which corridor, which ward, which bed, so that the body may be removed at sunrise. So many deaths, corpses stacked like plates, stored like linen, the Dead House completely full. Burials cannot keep up with deaths; the stink of rotted, putrid flesh is everywhere. The slow swing of her lantern with its single flicker of flame becomes a nightly occurrence in the wards. Were she an artist, she would not paint Christ washing Peter's feet in a golden bowl while the other disciples turn the pages of books, talk, wait their turn. Nothing like Tintoretto. Hers would be a chiaroscuro portrait of agony, blood, desolation, and death.

Slippers, Scarves, Jam

IN THE COMMON ROOM, FREEZING RAIN needles against the windows; hard winds off the sea shear through the cracks and broken panes.

"La di dah," crows Emma Fagg, a St. John's nurse. "Look at these, will you. Monogrammed linens. Some lucky soldier will have his saber wound bound in Lady Hoity-Toity's fancy hankie."

"What else?" Rebecca Lawford sorts impatiently through the boxes. The nurses crowd around the Christmas boxes from England, overflowing with gifts from *Times* readers.

"Look! Slippers, hand-stitched, dozens and dozens, from a Mr. Beadsworth. He writes that he and his children, for a Christmas project, have sewn these slippers 'for the brave soldiers of the Crimea.'"

"Oh God, ginger biscuits, my favorite! Tins and tins of 'em!"

"Keep away, Emma; they're not for us!"

"Jars of homemade raspberry and blackberry jams, orange and lime marmalade. Lord, can we not keep some for ourselves? I'd die for a spoonful."

"Loads of socks—dozens of shirts, too."

"Packets of money!"

"Look. A box from Balmoral, from the queen. She's knit scarves for the men to wear around their necks."

"How many? Enough for all?"

"Dunno. Lovely, though, aren't they?"

"There's a note."

Handed the note, penned in a small, firm hand, Florence reads it aloud.

> *I wish Miss Nightingale and the ladies to tell these poor, noble, wounded and sick men that no one takes a warmer interest or feels more for their sufferings or admires their courage and heroism more than their queen. Day and night she thinks of her beloved troops. So, too, does the prince.*

"Mrs. Bracebridge, we must make copies of the queen's note, post them around the wards. It will cheer the men. What's this now? A second letter?"

She reads it slowly.

"What, Flo, what does it say?"

"Not much. She wants copies of my hospital reports sent directly to her, and asks if the soldiers would like it if she sent each a bottle of eau de cologne."

"Rum would be better," mutters Mrs. Clarke, disappointed not to find any rum or gin in among the Christmas claptrap. She has managed to sneak a pair of socks into her apron pocket—for her chilblains.

Just then, a section of the roof, the weakest, blows off in the storm. As rain pours in, the nurses rush to lift the rest of the boxes, gifts from the well-meaning people of England, off the floor.

Private Letter

9 December 1854

Sidney,

Squalid. A word I say to myself multiple times a day. That this "hospital" is the Devil's own Kingdom of Hell is beyond doubt.

My two enemies, beyond filth and disease, are the purveyor, Wreford, and the chief medical officer, John Hall. Call me what you like—cook, housekeeper, scavenger, washerwoman, general dealer, and storekeeper, I keep meticulous records, fueling my case for proper food, bandages, medicines, mops, buckets, et cetera. Out of desperation, I have established my own storeroom in our living quarters, adding mistress emporium and brigadier general to my slew of titles, the last in reference to my futile attempts to cure some of the thirty-eight women of flirtatious behaviors and lack of sobriety. Instead of nightly sleep, I take my lantern and prowl among the wounded. I see God's tender mercies everywhere as well as His seeming indifference to suffering. A crisis of faith.

I have opened two special kitchens with supplementary boilers for sick cookery. When I arrived here, I found just thirteen great copper pots used both for boiling tea and cooking meat. As for vegetables, there are none. Last Saturday, I watched in disbelief as thousands of green cabbages were dumped overboard into the sea because no one was authorized to receive a shipment of cabbages! Scurvy is rampant among the men, and though I have seen with my own eyes bottles of lime juice in Wreford's storeroom, again, no one is authorized to distribute it! This is the unforgiving terrain I fight in, pen in one hand, mop in the other. We are doing better at keeping our patients fed, warm, and clean, though many still die of dysentery. For cholera, we have only tincture of opium.

I am more and more of the opinion that the so-called heroic medicines of the day—opium, arsenic, mercury, bleeding with leeches, et cetera—only hasten a man's death. Clean water, fresh air, laundered clothing, and wholesome food succeed far better at offsetting miasmic air, water, overall filth. I am of the minority in this opinion. Sanitation, hygiene, statistics—these are my earthly Deities.

Entre nous, we are in great want of hair mattresses or even flock, as it is cheaper. Our worst cases suffer terribly from bedsores. Can you not circumvent the "rat maze" and send supplies directly to me from London? I beg you to do so.

We are in an age of hemorrhage and gangrene. Every ten minutes an orderly runs to inform us, so we go cram lint in a wound till a surgeon can be sent for. As I write this, two ships more are loading at the Crimea. They will arrive with hundreds of wounded, dying, and dead. Then will come the operations. This morning, I saw one poor fellow, a Highlander, exhausted from hemorrhage, have his right leg amputated, then go off ten minutes after the surgeon left him. Almost before the breath left his body, he was sewn up in his own bloodied blanket and hauled off to the Dead House. Next, I watched an excision of the shoulder joint, superbly performed, and visited another poor fellow with two stumps for arms, another without an arm and a leg, another with paralysis in one eye, the other eye having been put out entirely.

All who can, come to me for tobacco. I have to tell them we have not a pinch.

Ever yours,

Miss Nightingale, barrack mistress, purveyor, clothier of the British army and general dealer in 6,000 shirts, 2,000 socks, 500 pairs of drawers, red nightcaps, slippers, knives, forks, spoons, *trays, tables, clocks, operating room tables, scrubbers, towels, soaps, screens, tin slipper baths, combs, red precipitate (mercuric oxide powder, excellent for murdering lice), scissors, bedpans, stump pillows, et cetera, et cetera.*

"Nightingale Power"

CHARLES HAS MISPLACED ONE of his felt bed slippers. As Selina searches for it under a stack of unread newspapers, both agree their Scutari adventure has lost its novelty. Flo has become a formidable force, so demanding they avoid her at every turn. "Nightingale power" is a much-used phrase around the hospital, a reference to her uncanny ability to procure whatever she wants by argument, persuasion, donations, use of her own funds, or other more mysterious, coercive, or stealthy means. But Selina has just shared a troublesome letter with Charles that cannot be ignored. Sitting up in bed, they discuss what to do, while Charles's slipper, having been found, rests beside its mate.

"I cannot read it to her; she will be in a rage, tap-tapping her foot before I reach the second line." Selina is referring to Florence's new habit of holding herself in a state of perfect stillness while one foot frenziedly taps out her irritation with someone's slowness, stupidity, or ignorance. She has changed. No longer the lovely, intelligent, sometimes moody young woman they had chaperoned in Rome and Egypt, she is snappish, unrelenting in her demands, indifferent to food, refusing sleep. She exhausts everyone. Beneath the bedcovers, they carry on a muffled discussion. Charles admits to missing his library, his men's clubs, his fine port and cigars. Selina cannot find a thing to sketch in Scutari that isn't gruesome, too awful for her pencils. Her job these days, as demanded by Florence, is to write down the last words of dying soldiers and mail them to their families back home. It depresses her no end.

"Still, it would be cold, Charles, to simply hand Liz's letter to her."

"Tell her outright."

"And say what? That a fresh battalion of nurses is due to arrive the day after tomorrow, if not sooner? With her constantly wishing she had brought half as many nurses over? That two or three would do?"

"Just give her the letter. Or when she is in the wards, leave it on her desk. Spare yourself her fury."

"Brilliant, Charles. I'll leave it for her."

"*Timeo Danaos et dona ferentes!* They conquer who believe they can! Poor poppet, your feet are ice! Snug over, let me warm them."

Private!

Slamming the letter down, in a rage, she snatches it up again. More nurses? More nuns? She is the superintendent; why was she not consulted? Because she would have said no. She will, in fact, say no. She rereads Liz's letter, addressed to Selina (and why to Selina, why not to her?). And why didn't he write her, ask her permission? Before she left London, he'd given his solemn word he would send no additional nurses unless she asked for them. She had not asked. She has, in fact, complained she would have done far better with half as many nurses.

She shapes her fury into privately intended, frigid sentences.

PRIVATE!

Barrack Hospital
Scutari
10 December 1854

Dear Mr. Herbert,

With regard to receiving & employing a greater number of Sisters & Nurses in these hospitals, I went immediately (on reading Mrs. Herbert's letter addressed to Mrs. Bracebridge, not to me!) to consult with Mr. Menzies, our temporary principal medical officer, under whose direct orders I now serve.

He considers there are already as large a number of nurses employed in these hospitals as can be appropriated & made consistent with morality & discipline. To maintain discipline among some forty women is no trifling matter.

He also considers that, were our numbers to increase to sixty or seventy, to keep order would be impossible. I so fully concur with Mr. Menzies that I will resign my position at once, if such a circumstance is forced upon me.

Our quarters are already inadequate. More nurses cannot be assigned. The sick are now laid up to our very door!

Had we come out with twenty instead of forty, we should have been less hampered with difficulties; the work itself would have been better & more efficiently done. As it is, ten of us do the whole work. The others simply run between our feet, trip and hinder us.

English people, it would seem, imagine Scutari to be a place with inns, hackney coaches & furnished houses to let. There is not a room in our cramped quarters that does not let in rain and cold when the weather is bad. We buy our miserable food through the commissary & are often without wood or coal for heat or cooking.

All this and more should explain the impossibility *of entertaining more nurses, particularly "ladies," here at present.*

Excuse confusion.

In great haste
ever yours

After she writes this letter, a terrible thought begins to take root in her. Had he taken advantage? Used her for his benefit? As war secretary, he well knew the public's growing outcry over the army's mistreatment of its soldiers, as reported in the *Times* by Russell and other journalists. He knew it might result in his downfall. He knew the system, rotten to the core, included him. Had he sent her as a decoy, as sentimental distraction? She thinks of Parthe, writing to her of her glorification in the press, the sobriquets like "Angel of the Crimea," "Lady with the Lamp," "Mother to Thousands" bandied about, the popular engravings of her, ceramic figurines in her image, false sanctifications—all some clever, even cynical, ploy meant to deflect public attention away from him and the misman-agement and corruption of the bureaucracy she is witnessing first-hand and fighting against at Scutari? Is she nothing but a sacrifice to salvage his political reputation and that of the army?

For the queen. For land and sea. For pride of empire. For that and that alone, a generation dies.

Five days later, a second letter:

PRIVATE!

Barrack Hospital
Scutari
15 December 1854

Mr. Herbert,

When I came here as your superintendent, it was with the understanding (expressed both in your handwriting & in the printed announcement you placed in the Morning Chronicle*) that additional nurses were to be sent only at my request and with the approval of the principal medical officer here.*

You came to me in your original distress, saying you were unable to find any better qualified person for the office, & that, if I failed you, the entire scheme would fail. Persuaded, I sacrificed my own judgment, & came here with thirty-eight females, well knowing that half that number would have been more efficient & far less trouble. I already knew that the difficulty—thirty-eight untrained women turned loose among three thousand men—of observing any order at all would be herculean. My experience now justifies that foreboding. I have toiled my way into the confidence of the medical men, and by incessant vigilance have introduced something like a system into the disorderly operations of these women. My plan has succeeded in some measure.

Now, at this point of affairs, you send a fresh batch of women, raising our numbers to eighty-six! To permit new women to scamper about the wards of a military hospital would be as improper as it would be absurd!

You have sacrificed the cause so near my heart. You have sacrificed me. You have sacrificed your written promise to the popular cry. You have advanced your own reputation by diminishing mine.

Under these circumstances, the only thing I can do is discharge twelve of the women I already have and fill their places with these new ones. In addition to the leaders of their delegation, Mary Stanley, your friend, and Reverend Mother Bridgeman, I shall have to shove twelve more into quarters already overcrowded & find a house in Scutari for the remaining twenty-two. Those twenty-two, impossible to employ in these hospitals, must wait to be employed at Therapia or elsewhere—or until you recall them.

Sir, you must feel I ought to resign. That must be your reason behind all of this. Therefore, I remain at my post only until I have provided in some measure for these poor wanderers. You will need to decide where the twenty-two nurses will be employed—at Therapia or elsewhere—or whether they are to be returned to England. You will need to appoint a superintendent to take my place, until which time I will continue to discharge my duties as best as I can.

Believe me, dear Mr. Herbert,
yours truly

P.S. Once more I refer to the deficiency of knives & forks here. The men are forced to tear at their food like animals. We are in dire need of Sheffield cutlery:

1,000 knives & forks
1,000 spoons

Send out immediately. I will do what I can in Constantinople to stop the gap.

Nightcaps and Chamber Pots

17 December 1854

THE *Egyptus*, ARRIVED FROM MARSEILLE, anchors off Constantinople. On board are fifteen Irish Catholic Sisters of Mercy, their Superior, Mother Mary Francis Bridgeman, twenty-four professional nurses, nine "ladies," and Mary Stanley, a friend of the Herberts' and head of the Protestant delegation of nurses.

Better forty-eight cabbages, forty-eight flannel nightcaps, forty-eight bottles of lime juice, forty-eight chamber pots. Forty-eight anything.

Walking back to the Barrack from the General Hospital, she stops on the British cemetery's promontory and, wrapped in her black woolen cloak, gazes across the Bosporus. She sees Topkapi, the sultan's palace, the gold-topped dome of Hagia Sophia, the Blue Mosque. Charles will be on board the *Egyptus* now, relaying her message: You are not welcome; you must turn straight around and return to England. The War Office, he is to tell them, has made a great mistake.

She will reverse her decision the next day, realizing that sending the forty-eight women back would create a political and religious uproar back home. She has to find room for them.

But for the moment, looking across the Bosporus, with soldiers by the thousands buried in rough rows and mass graves behind her, alone in the desolate silence, she surrenders, lets her animal-like rage be swallowed up in the salt air, screams until there is no sound left, only the bitter aftertaste of betrayal. He has put her life at risk to protect his reputation. She will never forgive him that.

Eventually, the "cloud of chittering locusts" (Charles's term) disembarks, crosses the Bosporus, and descends, unwanted, upon Scutari. Selina Bracebridge waits to greet them at the entrance to the Barrack Hospital. Florence is not there. She is busy directing two hundred Turkish workers in the emergency repair and restoration of a dilapidated wing of the hospital. Temporary lodging, she tells Selina, can be found for the Irish nuns at a convent of French sisters in Galata; the rest can be shelved at the ambassador's summer residence up the coast in Therapia.

Mother Brickbat

REVEREND MOTHER FRANCES BRIDGEMAN, commanded to make the acquaintance of Miss High-and-Mighty, to join her Nursely Majesty for lunch at the Barrack Hospital, is exasperated, insulted, ready to find a slew of faults. It has been nearly one week since she and her nuns arrived from London, eager to care for the wounded. Instead, they had been accosted on board the *Egyptus* by a portly blowhard in plaid pants who blew his nose every time she tried to speak, telling her she was to return to London immediately, mistakes had been made. The following day, a note signed by the same man, a Charles Bracebridge, informed her that this idea, notion, order, whatever it was, had been scrapped. They were to stay on. Lodgings would have to be found, as there was not a squeak of spare room in Miss Nightingale's quarters, where, Mr. Bracebridge wrote, even the roaches vied for space. Rooms were found at a French nunnery in Galata, a neighborhood in Constantinople across from the Golden Horn, and for five days, this is where Mother Bridgeman and her nuns have shelved, without a word of welcome from anyone.

Now she has paid her way in a caïque across the Bosporus to the northwest tower of the hospital, only to find Miss Nightingale missing, her nurses' quarters empty. Accustomed, in the convent, to being instantly obeyed by those around her—her will be done—Mother Bridgeman finds herself left to stew in a dreary sitting room, wondering if there is to be any luncheon at all, whether so much as a cup of tea will be brought to her by the old toad who grudgingly let her in, clearly irritated that her making of calf's foot jelly had been interrupted. Mother Bridgeman can hear her in the next room, grumbling about having to cook lunch for a papist meddler.

She walks around, hoping to ease her stiff, swollen knee, glancing into rooms off the cluttered sitting room, each more wretched and bad-smelling than the next. How does the Reverend Mother who is here, Mary Clare Moore, exist in such conditions? By comparison, the French sisters in Galata live extravagantly. Dairy cows, vegetable gardens, imported wines, clean, spacious rooms.

"Mother Bridgeman?" How had she not heard her come into the room?

"I apologize. I've been detained by a challenging case, a double amputation. I doubt he'll live. Do sit down. We have this one table, as you see. I'll check with Mrs. Clarke about luncheon."

A moldy lump of white cheese, a measly handful of cold potatoes, a dirty scrap of butter, warm beer in a bottle, a block of mahogany-colored beef marbled with maggots. All slammed down by Mrs. Clarke, smelling of gin, slapping about in house slippers.

As for the figure depicted in British newspapers—an angel, a saint, an ethereal, upper-class young woman, soft-spoken, gliding about with tender mercy—this creature—slipping into the room, stealthy as a cat, startling Mother Bridgeman out of her skin, is a far cry from that popular notion. Tall, yes, an aristocratic accent, yes, deceptively young and delicate-looking, too, but with shorn, unwashed hair, and from the moment she opens her mouth, ruling the conversation. A talking library of facts, statistics, numbers, this weird *not-woman* expresses no interest in Mother Bridgeman or her nuns, makes no inquiry as to their lodgings or nursing skills. Indeed, she acts resentful of half an hour wasted, eats nothing on her plate, shows impatience by constantly checking her pocket watch and tunelessly tapping her foot. The "saint" of Scutari is revealed as an unsexed creature of narcissism, self-regard, and icy ambition. A monster, not some sweet, feminine savior.

All this is abundantly clear to Mother Bridgeman as Miss Nightingale abruptly departs, leaving her to make her own way back across the Bosporus.

This misery of a lunch is the opening salvo to what will become a long, unresolved struggle between Reverend Mother Bridgeman and Scutari's Ministering Angel, who, without an instant's hesitation, privately names the churlish, insufferable, know-it-all nun "Mother Brickbat."

The Dead House

Christmas Eve 1854

THE DEAD HOUSE STANDS HALFWAY between the Barrack
Hospital and the British cemetery. Built to store bodies of
soldiers before they can be buried by Turkish grave diggers, it is a
simple, low-ceilinged structure of timber and stone.

In the snowy twilight, two women in hooded black woolen
cloaks walk toward the Dead House from the Barrack. They walk
rapidly, and, being of similar height, keep even pace. The snow,
falling steadily since morning, has stopped. Crosswinds that had
shrieked, blowing curtains of sharp, stinging snow this way and
that, have died down. They follow a fresh path of wheel tracks
left by a cart transporting that day's dead from the hospital, their
India-rubber galoshes squeaking in the packed snow, their breath
forming white plumes. Upon reaching the building, Florence uses
an iron key to unlock the door. She and Reverend Mother Moore
step into the Inspection Room. Behind this room is a small office,
deserted at this late hour. Beyond the Inspection Room and the
office is a windowless, unheated room where soldiers' corpses,
shrouded in filthy, once-white army blankets, await burial. Because
of the freezing temperatures, the smell is minimal. Accustomed to
the odor of death, the women take no notice.

She has brought with her two concertina lanterns. She lights
her own *fanoos*, lights the second, hands it to the nun. With flames
throwing fitful light and long shadows around the four walls
of the Inspection Room, the women stand a moment, hesitant,

before Florence steps up to the nearest body laid out on a rough wooden plank. Holding her lamp, she draws the blanket down until the young man's face is fully revealed. As she feared, as she had known, it is Albert Moone, infantryman, Ninety-fifth Derbyshire Regiment of Foot. She had held him in her arms once, Mrs. Moone's newborn son—that same wild copper hair—had rocked him to sleep and helped his mother on the day she had run away from her own home. Pulling the dirty blanket back over his face, she moves on.

Followed by Reverend Mother Moore, she enters the largest room. Dozens of bodies lie on planks, close together, in dismal, forgotten state. The smell is stronger in this room, but she moves among the bodies at the same deliberate pace. *Boys, mere boys, every one of them.* The wind outside shrieks, howls, as if keening. For what? Mercy? Vengeance?

Three days before, she had recognized his name on the wounded and casualties list. Albert Moone. She had searched for him, sat beside him during the amputation of both shattered legs, nursed him for the brief hours he lived. Haunted by his dying words, she had come to see him a last time.

"Do you come here often, Florence?"

They were walking the same path back to the hospital.

"Not often, no. But it is Christmas Eve, and those poor boys will never know another Christmas." *I came to see him, but I cannot bear to say I knew him. I must ask Selina to write to his mother. Another thing I cannot bring myself to do.*

"War is a terrible thing, Miss Nightingale."

"Man's creation."

"Not God's, surely, though it is curious how each side claims Him for their cause, each side prays to Him for victory."

"And each believes they are on the righteous side. The ones

justified to kill. Now and again, a patient shows me some token, a souvenir he's taken from the body of an enemy soldier. A pair of boots is most prized, but sometimes, almost with wonderment, they will show me a Russian crucifix or the icon of an Orthodox saint."

"You are not Catholic, are you, Florence? With your zeal, I should think you would be."

"Before I tell you why I am not a Catholic, not anything really, I must tell you I admire your calm temper. You never appear ruffled by crisis or irritated by opposition. You would make a far better administrator, a better superintendent than I. When I compare our qualifications, I am shamed. Were it not for you, this whole calamitous enterprise would be a failure."

"Come now. I do my little part, with you, quite frankly, as my model. Now you must tell me. Why is it you are not a Catholic?"

"It will seem blasphemous, but I attend no church, adhere to no one faith. I have, over time, formed a broad sense of the Divine. One can go not only to Christianity for worship but to Judaism, Mohammedanism, Buddhism, to the East, to the Sufis and fakirs, to pantheism, even to a grove of cedar trees or a field of grass for the right road to God. One can go to science, to the discovery of God's laws in this earthly world. To mathematics. I believe that numbers, marshaled into statistics, into use for the greater good, can reveal God to any one of us. Reverend Mother, I believe the universe itself is an emanation of God. And I believe we are best able to know the divinity within ourselves when free from dogma, superstition, and the theological splitting of hairs. Now I have surely offended you."

"Not at all, though I am a staunch Catholic in every fiber of my being. I find your views unique, and do not think it impossible that our Christian mystics, could they speak, might agree with you.

Since I have been here in Scutari, the words of Saint Teresa of Avila comfort me daily."

"What words are those?"

"'Suffering is the swiftest route to the Beloved.'"

"Suffering as a 'shortcut' to God?"

"A way of putting it."

"But if war, this war, 'smacks of murder,' as Mr. Bracebridge claims it does, how can such wholesale slaughter bring anyone closer to God? Those who die in my presence stretch out a hand, murmuring 'sister,' 'sweetheart,' 'mother,' naming some loved one, never once groaning or turning away. Most are scarcely sentient. They go off like animals."

"And God seems very far away."

"And far too slow in coming."

❦

After seeing his name on the list, it had not taken long to find him, to locate the ward, scan the rows of wounded for his copper-bright hair. He was pale from shock but conscious. She sat beside him, told him how she knew him. From Cromford.

"You will write my mother?"

"Yes, of course. I will send your pay, as well."

"That's why I joined."

"I know." *Why most do. Not for patriotism.*

"I didn't expect to die." Said with a faint smile. "I meant to return home. To the mines."

"To take your father's place?" Mr. Moone, she knew, had died some years ago.

"It's been hard for Ma." A long pause. "Miss?"

"Yes?" *Did he not remember her? Know her name?*

"Tell them." He was fading.

"Tell them what, Albert?"

"It's wrong. War. How they treat us."

A new surgeon, one she'd never seen before, stepped in with two assistants.

"This one's next. Sorry, lad, hold on tight. We'll have you fixed in no time."

As the amputation began, he closed his eyes, gently pressed her hand.

Commonplace

CANNON FODDER, BOYS USED UP, dumped in a common grave. Costing almost nothing.

The Lady with the Lamp feeds the monster, keeps the empire alive.

Complicit.

It's wrong. War. How they treat us.

There are times, walking these wards at night, I am almost healed. Away from those who belittle me, far from my own guilty, excoriating thoughts—here, in these wards, among the soldiers, offering them water or a word of comfort, in the smallest of these acts, I might glimpse the face of God. Receive and give love.

Letters Home

My dear mother and father,

I am very sorry not to have written before, but I was wounded in the Battle of Balaclava and sent from there to this hospital in Scutari, where I have been ill these last days with fever and complaint of the lungs. I feel considerably better now and hope you will write soon and tell me how everyone is at home. This letter is being taken down for me by a Miss Nightingale, who sits by my side. She is a nurse and sees to it I lack for nothing. I am a little tired now but send you all my love. May it be God's will that we be together again one day soon.

With greatest affection and love,
Henry

P.S. I have enclosed a lock of my hair for Mother.

Dear girl, my dearest wife,

You must always know I have never gone one day without thinking of you. How is it with our little boy? Never let him forget Papa loves him.

As I am unable to, these words are being written down by a kind nurse, her handwriting, as you will see, is far better than mine. My leg has been bad since surgery; my fever has returned. I pray I will soon recover and return to you and to our home when this war is over.

My eternal love,
Your "Danny"

PART TEN

Ministering Angel

January–February 1855

*She is a "ministering angel" without any exaggeration in these hospitals,
and as her slender form glides quietly along each corridor, every poor
fellow's face softens with gratitude at the sight of her. When all the medical officers have retired for the night and sickness and darkness have
settled down upon the miles of prostrate sick, she may be observed alone,
a little lamp in her hand, making her solitry rounds.*

— John MacDonald, Crimea Fund manager,
Times, 8 February 1855

Dear Mr. Herbert

25 January 1855

As to your inquiry regarding the forty-eight Catholic sisters and Protestant nurses and ladies sent over by you last month, it is true. I do not wish them here, but neither can I return them without an uproar in certain political parts back home. Of necessity, I have settled on this plan of distribution:

—19 nurses have returned home

—8 to Balaclava

—16 to the hospital at Koulalee

—41 here at Barrack

A total of eighty-four independently of Reverend Mother Bridgeman and Mary Stanley, your friend, whose thought had been to leave for home as soon as she delivered this second party of nurses and has elected to stay on indefinitely. Mary is not an ally, but has taken on the character of treachery. At present, I will say no more.

Aside from the ongoing "religious wars"—meaning Mother Bridgeman's insistence on placing the authority of the Roman Catholic Church above mine, as well as her alliance with Dr. John Hall, returned to replace Menzies, the two of them obstructing my every wish—aside from that tempest in a cracked teapot, my chief trouble continues with the purveyor's stores, with the purveyor himself.

Thanks to Wreford, anything I ask for is nowhere to be found. My daily forages in his purveyor's storeroom turn up—nothing.

Ever yours, in haste,
Florence

P.S. Below articles paid from the Times fund—all are in my personal storeroom:

Flannel shirts 2,274
Cotton shirts 2,216
Socks 1,074
Drawers 472
Nightcaps in proportion
Slippers in proportion
Plates and tin cups in proportion
Knives, forks & spoons 250
Wooden trays 86
Tables 24
Forms 48
Urine pots in proportion
Clocks 6
Operating tables 2

Chloride of Lime

1 February 1855

Dearest Mother,

A word to say we are all right, we have no cholera & that God is worth laboring for. I will work for these miserable hospitals as long as I have power to do so.

Your mind seems sorely troubled about chloride of lime. Do you not suppose that a scavenger such as I am, daily raiding the purveyor's storeroom, would not have found sacks of chlor. of lime to put down in every corridor? Do you not picture me overseeing the fatigue parties that cleanse those places that require disinfecting? Alas! I am both purveyor and scavenger; I am everything to these colossal calamities, as the hospitals of Scutari, both Barrack and General, will one day come to be called in history.

S. Herbert has borne me out gallantly in my commissariat reforms. I have almost forgiven him his "December offense," telling him it was less than a peccadillo.

I do read your letters. I do not read the Times. Your letters mean a great deal to me in a place where envies & emulations & petty jealousies interfere with the lives of men.

Ever yours, dearest Mother,
Florence

P.S. I keep a Greek tortoise beside my bed. He sleeps in a wooden crate packed with straw. He is named Jimmy, after a drummer boy of the Seventy-seventh Regiment of Foot who brought him to me. Jimmy trundles behind me in the wards and lets the soldiers scratch his neck. He is not Athena, he does not curtsy, but he is nearly as wise.

"See, Jimmy, I sing your praises all the way to England." She watches him extend his stalklike neck to be scratched and sighs.

Stabbing the sharp point of a pen into the glass well—the ink a half-frozen sludge—she writes another report for the War Office and the queen. Casualty numbers, cholera, frostbite, gangrene numbers, amputation statistics, the all-important requests for slippers, shirts, arrowroot, sago, spoons, chloride of lime—a slow, never-ending march of needs.

Committed to reform, I wonder, in my despair, if revolution is not the better way. I have not yet forgiven Sidney, though I remember the Savior's words: "Forgive them, Lord, for they know not what they do." I helped Albert Moone die by making him fit enough to fight again. Along with hundreds, thousands, like him. Who knows what we do, for what acts each of us will need to be forgiven?

Give me the honest innocence, the brutal law of animals.

Mortality

5 February 1855

Mr. Herbert,

At the beginning of January, we had 2,500 men at Barrack Hosp'l, 1,122 at General—total 3,622. As of yesterday and the day before, February 3 & 4, hundreds more landed from the Golden Fleece. All were stretcher cases. The mortality is frightful; it exceeds anything we have yet seen—thirty in the last twenty-four hours in this hospital alone. One day last week it was forty, and the number of burials from Barrack & General seventy-two. We bury every twenty-four hours.

I shall miss you at the War Office, since Lord Palmerston has become prime minister and Lord Panmure has been appointed in your place. I have lost my dearest confidant, and must hope that your orders, as you left them, may yet be carried out.

Yours,
FN

19 February 1855

Dear Mr. Herbert,

I am able to report a decline in mortality. In the last twenty-four hours, we have lost only 10 out of 2,100 here at Barrack. Mother writes that you have already stepped down from your new position as colonial secretary. She says you will remain an MP.

Arrangements here continue to be of the Elizabethan era. Summer will soon be upon us and then shall we cry, as we complained when winter came, "Who'd have thought it? Here is hot weather!"

I trust you are well

—FN

PART ELEVEN

Let Us Live in Our Dead

March 1855

Three thousand, alas! dead in January and February alone. We have endured in Grecian silence, we have folded our mantles about our faces. We have died in silence without complaining.
—Florence Nightingale

I must say—there is nothing like a hot dinner!
—Alexis Benoît Soyer

Mrs. Seacole

6 March 1855

A STRANGE STORY I PUT DOWN in my journal.

Yesterday, Selina found me, as usual, slaving at my desk. Approaching me, she looked bemused but wary. A visitor, she said, a British nurse from Jamaica who wished to meet with me. She was right to be wary. "I haven't time," I snapped. But Selina stood her ground, wouldn't leave. "Well?" I looked up. "What does she want?"

"Her name is Mary Jane Seacole. She says she has come from England at her own expense to help nurse the soldiers."

Before I could ask Selina if she had lost her mind to even come to me with this—hadn't we sent nurses away and weren't we still overrun with them?—she raised a hand as if to quiet me. "I know, I know. I told her we have a sufficient number of nurses already, that we are in need of no more. Apparently, she knows that and is on her way to Balaclava to begin work of her own. I simply thought you might want to meet her."

"Jamaica? Then she must be black. And on her way alone to Balaclava?" For no other reason than curiosity, I did want to meet her. I sighed. "Put her in our spare room for sick nurses, and tell her I will be there in a quarter of an hour."

And so I met Mary Jane Seacole, a woman of around forty, dark-skinned and possessed of the most unusual eyes, shining with intelligence and something else, something rare in this place, so rare that I'd nearly forgotten it—a natural good humor. I liked her instinctively. When I asked if she had eaten that day, she answered she had not, so I ordered dinner brought to her, and invited her to stay the night. I would also see to it that her breakfast was prepared for her before she sailed for Balaclava in the morning.

In the brief time we spoke, I learned she had met with Sidney Herbert, then with Liz, in London, that each had told her there was no need of additional nurses at Scutari (both no doubt still smarting from our recent skirmish). They informed her no money was available from the *Times* fund to pay her passage here, a falsehood likely told her due to the color of her skin. Nothing provable, but expected. Unsurprising.

I asked her intentions once she reached Balaclava, and she answered with a lively determination. She meant to build a hotel for the officers, have food and drink available for them, and, as often as she could, go to the tents and fields to care for wounded soldiers. "Drink?" I asked, showing disapproval. "Why yes, a bit of rum or porter can be a great comfort to fighting men. In the right proportion, it is as healing to body and spirit as food and medicine." I said nothing, though I could not have disagreed more. "What medicines do you use?" I asked. She said she was descended from a line of Jamaican and West African doctresses, including her own mother, a healer who used traditional herbal medicines and ran a boardinghouse in Kingston that cared for convalescent army and naval men. By now, I had invented an image of a "hotel" for officers in Balaclava, an atmosphere of general drunkenness and dissolution, and though I greatly disapproved of her attitude toward alcohol, I was intrigued by her use of herbs for medicine. Clearly, I would never welcome her here at Scutari, not with my strict rules and prohibition of alcohol; still, I could not help but like her and feel she liked me a little, too—after all, we both cared about helping soldiers, both of us were unmarried by choice (I asked), and both of us were dedicated to nursing. As much as we had our differences, we had these in common.

Her dinner was brought in, and as she thanked me for it, I could see how tired she was, so I stood to say good-bye. Before I left, we had the most extraordinary exchange, perhaps the real reason for my taking time to preserve this story in my journal.

"Who is it you work for, Miss Nightingale?" she asked.

"For the British government. The army, specifically. Why? Whom do you work for?"

"Myself. And those soldiers who have need of me. I answer to no government."

"I see."

"Do you? Do you see that by working for the government you are part of a class system that oppresses the poor and keeps those like myself"—here she pushed up one sleeve of her dress, exposing the skin of her arm—"enslaved?"

I wanted to protest, to tell her about my grandfather, his life's work, abolishing the slave trade, but it seemed irrelevant—no, not even that, but . . . but what? A sign of my privilege.

Eating her dinner, she looked up at me and smiled. There was no judgment in what she had just said to me; that was what was so extraordinary. She was not condemning me. She had simply spoken the truth.

"Yes, I suppose I do see," I said quietly. "But I am doing my best to change that system from within."

"Through reform?" Another thing about her. Her voice. Intelligent, calm.

"Reform is slow work, but I have always believed in effecting change from within."

"Even in a system that allows women no power?"

"I have had the advantage of family, of means. I use those."

She put down her fork, took a drink of water. Looked at me with a warm expression, almost as if we were friends.

"We work from where God has put us, Miss Nightingale. I am poor, an outsider because of my race. Aside from the disadvantage of being a woman, you have boundless privilege."

"Perhaps. But does not an outsider, such as yourself, perceive the problem most clearly?" Even as I spoke, I heard the falseness of my words. Her burden was heavier than mine, yet her bearing and grace far greater. She would say one more thing that would nag at me. Shift my perspective.

"So long as men are born, generations of war hunger—war itself—will be with us."

"I hope not, Mrs. Seacole. Truly, I hope not."

I stood and bade her good night. A feeling of affection passed between us, a mutual respect I would not soon forget. That night, I prayed to become a better person despite the challenges I faced. I prayed for Mrs. Seacole to be well protected. It was clear to me God had called her, too.

The Sanitarians

Barrack Hospital
8 March 1855

IN THE COMMON ROOM, the members of London's Sanitarian
Commission respectfully introduce themselves. John Sutherland, the commission's head, a Scottish physician, fashionable in
a plaid frock coat and wool cap. Less stylishly attired, Sir Robert
Rawlinson, Esq., civil engineer. Dr. Hector Gavin, another Scottish
physician. Not present, delayed, is an inspector of nuisances from
Liverpool, along with his assistant and the commission's secretary.

Dr. Sutherland removes his leather-billed cap. "I speak for all
the commission, Miss Nightingale, when I say we are most hon-
ored to make your acquaintance. Every drawing room and parlor in
London is filled with the most reverent speculation about you. On
behalf of Lord Palmerston, Lord Panmure, the War Office, and the
British army, we are here to serve you."

"In sanitation, primarily." That is Dr. Gavin, rumbling from the
corner, hoping for permission to light his pipe.

She waves her hand. "Too much fuss over me, gentlemen—
it distracts from critical issues of hygiene at Scutari. Conditions
here are appalling; the dead outnumber the living. In the last
months, I have organized my nurses, improved the supply system,
established general cleanliness. Still, the crisis is catastrophic. It
is nearly beyond me."

Mrs. Clarke brings in a tray of tea, a loaf of soft white bread, half a jarful of gooseberry jam, left from Christmas. Shuffling behind is Jimmy.

"Heavens, what a droll creature!" Dr. Sutherland says, gratefully accepting his cup of tea, sitting down at the table.

"He will end up in my next pot of soup," Mrs. Clarke mutters.

"Jimmy is a Greek tortoise. *Testudo graeca*. I named him after the Scottish drummer boy who found him on the battlefield at Inkerman and brought him to me. Mr. Gavin, is it? Light your pipe, I don't mind."

"Does he bite?" the engineer, Robert Rawlinson, asks.

"Never, though he might like a nip of your bread. I take him into the wards with me. Pets can be wonderfully healing for patients." Florence plucks Jimmy off the floor, sets him on the table.

Dr. Sutherland lets the tortoise nibble a bit of bread from his fingers.

"Extraordinary."

"Humph." Mrs. Clarke pads off, a haze of gin strong about her stolid person.

"Mrs. Clarke has worked for me several years. I'm afraid life at Scutari has been hard on her."

"No offense." Sutherland tears off another bit of bread. "With your permission, Miss Nightingale, we would like to begin work straightaway."

"You have it. How will you begin?"

"With a thorough inspection. Our Liverpool man, the inspector of nuisances, will see about the waste systems. The rest will inspect drainage systems, water pipes, methods of air circulation, trash removal, disinfectant methods, and so on. We will start at Barrack, move on to General, then off to the smaller hospitals in Balaclava and so on. Devil take it! He bites!"

At the sight of Sutherland sucking on his finger, scowling at the tortoise, she laughs.

"You must not report Jimmy to your inspector of nuisances. Mrs. Clarke might make good on her threat to turn my little friend into soup."

"Not at all, he's safe. But he does give a nip, the old codger!"

⁓

Early the next morning, Drs. Sutherland and Gavin, Mr. Rawlinson, and the two experts from Liverpool begin their inspection of the Barrack's great quadrangle, its four towers and central courtyard. At one time a Turkish army barracks built on top of a burial ground, now an English war hospital on top of a cesspool, Scutari presents the sanitarians with dozens of main and ancillary buildings in desperate need of repair, contaminated water supplies, and drainage systems broken down. The first task, they agree, is to hire workers to unclog the sewers. From a large pipe that carries water throughout the entire hospital, they drag the rotting carcass of a horse. After the horse emerge dozens of dogs, rats, and other organic debris, badly decomposed. Cartloads of refuse are hauled out from beneath the hospital's floors; clogged sewers are flushed out. In the central courtyard, they discover human excrement from open privies seeping into nearby water-storage tanks; the privies are cleaned, sealed off from the water tanks. Inside the hospital, windows are installed, vents put in the roof to improve circulation. As the rotten flooring is torn up, hundreds of rats' nests are uncovered. Ceilings and walls are whitewashed with quicklime, woodwork scrubbed down with chloride of lime. Patients' waste pails and trash begin to be removed and emptied daily.

⁓

Returning to the Barrack from hospital inspections in Balaclava, members of the Sanitary Commission are in shock from what they have seen. Sitting in the common room with the others, John Sutherland speaks to her first.

"It is an unparalleled calamity, Miss Nightingale. In this severe winter, the soldiers have had no tents, or if a tent can be found, it has no flooring. The men wrap themselves in wet, befouled blankets and sleep in mud. The trenches fill up with ice and freezing water. Men's boots freeze on their feet, and when the boots are boiled off, huge patches of skin come off with them. We saw no ambulance vans, few mule litters. What we did see were Turks, hauling the wounded on their backs to the harbor, where they had to wait hours, often days, to be evacuated. It was the bleakest sight I have ever seen and one I hope never to see again."

"The men come to us with frostbite, as you describe, Dr. Sutherland. With gangrene. They die less from battle wounds than from dysentery, diarrhea, fever, foul air, preventable mischiefs. They die by the thousands. This January, we had one thousand out of one thousand one hundred and seventy-four men from Balaclava die. In February, the fatalities numbered five hundred and twenty."

"Weren't two smaller hospitals opened last month?" Dr. Gavin asks.

"One in Smyrna, another in Renkioi. These two are emergency hospitals over which I have no authority."

"What? Why is that?"

"My authority is limited to the Barrack Hospital. Mr. Herbert never expected the war to last this long, so the written terms of my superintendency, as he drew them up, are vague. They do not mention hospitals in Sebastopol, Balaclava, or anywhere else. Dr. Hall—I believe you met him—has taken full advantage of that vagueness by obstructing my authority. He is completely against me. Not only against me but against having any female nurses in the army."

"And the French?"

"The French have established excellent military hospitals here; their hospitals put ours to shame. In my opinion, to patch up our current system is not enough. Overall reform of the army's entire hospital system, root and branch, is what is needed."

The engineer, Rawlinson, speaks up.

"Might I add a personal observation? Your rats here at Scutari are most impressive, but those at Balaclava are of a size and appetite not to be believed."

Everyone laughs.

"I hope to see for myself, Mr. Rawlinson, and soon. When the weather improves, I intend to sail to the Crimea."

"Balaclava's rats will fall into rank to greet you." Dr. Gavin puffs on his cigar.

"Whole regiments," the mostly silent Rawlinson adds.

"With pipes and drums," Dr. Sutherland says, building on the joke.

"The Ninety-third *Rattus rattus*." Dr. Gavin chuckles, then puffs a ring of smoke.

"Stop!" Florence laughs. "When do you gentlemen sail for home? I have not laughed since arriving here. I shall miss you."

"We have several other hospitals to inspect and make recommendations on, then a final inspection here at Barrack. Several weeks, I expect."

"Then you may encounter another visitor on his way here and, from what I hear, at his own expense."

"Do we know him?"

"Alexis Soyer? He is a French chef from the Reform Club. In Dublin, he set up soup kitchens during the worst of the famine. He was appointed cook for the queen's inaugural luncheon and managed to feed some two thousand guests. From what I understand, he is a celebrity."

None of the men had heard of him. "Well, what do you expect?" Dr. Gavin quips through a cloud of tobacco smoke. "We sanitarians either have our heads stuck up sewer pipes or down drainage holes."

"And he comes to Scutari to . . ." Rawlinson sounds mildly suspicious.

"I was told he saw an article in the *Times* exposing the scarcity and poor quality of the soldiers' food. He arranged a meeting with the prime minister, asked permission to fix the men's diets and thus, by cookery alone, win the war."

"Just what is needed! A wartime minister of pots and pans."

"*Des pots et des casseroles!*"

"Ah, Miss Nightingale, better conceal your tortoise!"

"From what, Dr. Sutherland?"

"*La* soup tureen! You must not let your little fellow be boiled into a green broth."

"Let us not forget *les ratons*! *Les Scutari-ats*. Surely monsieur will dice those gnawers into tarts and pies!"

"Stop, do stop!"

Dr. Sutherland passes her his handkerchief.

"Gentlemen, be proud! We have amused Miss Nightingale."

Alexis Benoît Soyer

*D*IABLE! *PARBLEU! NOM D'UN CHIEN!*
Where does this burst of Gallic profanity come from?
From a potbellied Frenchman of medium height with the sensual,
delicate air of a gourmand. A well-larded specimen of flesh fopped
out in outrageous fashion—high boots of African ostrich, silk
harem pants, a lavender stripe down each leg, a loose linen shirt
topped by a coat like a painter's smock lined with scarlet and white
stripes. Topping this flamboyant ensemble, a beret of scarlet velvet
with a long tasseled tail. Master chef Alexis Benoît Soyer, whose
recettes for brochettes of kidneys with sultana sauce, young rook
pudding, rarebit à la Soyer with champagne and eels stewed white
are imitated, coveted, stolen, has arrived in Constantinople accompanied by his valet, assistant, and amanuensis (aside from splash-
ing the occasional legal document with the practiced letters of his
name, M. Soyer is illiterate). It is to Julien these curses and insults
are addressed, but as they are a constant occurrence, they drop off
him harmlessly, like limp asparagus spears.

"I have found them, monsieur. Your cooking spoons."

"Under my nose, eh? Cod's head, repulsive box of bones."

"*Merci, monsieur.* Shall I accompany you to the Barrack?"

"Of course, dunderhead. You can see the ugly towers from here.
We'll leave this so-called Greek restaurant where we have snored
cheek by jowl with strangers, clasped our overcoats to our chests
and flailed off vermin. We decamp to Scutari. Napoléon was
never more correct—an army marches on its stomach—though he

339

should have gone further and said an army marches on a stomach fed on the *recettes* of Alexis Benoît Soyer. Do we agree, Julien? The belly governs the world."

"Is that him?" Sister George whispers, pressing close to Florence. "He cuts a dash. But who is the skeleton flickering around him?"

"His assistant, I hazard. Yes, that is the great Soyer. Plump, isn't he? A soaked raisin. He's come at his own expense. Our little Crimean catastrophe has inspired him."

"Do we introduce ourselves?"

"Let's spy another moment. Fat peacock. I like him."

Raw Meat, a Table Leg, Some Buttons

"*LA VACHE!* WHAT IS THIS? Three copper cauldrons? For what? To brew tea and boil meat? How is the meat cooked? You show me, please?"

Soyer looks on, incredulous, as a pimple-faced orderly wrestles a block of raw beef onto the wooden leg of a chair, fastens it with string, marks the meat with an object he can identify—a nail, a string of buttons, old knives, forks, scissors, pieces of red cloth cut from an old jacket—in this case, a fork and a button.

"What is this you are tying onto your block *de boeuf*, monsieur?"

"A pair of old snuffers, sir. Candle snuffers."

"*Sacré bleu*, they're filthy with wax and burned wick."

"They've been boiled so often, sir, I suppose they're clean enough."

"Fine logic. So. You throw skewers of raw meat into the pot along with all this other rubbish? *Fils de pute!* The water isn't even boiling."

"It cooks all the same. Some less than the rest."

Suddenly, the two orderlies answering this odd Frenchman's questions grow quiet. One doffs his felt cap. Soyer turns to see what the fuss is about.

"*Alors, madame!* I have not offended your sensibilities?"

"Not at all, monsieur. We are glad you are come. May I introduce Sister George? She is one of my best nurses, so excellent, in fact, that I call her my Cardinal."

"*Enchanté.* And this duke of limbs is Julien, my necessary."

"A pleasure, Julien. Monsieur Soyer, how have you found our kitchen?"

"I am inquiring, Miss Nightingale, how the meat is cooked."

"Inefficiently. The beef—sometimes it is lamb—comes out of the pot raw or overcooked. Often, the patients are given only bone and gristle. The 'soup' that follows the meat is indescribable."

"I notice it is eleven o'clock, and the patients in your wards have not yet eaten?"

"They are not served, most days, until past one o'clock. The entire process, beginning to end, is a chaos of unwashed dishes, maggot-filled meat, hard bread, and cold soup."

"Something I will remedy, I assure you. Will you and the holy Sister join me on the next round of meal serving? I wish to observe everything."

"Of course. Dr. McGrigor can join us, as well. He is one of my few allies, and believes, as I do, in the benefits of wholesome food."

"Food must never be 'wholesome,' Miss Nightingale. Food must be exquisite. Luscious. Succulent. A man disappointed in what he eats will console himself with something to drink."

"That is more than true here. Drunkenness is rampant. My God, how they drink! It is a plague."

La Tortue

"And where is the little fellow?"
Florence reaches deep into her apron pocket.

"*Voilà! Jimee! Le soupe de tortue!* A little like veal, a little like lobster, all spiced with clove, lemon, cayenne, two or three splashes of Madeira . . ."

"Monsieur Soyer! Jimmy is a pet."

"A pet *soupe?*"

"No! The patients enjoy him. He is a sort of mascot."

"*Quel dommage.* Criminal to leave such a dish untasted. Ow! *Merde!* He has just bitten my finger. Nasty little brute."

They stop between pallets in one of the wards. Soyer stares down at a blond-haired young solider, his only visible injury an amputated foot.

"Young man. I am sorry about your foot, but you look otherwise to be in splendid form. Can you tell me what dinner you dream most of, what food you would eat tonight if you could?"

"Oh, sir, I would have two broiled kidneys, a plate of scalloped oysters, a chop done rare, two taters, and a bottle of port."

"*Bien.* But did you know eating a broiled kidney at night is a guarantee of nightmares? Miss Nightingale? Why are these men eating their meat before their soup?"

"Because they have only one bowl apiece. A tin basin."

"Hideous. But why not cut the meat into little pieces, pour boiling soup over it, thus keeping the meat warm?"

Dr. McGrigor nods. "Capital idea! Soup comforts the stomach

343

and disposes it for better digestion of the meat and potatoes. Mr. Soyer, I've seen these men swallow their food whole, without masticating it. That cannot be healthy."

The blond soldier speaks up. "Because the meat is tough as a mule's hoof, sir."

"*Précisément.* Tomorrow, I will demonstrate how to make a soup using the same ingredients but in different order. A tasty soup, not scum. Julien! Julien is my headman. An oaf, but I must have him with me at all times."

"*Oui?*"

"Take this down: four pounds of meat, a quarter pound of barley, some mixed vegetables—dried if there are no fresh— salt, pepper, and, if supplies allow, a little sugar and flour. *Voilà.* Miss Nightingale, Doctor McGrigor, I share a terrible discovery. When I asked your kitchen men what they did with the fat that rises to the top of the boiling meat, they answered that they threw it out! 'Why?' I asked. 'We do not like it,' they said. Stupid, headless fellows. I suggested they try skimming three inches of white fat off the top of a cauldron of boiling beef; they will find it better to cook with than that rancid snot from Constantinople. Where do these half-wits come from? I had to tell them what a chef is! I must find two or three real cooks to teach them. I also need carpenters and an engineer to rebuild this kitchen. I will need a charcoal stove, an oven, a storeroom, a larder, and a chopping block. Tomorrow, I review convalescent diets—we must have broths of chicken, mutton, and veal, beef and mutton teas, rice water, lemonades, arrowroot, sago, calf's foot jelly, barley water, rice pudding, macaroni, all digestible for the sickest patients. Once I achieve my success, I will sail on to Sebastopol and take the Soyer stove with me. I described the stove in my latest book, *Soyer's Shilling Cookery for the People*—you have it? I shall give you each a copy. In it, I outline a system of plain cookery and domestic economy for the laboring classes. I teach that religion liberates the soul, education elevates the mind, and food heals the body. If the morals of a people greatly depend upon what they eat, then how much more true for men on battlefields? Hippocrates, that Great Physician, spoke the truth when he said, 'what pleases the palate nourishes.' And God, Great Architect of Heaven, has put the good of men's stomachs first."

PART TWELVE

Balaclava

May 1855

Rather, ten times, die in the surf, heralding the way to a new world, than stand idly on the shore.

—Florence Nightingale

Herrings

Balaclava Harbor
On board the *Robert Lowe*
5 May 1855

"MOTHER OF GOD! LOOK AT 'EM. Packed in like herrings!"
Charles Bracebridge is on deck, Florence's binoculars
pressed to his eyes. With an incredulous expression, he returns
them to her. "Impressive, what. Maritime power. And between
Balaclava and Sebastopol are the battlefields."

Putting the binoculars to her own eyes, she adjusts their focus.
War? It looks more like a festival at sea. She clearly sees the port,
the buildings of Balaclava beyond the crowded harbor, and, to the
west, what must be Sebastapol, the Russian naval yard, under
siege by the French and the British for half a year now. This is
where the most terrible battles have been fought. Alma, Inkerman, Balaclava with its inglorious charge of the Light Brigade.
This is where the thousands of casualties come from, three hundred miles from Scutari.

She is so tired.

Since they left Scutari five days ago and boarded the *Robert
Lowe*, she has fought off an unrelenting, marrow-deep fatigue. She
has filled hours of sleeplessness with letters home and detailed
reports to be sent to London. She tears through paper faster than
nurses use up bandages. All her actions begin with paper, pen,
and ink. The compulsion to write. Sometimes she wishes she had
never been taught to write, could not write at all. Could remove

her unquiet brain, like a hat, with its analyses, facts, and calculations. Its resentments and worries. She is so very tired.

"*Alors, zut,* madame! War is a busy place. Not unlike commerce."

"Indeed, Monsieur Soyer. Men flock to war as they do to market."

"War is like a terrible picnic. An obscene holiday. Look past these ships, what do you see in the cities and camps? I see stomachs. I hear the intestines of generals and infantrymen. Beneath opposing uniforms and nations, all innards are the same. I see my little stoves winning the war."

"I see suffering and death, monsieur."

"How sad, madame, to see only that." He claps his hands. "I will set up my little kitchens, turn water to champagne! Oof, my ears. What was that?"

"Gunfire, monsieur. Part of the holiday, your picnic." She smiles wanly. The thought of food nauseates her, though if there is a Great Kitchen in Heaven, may Alexis Soyer one day be in it, working his magic.

"Blasted herrings, what? All come to see you, Flo." Charles honks into his handkerchief. "Catch a glimpse of the Nightingale. Lady with the Lamp." Recovering from a cold, he is missing his wife's little attentions. Florence has left Selina in charge of the "bear garden," relying on her to maintain order, keep the liquor locked away from Mrs. Clarke, Eliza Forbes, and God knows who else. She has instructions to discourage certain nurses from moving flirtatiously about the wards and, above all, to stop Brickbat's nuns from praying for deathbed conversions.

The *Robert Lowe* comes nearer the harbor. With her binoculars, she makes out individual faces among the blur of spectators smashed against the ship's railings, many with their own binoculars raised and pointed at her. She recognizes no one. *Celebrity. Impersonal. Nothing to do with me. What are they looking at? What are they looking for? To better themselves? No. They wish to see a freak, a sentimental story, an upper-class young woman sacrificing every privilege to nurse the common British foot soldier. But is not every person drawn to the good, drawn to God? Or is it enough to simply stare at the ideal and boast later of having seen it? Of all people, I deserve no celebrity. I want none. I am, in fact, part of the larger problem. The larger sin. I patch boys up and, if they live, see them off to battle again. I am as much a murderer as any elite officer in this hellish enterprise.*

"Are you well, Flo? Does the gunfire bother you?" At her side, Charles is solicitous. He is like some great shaggy dog, blundering in his affections, protective, loyal. Wouldn't harm a flea.

"No, it doesn't bother me. I am eager to see the hospitals, but I want to meet with Lord Raglan first. As commander in chief of the British army in the Crimea and as my friend, I owe him my regards."

Lord Raglan, a man nearing seventy and ill, weighted to the ground with war medals and honors. An English military hero who has proved himself utterly incompetent in this war. One hundred and ten men killed, 160 wounded in the Charge of the Light Brigade. Four hundred horses lost. All because of an order too hastily written, illegible, misinterpreted, wrongly carried out. Lord Raglan's infamous order. Still, he is an old friend who defends her cause, and so she will see him.

But Raglan is not in his headquarters, not anywhere to be found, so with a guide, she and Charles ride on horseback to view a mortar battery. As they pass through the tented encampment of the Thirty-ninth, great numbers of soldiers turn out to cheer her. Hip hip hooray for Miss Nightingale. Hip hip hooray!

Today, as I rode away from the men of the Thirty-ninth, there was nothing empty in that cheer nor in the heart that received it. I took it as a true expression of true sympathy—the sweetest I have ever had. A full reward for all I have gone through. In all that has been said against and for me, no one soul has appreciated what I was really doing—none but the honest cheers of the brave Thirty-ninth.

Next morning, still feeling tired, as if her arms and legs were made of lead, she travels by horseback with Charles and Alexis beyond the Russian artillery range, where they survey Sebastopol from a high vantage point. At the impressive sight of the twenty-square-mile British encampment with its 150,000 soldiers, its row upon row of dazzlingly white tents, Soyer bursts out, "No need for gunpowder, *mes amis!* Why sacrifice lives to gunpowder and cannon when a failure of cuisine will destroy them all!"

"Take that up with Lord Raglan," Charles replies good-naturedly. "I'm sure he'd like to see his army, its regiments, guns, horses, and cannon, replaced by kitchens and a few of your famous stoves."

Before remounting the little mare she'd been given to ride, she retrieves a minié ball discharged from some soldier's musket. She pockets it, then picks a handful of wildflowers to enclose in her next letter to Parthe. Uproots a fistful of bloodstained grass, a souvenir for herself.

Parthe!

A most wonderful sight, looking down upon Sebastopol, shells whizzing right & left! I have enclosed some little flowers—here, it is the most flowery place you can imagine—a red tormentilla, some yellow jasmine. And something else I picked up from earth plowed and shot with shell—a new sort of bullet invented by the French, a minié ball, used to great effect, I am told, with a rifled musket. I have treated many a hideous, disfiguring wound from this harmless-looking scrap of soft lead.

∽

In Balaclava, she tours a former Turkish school, now a hospital, as well as Castle Hospital, a row of wooden huts on the Genoese heights. Soyer, wearing a white tunic, loose white pants, a blue velvet cap edged in gold binding, accompanies her everywhere. They agree the hospitals' kitchens are in dire need of reorganization; it will take months to bring them close to the same level of order she has achieved in Scutari. But here, her authority is crippled. The army gave permission for her to visit the Crimea not as superintendent of nurses, but as "Almoner of Free Gifts in the British Hospitals in the Crimea," a meaningless title awarded her by the Crimea's purveyor in chief, David Fitzgerald, and her old nemesis, John Hall. When she met with Sir John McNeill and Colonel Alexander Tulloch on board the *Robert Lowe*, men hired by the War Department to inquire into the supply system, she had nothing but praise for their success in procuring fresh meat for the soldiers three times a week as well as steady supplies of bread from Constantinople. Only by meeting with men like McNeill and Tulloch and receiving three cheers from the soldiers does she feel strong enough to fight men like Fitzgerald and Hall, who dislike and obstruct her, spread scurrilous rumors.

"The thing is," she confides to Soyer over dinner on board the ship one evening, "they are polite enough to my face. But behind my back, they block my requests at every turn. They are the worst kind of enemy."

"Unless a woman is subtle enough to disguise it, she will never be forgiven for being more intelligent than a man. You, my friend, are more intelligent than most men, most women, as well, and the deeper source of your power, *à mon avis,* is not so mysterious. It is"—he kisses his fingers—"entirely due to *mon superbe coq au vin.*"

∞

Though there has been a small outbreak of cholera at the General Hospital, she waves off Soyer's warning not to expose herself to contagion. "What good am I, Alexis, if I cannot nurse the sick?"

On May twelfth, her thirty-fifth birthday, she spends the day at the hospital, sitting with nineteen-year-old Henry Thomas Hunt, a soldier from Norfolk, dying of cholera. Makes him as comfortable as she can. He dies without complaint, his hand in hers. After the body is removed by orderlies, she pens a letter to his mother, encloses a lock of his light brown hair, the crucifix from around his neck. In his last moments, he had lifted up both arms and cried out for his mother. A curious thing, but on battle-fields and in hospitals, most soldiers who are dying cry out not for sweethearts or wives, but for their mothers, the root and source of their brief existence.

To Mrs. Maria Hunt,

I grieve to be obliged to inform you that your son, Henry, died in this hospital on Sunday last. His complaint at first was chronic dysentery, then cholera—he sank gradually from weakness, without suffering. Everything possible was done to save him and keep up his strength. He was fed every half hour with the most nourishing things he could take & if there was anything he had a fancy for, it was taken to him immediately. He spoke much of his mother & gave us directions to you in his last moments. . . . His greatest anxiety was that his mother should receive the pay due to him & that she should know he had not received any more pay since he had been out. You may have satisfaction in knowing he had the most constant and careful attendance from the doctors & the nurses. He died peacefully & as sorrowful as this news is for his bereaved mother, may she find comfort in knowing his earthly sufferings are over & in the hope that our Almighty Father will receive him into a better world than this.

Yours most respectfully,
Florence Nightingale

Struck Down

Balaclava Harbor
On board the *Robert Lowe*
13 May 1855

WHEN CHARLES COMES TO SEE why Flo did not appear for breakfast, he finds her still in bed, whispering for Dr. Anderson. "I am not well, Charles," she says. Alarmed, he rushes off in search of Nurse Roberts, asks her to sit with Flo while he goes in search of the doctor.

Arthur Anderson, principal medical officer, boards the ship, enters Miss Nightingale's darkened cabin. An hour later, a stretcher is brought on board by four guardsmen. Soon after that, Miss Nightingale is carried off the ship and taken to a private hut behind Castle Hospital.

The news spreads like wildfire through the camp.

Miss Nightingale, their Ministering Angel, their Lady with the Lamp, is near death.

Her fever spikes in the mornings, climbs still higher in the night. She is soaked with sweat, delirious. No visitors are allowed, but soldiers heap wildflowers outside her door. Several times a day, Mrs. Roberts steps outside the hut to speak to Charles. Dr. Anderson has told her, and now she tells Charles, that Flo's is the worst case of Crimean fever he has ever seen. When Alexis Soyer shows up with a healthful concoction of soup, Mrs. Roberts thanks him, knowing Florence will leave it untouched. She cannot sit up, cannot eat. When Dr. Anderson asks that Florence's hair be cut to help cool her brain, Mrs. Roberts takes a pair of sewing scissors and cuts her patient's golden red hair up to the hollow of her neck.

One day, with a violent rainstorm adding oppressive humidity to the heat, Mrs. Roberts soothes Miss Nightingale, wiping her face and neck with a damp cloth.

"What, dear? What are you saying? Is there someone you wish to see? Is he among the troops, in one of the hospitals? Would you like me to send a message?"

Her eyes slew wildly. "But he is here. Beside my bed. Can't you see?"

There is no one but the two of them in the dim, stifling hut.

"Here? Oh yes, I see. What do you wish to tell him?"

"Write it down. You must write it down, Mrs. Roberts. He must know it. That I love him. Have always loved him."

"I will, dear. I will."

A double rap, firm as an order. Mrs. Roberts leaves her sleeping patient, opens the door.

Out in the muddy yard, sitting upright on a magnificent gray horse, is an officer wearing a gutta-percha cloak and rain hat. Standing nearby, holding the reins of a second horse, is a man of lesser rank. Opening her umbrella, she goes out to speak to the officer.

"She cannot be seen. You are?"

"A soldier. One who has traveled a long way to see Miss Nightingale."

"I'm sorry, she can have no visitors."

"My name is Raglan. Your patient knows me well."

Inside, taking his rain-darkened cloak, she sees the empty sleeve pinned to his shoulder. The loss of his arm at Waterloo, she recalls reading about that.

He sits silently beside her, and after half an hour, leaves. In less than a month, Lord Raglan himself will be dead.

Charles struggles to write Sidney Herbert, to warn him of the likelihood of Florence's death. At the same time, Lord Raglan boards the *Robert Lowe* and comes to Bracebridge's room with a specific order. "Delay any telegram to her family until there is some hope of her recovery."

He leaves. Charles, sighing heavily, continues his letter:

> *I believe she got the disease from the time she spent at the bedside of a young soldier dying of cholera—though I repeatedly warned her. She only laughed, saying she had been around disease too much and had no fear of contagion. She has never been strong, and now this vicious "Crimean fever," combined with her terrible exhaustion, the damnably hot weather, and a relentless opposition to her views—all these threaten to fell her great spirit.*

He posts the letter but waits, as Raglan had asked, to inform her family. On the tenth day, the fever breaks; the worst of the crisis is over. He sends the Nightingales a telegram saying she is "convalescing," writes another letter to Sidney Herbert saying she is "out of danger." He does not offer Dr. Anderson's opinion that the convalescence will be long, and she may never return to full health.

To Parthenope, he writes more honestly:

> *Flo is unable to feed herself, unable to speak above a whisper. The slightest exertion exhausts her. But your dear sister lives, she will return home, and for all who love her, that is the main thing.*

The soldiers no longer openly weep or walk about the camp

with grief-stricken faces. There is talk of where she will go to con-
valesce. England? Switzerland? Geneva with the Bracebridges?
When asked, she gives a single firm answer. She will continue to
work in Balaclava. Discouraged by Dr. Anderson, she agrees to a
compromise. When she is able, she will sail back to Scutari and
resume her work there.

Charles, after allaying his terrible fear of contracting cholera
by galloping his horse back and forth across the charge line of the
Light Brigade, fires off a message to Selina:

*Come at once, dear, and take Flo back to Scutari with you.
You must find a house for her to live in. She cannot return to
the northwest tower, to that wretched piss hole. Mrs. Roberts,
her nurse, must stay with her, as well.*

PART THIRTEEN

Scutari

June 1855

Weary Old Riddle

"Your hand, Mrs. Roberts. Give me your hand." Her voice is scarcely audible. "You have nursed me as if I were your own child. You have saved my life."

What is there to say? She would give her life ten times over for Miss Nightingale.

In the pleasant two-story house Selina Bracebridge has rented for them, the opened windows in the sitting room let in a cool morning breeze. Elvira Roberts, who sleeps on a cot beside the sickbed, waits until her patient is asleep, then goes into the kitchen. Miss Nightingale has begun asking for tea. Whenever she wakes, a cup of warm tea is by her bedside, along with any spoonful of broth or calf's foot jelly Mrs. Roberts can coax her to take.

As she listens to the twittering of goldfinches in a nearby laurel, to the cooing of doves further off among the oaks, Mrs. Roberts wonders if her patient has any memory of that night on board the *Robert Lowe*, when, sweat-soaked and delirious, she had raved on about a man standing beside her bed. *Master.* A man she loved who wasn't there.

Life is a weary old riddle. Yet how fiercely we cling to the least shred of it.

To Parthe from Selina B.

I accompanied Flo back to Scutari. She was carried off of the ship on a stretcher by four guardsmen, who treated her with extreme care. As of yesterday, she is settled in a small, pleasant house I found near the Barrack Hospital. Mrs. Roberts, an older nurse from St. Thomas's Hospital, stays with her.

I visited this afternoon, and found Flo looking very nice indeed. Her hair is quite short; she sits up and walks a little. She wears a plain white cap and has the gentle, almost childlike look I remember of old. . . .

Not the whole truth, but why give discouraging news to Parthe, who will share this letter with her parents? I had actually found Flo with a ghastly pallor, emaciated, the bones in her hands and face standing out. She eats nothing but a little jelly and tea and can only stand a moment before her legs give out. Her first lucid words to me were of needing to return to work, insisting the nursing enterprise at Scutari would collapse without her. Perhaps she is right.

I resume my letter.

Lord Stratford, the English ambassador, has offered Flo his summer residence in Therapia for her convalescence. When she has strength to travel, I think it best she go there with Mrs. Roberts for at least a month, though so much tranquillity may prove impossible for your sister. Already, she insists on a full workload; if she is not slaving for her cause—hospital reform—a kind of panic sets up in her, a snappishness. She must work. In my life, I have never seen anyone so driven by the need to achieve for others—it gives her strength, but it has also nearly killed her. I do not understand the source of this compulsion, but I know this—Mrs. Roberts and the doctors here agree she requires a lengthy convalescence. In Therapia may she find, if only for a moment, the rest she needs.

Yours,
Selina

The truth is, if no one stops her, she will work herself to death. Twice, out of concern for her, we have postponed leaving. We cannot wait any longer. Charles embroils himself in controversies, offends others. I am unwell and long for my sketchbooks, my art. We cannot keep pace with Flo; we do not have her tenacity, her zeal for reform. We cannot love the soldiers as she does. They are birth sons to her.

I need to close the chapter on this "misadventure," this corrupt, bloody business of war. War ennobles no one. We are scratched and mauled by it. We have had enough.

PART FOURTEEN

Therapia, Turkey

July 1855

Âmes Damnées

IN THIS COVE, ONE OF THE MANY small sheltered bays between the Marmora Sea and the Bosporus, here in the summer villa of Lord and Lady Stratford, she has no company but the quiet presence of Mrs. Roberts, no sound outside the opened windows other than the rhythmic lap of seawater, cool breezes riffling the tall, slanting stone pines and broad-limbed chestnut, the Oriental plane tree, the Judas tree with its profusion of magenta blooms, the restless, piercing cries of the *âmes damnées*, lost souls, tiny birds skimming low above the sea, seeming never to alight anywhere. Nothing to see but shoals of silver porpoise arcing out of the bay and the colors of the sunrise or sunset, saturating the calm sky with shades of orange, red, violet.

She stands before a set of open French doors, listens to the stillness of another long night, broken only by the call of an owl hunting for prey.

She spends her days outside, in the dappled shade of the plane tree's light green, maplelike leaves. Leaning against the divan's soft cushions, drifting as if in a boat, a dahabiya, lost between sleep and dream. The weakness of her body imposes an indolence on her, a languor, a delicious doing of nothing at all. It is like being a child again, open to all the earth's wonder. The changeable colors of the sky, the gloss of the sea, the healing green of trees and fragrant shrubs, the sunlight, golden, glinting, sparkling . . .

"Three things remain with us from Paradise: stars, flowers and children." Dante. How long have I read only supply lists, letters from

369

bureaucrats, administrators, letters turning to dust the moment they are read? My letters, too. Nothing but dust.

In Therapia, she grows stronger, and one day asks to walk to the shoreline. Leaning on Mrs. Roberts, she fights a whirling in her head and roaring in her ears, a stonelike fatigue that flares into pain. Setting one foot in front of the other, it takes an eternity to walk the short distance to the shore and back. The next day, she does it again, and the day after that, until she is walking on her own, going longer distances, walking in the cool dusk, beyond ordinary time.

But Paradise always recedes for those in human form. She wakes one morning with the old need, the compulsion, to write. A letter to Parthe first, thanking her.

> *Mrs. Roberts has read "The Life and Death of Athena, an Owlet from the Parthenon" to me over and over. We laugh and cry together, admire your words and illustrations. How good you are, Parthe, to have created this tribute to little Athena, still so missed and looked for, still so loved.*

More formal letters to army and War Office officials. Letters to Selina and Charles. A brief, formal letter to Sidney.

After that, she writes in her commonplace book. Arranges her thoughts. As she had once made her child's lists of seashells, dolls, books to be read, coins collected, she shapes her surroundings, orders her world, is soothed and made whole again by words.

Commonplace

MAMA WRITES THAT I MUST PRACTICE the art of patience. But is not action a prayer? If I see a man by the roadside, begging for food, do I hurry past so as not to be late to church, or do I stop and tend to his hunger? Which is the better worship?

And who, really, is Mrs. Roberts? She has never left my side, has risked her life to save mine, and seeks neither money nor praise. Yet there is some impenetrable barrier about her person. Like a cloistered nun, she has erased herself, become pure quality without the weight, the shallow dross of personality.

White Ribbon

S HE RESTS ON THE DIVAN, sunlight dancing through the leaves of the plane tree, the branches of the chestnut and sycamore. She hears the murmuring of the sea against the pebbled shore. This evening, she will walk farther, to the tall, straight rows of cypress. Trees pointing upward to immortality. Dark spires of grief.

∽

"Miss Nightingale?"

It is Mrs. Roberts with her tea and a spray of lavender from the garden, its silver stems loosely bound with white ribbon.

PART FIFTEEN

Aunt Mai's Letters

No Pictures, No Portraits, No Parades

15 September 1855
Scutari

William, dearest brother,

I send this private report on your daughter—enclosed are separate letters, with gentler sentiments, for Frances and Parthe. When I arrived in Scutari two weeks ago, I found Florence much changed. The summer had been intensely hot, humid, with daily tropical-like rains, a "steam bath," as Flo described it. To give relief, she shaved her head. The sight, at first, shocked me. The Crimean fever has greatly aged her. A wisp of bangs across her forehead adds an odd, childish look. Her form is wasted away, her strength uncertain—crossing a room, her legs suddenly give way and she must sit down. She has periods of uncontrollable restlessness and does not sleep. I have found her working at her desk at 1:00 A.M., sometimes as late as 3:00 or 4:00 A.M. She eats next to nothing, her spirits are often irritable or depressed. This fever, this war, has taken much of your child's gentler nature.

The Bracebridges returned to England at the end of July—perhaps you have seen them? The French chef, Alexis Soyer, fell ill with dysentery and returned to Paris. The Sanitary Commission, which did so much to improve these hospitals, has left along with Mrs. Clarke and a number of the nurses. The siege on Sebastopol has ended; the Russians withdraw their troops. Flo believes the end is in sight and will return to the Crimean hospitals as soon as she is able.

As for the hospitals here in Scutari, mortality has fallen to 2 percent. In one year, your daughter has accomplished a herculean task, though it nearly cost her her life.

Last month, she presided over the opening of what she calls the Inkerman Café, a house between the two hospitals where soldiers can go to read books, study, hear lectures. Her intent, establishing this place, is to reduce the rampant drinking and idleness that gives these soldiers a bad reputation. She has established a means, too, by which they may send their pay to their families instead of squandering it on porter and rum.

Whenever we walk out together, I see the soldiers' outright adoration of "Miss Nightingale." They give crisp salutes, break into boisterous, spontaneous cheers. This gives her strength to accomplish even more for their benefit. I wish you could see what I see, William. You would be amazed at the extraordinary effect your daughter has had in this part of the world. I know of no woman like her.

The thousands of soldiers who have lost their lives are never far from her thoughts. I am convinced their deaths are what drive her. These infantrymen and common army soldiers are sons to her, no less than had she given birth to every one of them herself.

Great Affection,
Mai

1 December 1855
Scutari

Dear Brother,

News of the establishment of the "Nightingale Fund" has reached us. That Lord Panmure, Sidney Herbert, the Lord Chief Justice, the Speaker of the House, and some seventy other individuals of distinction have formed a committee to create a national fund to train female nurses and one day establish a school for nurses—for so long Florence's vision—and that the public so generously pours money into this fund, is magnificent! Even Flo, always so hard on herself, judging her efforts to improve patient care in the military hospitals a failure, is lifted by this news. "Perhaps life is sweet after all, Aunt Mai," she said when I had finished reading aloud news of the "Nightingale Fund."

She has not enough strength to administer these funds herself at present; perhaps the committee, or select members, Lord Panmure or Sidney Herbert, will help once she returns home. For now, we rejoice. That she is loved at home and revered by the soldiers in Turkey and the Crimea, even while being opposed at every turn by the "petty mid-dleman" of a disorganized bureaucracy; to have this fund and, with it, all the money needed to establish a school for nurses in London—the first of its kind!—raises her spirits no end.

Affectionately,
Mai

20 December 1855
Scutari

Dearest Brother,

Florence has received the queen's gift and worn it to Lord and Lady Stratford's Christmas party. It is a beautiful brooch, designed by Prince Albert, and on one side says "Blessed Are the Merciful." The brooch arrived with an invitation from the queen. I give you Her Majesty's exact words: "It will be a very great satisfaction to me, when you return at last to these shores, to make the acquaintance of one who has set so bright an example to our sex."

With this terrible war finally ending and Florence's work being rec-ognized in ways that will make her name endure forever, should we not all be grateful and proud?

Happy Christmas,
Mai

April 1856
Scutari

William, dear brother,

   This will be my last letter before returning home. We have no specific date, as Florence refuses to leave until every last detail is attended to, but she implies it will be this summer, perhaps as soon as July.

   One obstacle to her work has been the ongoing disagreement over the breadth of her authority as superintendent. As a result of Colonel Lefroy's private report to Lord Panmure on the deplorable condition of military hospitals here (he visited last October), Florence has been granted full superintendancy over all the hospitals in this region, including the Crimea. This gives her what she has long asked for, full authority, now and in any future wars. From now on, all army nurses must answer to a single superintendent. Our Flo has won yet another battle! That is how I see it, a victory—but perfectionist that she is, Florence insists her "achievements" in the Crimea are but the starting point for a much larger mission, what she refers to as "God's work."

   She has gone several times back to the Crimea, with the army giving her a buggy to travel between hospitals and camps. As with Scutari, she has established reading rooms for the soldiers and ways to post their pay home to their families. With her powers now consolidated and the war closing down, she is writing up final requisition reports as well as letters of character reference for each nurse, insisting on seeing each one off. As soon as the Treaty of Paris was signed this past March, the Sisters of Mercy, with Mother Bridgeman (whom Flo never tired of calling "Mother Brickbat"—they clashed because they were too alike) left as well.

   I foresee our being able to leave by this summer. Florence is adamant her return be unadvertised, without fanfare. "No pictures, no portraits, no parades." Her words. We are to return to England disguised as Mrs. and Miss Smith. I hold out hope for early summer, but she vows not to leave until every last living soldier has gone home—so it may be more August than June.

Do you know if Parthe received Flo's amusing letter about slaying rats? I have witnessed such encounters myself. Horrifying skirmishes, yet strangely comical, too.

Your devoted sister,
Mai

PART SIXTEEN

Rattus, Rattus!

How the mighty have fallen! The weapons of war have perished!

—2 Samuel 1:27

Un Petit Drame

Dearest Parthe,

In good spirits and fair health, I enclose this little drama, un petit drame, *for your entertainment. Perhaps you will write it as a book with illustrations? This will be my last letter from this part of the world, a brief tale of me—scruffy terrier—at war with a rat!*

FINIS!

Scene: hut in the Crimea

Time: midnight

Dramatis personae:
- *— one sick nun, stone deaf*
- *— me, the hut's only other occupant but for one fat rat lounging on a rafter over the sick nun's head*

Enter: me, lantern in one hand, broomstick in the other

Action: Broomstick employed, bloodied, enemy hurled out of hut. Nun oblivious, asleep and snoring.

Closing line: If there is anything I "abaw," it is a Rooshan & a rat!

Moral: Let us defend the deaf and the sick, especially those who sleep and snore through the heroic slaying of Rattus rattus!

Affec.
Flo

PART SEVENTEEN

Derbyshire

Lea Hurst

August 1856

HAVING REACHED HER DESTINATION, Whatstandwell station, she steps off the train, the hood of a black cloak hiding her cropped reddish hair and gaunt face. She finds a waiting cart, hires its driver. The moment she sees the tall brick chimneys spiking above the familiar green canopy of birch, oak, and sweet chestnut, she asks him to stop. Dropping her carpetbag onto the dusty road, the driver pockets the coins without a word, turns his weary draft horse back to the station.

Thank God he did not know me. So far no one has recognized "Miss Smith." I deserve no celebrity, want no fame.

She picks her way down the late-summer pasture, bee-loud, thick with ox-eye daisy, meadowsweet, blue cornflower. She'll go to the kitchen door, surprise Kitty or Hannah. Mrs. Gale, gone ten years. Miss Christie, too. Childhood, such a distant, curious realm.

From the shock on Kitty's face, she must look ghastly. Skin and bone, thinning hair, most of it fallen out. At Euston Station, she had begun feeling feverish, less than lucid, every bone in her body on fire.

A servant she doesn't remember carries her carpetbag upstairs. Mrs. Nightingale, on hearing the news, rushes down to find her daughter slumped over the kitchen worktable. Following behind Frances, Parthenope bursts into tears. Flo looks awful—her cloak stained, torn, her neck thin and white as cuttlebone—though she still wears the bracelet they had given her, strands of Mama's, Papa's, and Parthe's hair plaited together. But her sister's hands—the long, graceful fingers that had floated over the keys of the pianoforte, are red, roughened, with crescents of grime beneath the nails.

William clatters downstairs. Hearing his deep, familiar voice, she attempts to stand. Lifting her up in his arms, he climbs the stairs, carries her to her old bedroom, where Hannah, after closing the drapes, undresses and puts poor Miss Nightingale—*a shadow of herself*—to bed. She will lie feverish, scarcely breathing, for three days.

✍

Crimea? Scutari? Wandering foul, byzantine passageways, lost in dark, flooded corridors, passing rows of men on filthy pallets, begging for water, their hands reaching for her. Pulling her down.

The sheets, soaked with fever sweat. Blurred shapes—a desk, a chest of drawers, a door opening into a dark house where people sleep undisturbed. Get up, prepare for night rounds. No. I am home. At the window, I push apart the heavy curtains. A full moon shines low, so gravid, I try to touch it through the glass.

A sound. Turn to see someone living, the copper-haired boy from Cromford, Albert Moone, standing tall and straight in his common soldier's uniform. Take a step, only to see him dissolve into cannon smoke. The room empty again, haunted and dark.

In the hallway, I climb familiar stairs to the third floor. The nursery, outlined in moonlight, looks untouched, everything in its place, as if Miss Christie might enter at any moment, take up her accustomed place in the bittersweet drama of my childhood. Standing at the window, looking toward the black edge of woodland, it comes back, as if I were a child of seven again, an afternoon in late autumn when I ventured alone into those same woods to search for stones and came upon the dying hare—my first encounter, my first taste of suffering.

PART EIGHTEEN

Rose Diagram

The true foundation of theology is to ascertain the character of God. It is by the aid of Statistics that law in the social sphere can be ascertained and codified, and certain aspects of the character of God thereby revealed. The study of statistics is therefore a religious service.

—Florence Nightingale

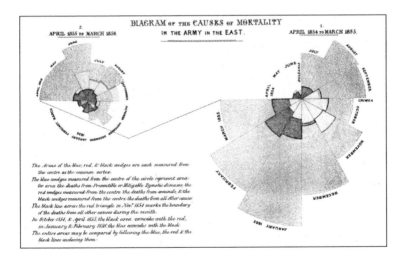

Ash

30 Old Burlington Road
Mayfair
London
July 1861

"THIS MORNING AT THE STATION, I watched a train pass on the opposite track. It had a black-and-gold hearse on it and I thought, *now there is the only carriage I shall ever want.*"

"Fiddlesticks, Sidney. You'll live to be one hundred."

"No, it is you who will live to be one hundred. You are indestructible."

"Nonsense. I have been dying since Crimea."

Even ill, Sidney Herbert is handsome, strikingly so, though his dark hair has thinned and his fashionable clothes hang loose on him. Bringing the coffee cup to his lips, his hand trembles so badly that he has to use the other hand to steady it. Illness is written all over him; exhaustion, pallor, pain. He sets the cup down with an effort, and in a familiar, elegant gesture, one she has seen countless times, runs a hand through his hair.

"What does Bence Jones say?" Henry Bence Jones, their old friend from St. George's Hospital, has diagnosed renal sclerosis—Bright's disease. Sidney is under his care.

"Not much. Retire. Leave public life. Go home to Wilton. Rest. I prefer to work here in London, take my Christchurch Remedy."

"What is your Christchurch Remedy? I have never heard of it."

"A mix of camphor and chloroform. You inhale it in one nostril, then drink several glasses of brandy. Keeps me on my feet like nothing else. Enough brandy and I am ready to crank down to the office and work. Still, the game is nearly up, Flo. I may try the water cure at Malvern."

For six months, she has prodded, chided him. Criticized his forgetfulness, his disorganization, been impatient with his chronic sleeplessness even as she approves the tremendous speeches he delivers in Parliament on her behalf. Dozens of speeches. The truth is, she is terrified, and constantly writes Lady Herbert, recommending remedies.

> *Take it from an old nurse who knows, Liz. Sidney would do well to ignore his doctors, take only beer and beef, no sauces or acids. Will you see he wears a flannel belt around his waist, does not go out nights, sleeps in the country, away from London's foul air? Make sure he takes plenty of exercise. Henbane is good to add to Bence Jone's prescription of ammonia, chloric ether, steel, and glycerine (tho bark is good, too). Avoid like the plague those doctors whose grim pronouncements produce the very disease they seek to cure!*
>
> *I am glad to hear he slept "like a top" over the weekend, and even managed to do a bit of riding.*

For five years, since the end of the war, she and Sidney have worked side by side in her "Little War Office," the name given her Burlington Street flat by those members of Parliament who frequently visit her there. On returning from the Crimea, she had declined the queen's invitation to live in Kensington Palace, reluctant to be too much in the "royal pocket." She prefers to live modestly, close by the houses of government, where she can easily receive visitors. Bedridden much of the time, she rarely leaves her flat.

Until today, he has never spoken of his illness, toils almost as hard as she does to see that her plans for hospital and sanitation reform are approved. Only the misfortune of having a "weak constitution," as he puts it, prevents his name from being put forth for prime minister, as so many had once foreseen, hoped. She is certain he will one day enter the annals of British history as a respected and honorable politician. Knows it is he who comes closest to secular sainthood, not her.

Since the war, they have worked as two halves of one brain, she organizing facts into reports, arranging statistics into visual diagrams, he writing and delivering thundering speeches in the House of Commons, arguing for Florence Nightingale's public and army hospital reforms. (*Two hundred speeches in 1860 alone, each shortening my life. Yet, for your sake, Flo, I would gladly give every one of them again.*)

"We work as one, Sidney. As two men work in unison, striving for the common good."

"Not two men, never as two men. But in unison, yes."

Neither has ever spoken of the bond between them. Not in all the weeks, days, and hours of working together in the Little War Office has the first awkward, compromising word been spoken. Her first-floor room, turned into a spartan office space, is papered over with precise diagrams, charts, projections. (*A visual pattern, like my Rose Diagram, conveys information better than a dozen articles. Statistics turned into diagrams are a kind of art. They possess persuasive power, are superior to words.*)

Centered beneath the window overlooking Burlington Street is the shabby brown divan he takes his naps on. There are two desks and two chairs, a few extra chairs for visitors. In this austere room, they work to move a sluggish government, made up of privileged men resistant to change, toward some national conscience, some compassionate policy of public health. It is reform work. Slow, tedious, bloodless. Not violent like war, less dramatic than revolution. In fact, boring.

"Your kittens, Flo, how are they?" Someone in government, knowing her fondness for cats, has given her two Persian kittens; he has yet to see them.

"Rambunctious."

"Do they have the Persian's blue eyes?"

"Brilliant blue. I don't know where they've gone off to. Yesterday, they knocked a Chinese vase off my bedroom mantel, then looked so contrite and pitiful, I forgave them."

From habit, their talk returns to the business at hand. The immediate financial cost of hospital reform. As usual, she is hard on him, a little unfair, saying he too easily lets himself be beaten down by bureaucracy. As he stands to leave for another appointment, wrapping the scarf Liz had knit for him around his neck, she further accuses him. "No man in my day has ever thrown away so noble a game with the winning cards in his hands. You disappoint me."

Unkind, he thinks, *but she is desperately frightened of losing me.* The moment he leaves, she will send a remorseful apology. She has done it countless times.

"You must get well, Sidney. Without your reputation, my work—our work—is in danger of going unfinished. Without you, our cause is weakened. I have never believed in fatal disease in myself. I will not believe it in you now."

"Obstinate Flo, unreasonable woman, listen to me. There are a dozen others qualified to take my place. Any one of our friends on the reform commission—Sutherland, Alexander, General Storks, even Andrew Smith, why not Smith? Sutherland in particular could carry your banner forward. In time your reforms will be accepted, but government, as you know, is glacially slow. And look,

you've published a rattling fine book, *Notes on Nursing*—I hear it
outsells Dickens! And your School of Nursing at St. Thomas's, the
first of its kind for women, looks to be a smashing success. Surely
these triumphs, outside our tedious work in government, give you
satisfaction."

"No. In most things I have failed. And there is no one on Earth
to replace you."

"You put too high a value on me. You always have."

"You are a man of exceptional courage and character."

"Good Lord, no. You have the wrong hero. I am full of
self-interest."

"Everything that is good and honorable I have learned from
you. In past days, you know, I privately called you 'Master.'" She
cannot admit that, sometimes, she still does.

"Flo, there is only one of you in this wide world." He loosens
the scarf from his neck, unbuttons his greatcoat, sits back down.
Whether she accepts it or not, he has little time left.

"May I talk openly?"

"Death. You are about to speak of death."

"Yes, but no. I'd like to know your thoughts on God, actually."

"My thoughts or my opinion?"

"Liz says you are a modern mystic. I would call you a pagan.
You do not attend church, do not adhere to any religion or sect of
religion; you embrace and dismiss them all. I'd like to know your
honest thoughts on God. It is the same question I put to you years
ago, at Wilton House."

"Mystic, pagan. Labels that miss the real question. I see God
less as a being, more as a sublime force, an intelligence running
through all life. When I was young, I interrogated God the Being.
I demanded answers from Him. Receiving none, I grew disillu-
sioned and turned to science. Mathematics, geometry, statistics. I

discovered in numbers a divine, if impersonal, ordering of infinite complexities. Laws that were genderless. I still see that. I have come to believe it is our task to discover those laws and learn to live in harmony with them. As for God's 'voice,' I heard it when I was sixteen and only three times thereafter, though at Scutari, as I sat with dying soldiers, I began to receive inner guidance, was able to sense what was asked of me, what to do and say from moment to moment. I came to rely almost entirely on these 'impressions' and less on fixed tenets of religion. It is simple, really. Beyond the body, in the depths of our spirit, God waits for us to hear Him."

He is slumped back against the divan. *Did he hear what has taken me a lifetime to learn?* Seeing him with his eyes closed, she admits what she has seen countless times in others. A shadow, closing in.

"I have written Liz with new remedies, Sidney. An astringent, gallic acid, may do some good."

He opens his eyes. "I will try whatever you suggest. It isn't that I am eager to die, more that death seems inevitable. I am trying to come to peace with it."

"Stop. I won't have you talking of your death."

"What shall we talk about, then?"

"Of what we have achieved. Of all that remains for us to achieve."

"No, not that. I'm tired of talking. Come, sit beside me."

On the divan, where he has sat hundreds of times, recording notes, writing drafts of future speeches, lying down for an hour's rest, they sit close, not speaking, their hands touching.

༺༻

She is writing out yet another remedy, a prescription to send Liz, when a letter from a Dr. Williams—a name she doesn't recognize—arrives.

2 August, 6:00 P.M.

All is over! Lord Herbert breathed his last about eleven this morning, half an hour after I got there. He had a convulsion in the night and was thought to be sinking, but rallied after and was quite sensible—he took leave of them all—was quite aware of his approaching end. Except at the last, he suffered no pain. When I asked, he said he had some pain in the chest—the death pang—but it did not last and he passed away quietly. A telegram from Lady Herbert, requesting I acquaint you with her husband's death, awaited my return home. I have lost no time.

❧

Papa,

Few people will ever know what I have lost in my dear Master. Indeed, I know no one but myself who had so much to lose. No two people pursue together the same object as I did with him. And when they lose their companion by death, they have, in fact, lost no final companionship. Now he takes my life with him. My work, the object of my life, the means to do it, all in one depart with him. Papa, I, too, should have died.

Parthe,

I am told his last words were of me. "Poor Florence! Poor Florence. Our work unfinished." No one understood him but me. No one loved & served him as I did.

I am his true widow.

I cannot bear to look down Burlington Street in the direction from which he always came to me. I cannot bear . . . any of it.

❧

Concerned her sister had not attended Sidney Herbert's service at the small church in Wilton, Parthenope makes the three-hour journey to London, then to Burlington Street. She finds her upstairs, asleep. Every window is flung open, papers and books are scattered, embers smolder in the hearth. Bending down to read what is written on a partly burnt scrap of paper, Parthe watches as the curious word—*Master*—scrawled in Flo's strong, singular hand blazes, then softens to ash.

Epilogue

If I could give you information of my life it would be to show how a woman of very ordinary ability has been led by God in strange and unaccustomed paths to do in his service what he has done in her. And if I could tell you all, you would see how God has done all, and I nothing. I have worked hard, very hard, that is all; and I have never refused God anything.

—Florence Nightingale

Edison's Phonograph

Little Menlo, Upper Norwood
Surrey, London
July 1890

Having left a cup of lukewarm tea and plate of day-old scones on a side table, Colonel Gouraud's valet leaves, the slish-slish of his slippered footsteps fading off.

"Silk beast," Johnnie Johnston hisses, jaw clenched, battling the ends of his bow tie. The tie, brand-new, is stiff and uncooperative. "Bingo." He draws himself up to triumphant height before the looking glass, pats his water-slicked hair into place. That should pass muster with the old bat. According to Gouraud, she is a recluse, deaf and bad-tempered. What does it matter, except to his male pride, how he looks anyway? Isn't he just one more swell on London's streets, on the lookout for fast money and backstreet adventure? Oh, but what an adventure he will *not* be having today.

Holding the cup at a safe distance from his expensive new morning suit, slurping down tea, he uses his free hand to pluck up a stale scone while surveying Colonel Gouraud's recording equipment. Shipped from Mr. Edison's studio in New Jersey, the new phonograph has a stumpy yellow beeswax cylinder, a detachable black trumpet mouthpiece, and a wood carrier top with *Edison Standard Phonograph* in tendriling black letters across both sides.

Looking from the window down to the street, he sees one of Gouraud's hackney coaches waiting. Swivels his head in the mirror, a final preening, wonders what Maud will think of his new look. Maud of the unbending waist and iron disposition, though for him, she has turned pliant as a lily. He folds in the trumpet, buckles shut the case. Onward. Record the old bird (Nightingale, ha ha!), hope for an amusing story to impress Maud with at the dance later tonight.

"West End, 35 South Street, Mayfair," he calls up to the driver, sliding the invention that is supposed to capture the old bat's voice for all time across the leather seat before climbing in himself.

Gripping the phonograph, Johnnie Johnston gazes up at the nondescript building. He'd been warned to expect cats, a great many cats. Sneaky beasts—he's never liked them. Mercurial and sly, like more than one woman he's run across.

He'd been warned to be quick, that she never sees anyone for more than a quarter of an hour. She'd famously turned away the queen of Sweden, saying she had too much work to do. Gouraud had only managed to get her to agree to be in Edison's celebrity series by assuring her that her voice, recorded for all time, would raise money for veterans of the Crimean War, the war that had made her into an English icon, an uncanonized saint. She would only do it, she told him, to help those heroes of Balaclava still alive, eking out their last days in poverty, sleeping in workhouse coffin beds, on the streets, or crowded into the Royal Hospital Chelsea—of late, there had been a number of indignant editorials in the newspapers.

I'm still steamed about the fast one Gouraud pulled on me, Johnnie Johnston thinks, opening the street door into the building's dingy foyer. He'd originally been assigned the great Arthur Sullivan; that's what he'd boasted to Maud—Sullivan, composer of *H.M.S. Pinafore*, *The Pirates of Penzance*, *The Mikado*. When that fell through, he'd been promised Lord Tennyson reading "The Charge of the Light Brigade." But no, here he is, about to deal with a "battle-axe," Gouraud's very words. "And for the love of God," the colonel had added, "keep an eye on her damned cats. She'll skin your hide if you stir a hair on any one of 'em." He scowls down at the fat white Persian bumping amiably against his calf, while its twin, haughty and cross-eyed, glares from the top of the staircase. Swiping back his own hair, exasperated, he trudges up the three flights. For someone as ambitious as Johnnie Johnston is, meeting some seventy-year-old spinster who'd had something or other to do with women's nursing and, worse, sanitation, centuries ago is of less interest than the butt end of a flea.

Blinding whiteness. Every window flung open. Birdsong. Sun lighting up books, papers, journals. White walls, white ceiling, blank. At the center of so much glare, a bed of white linens, white pillows, a white counterpane. Stubbed in its snowy center, her, he supposes, a stern, glacial bloom. The bed itself is heaped with sloping hills and columns, slipping stacks of paperwork, an avalanche warmed by sunlight, brightened by morning air flooding in from the open, curtainless windows. *The Alps*, he thinks. *An Alpine sanitorium.*

Before the nurse can shut the bedroom door, cutting off his view, Johnston takes it all in. The arctic atmosphere, the mountains of paperwork, the dazzling sunlight.

From behind the closed door comes a voice—silvery, aristocratic, decisive.

"Take a seat, young man."

He does, but not before drawing out his new pocket handkerchief and snapping away the mat of feline hair coating the green divan. He sits down, wedging the phonograph between his feet. Her sitting room is just as white, the walls as bare but for the engraving of a man, framed and hanging beneath an ugly crucifix made, she will inform him, from Russian shrapnel and musket balls. Beneath the cross, beneath the portrait, are half a dozen tea-cups set out on the floor, some with bits of meat, others glistening with water. An enormous cat, an orange tortoise, leaps from the floor onto the back of the divan, bangs its rocklike head against the side of his neck, purring obscenely. Another, black with white paws, weaves dangerously between his legs. He tries not to shudder. "Scat, you," he mutters, peeling the creature off his trousered leg. Back it comes, persistent.

From behind the bedroom door, he hears a series of melodic, high-pitched whistles. Birds? Imitations of birds? The nurse? Later, she will tell him she feeds a dozen or so birds every morning, whistles them to her windowsill. Wood pigeons, house sparrows, starlings, sometimes a song thrush or raven.

It is all pretty dreadful up to this point, until the door finally opens and she comes into the sitting room, leaning on the arm of her nurse. She is wearing an old-fashioned black dress with a white collar, a lace head scarf tied beneath her chin. And something else he had not anticipated: She is fat.

Rumors are poor substitutes for truth. The Angel of the Crimea is not impaired or bad-tempered in any way that he can tell. She has, in fact, the most piercing gray eyes—eyes that take him in at a glance, take in the full measure of his (admittedly callow) character, dismissing and engaging him at once. He has the eerie feeling she knows everything there is to know about him, sins and all, yet holds no judgment. An unsettling, if hopeful, sensation.

She isn't as wicked as he'd been warned. Not by half. She straightaway apologizes for keeping him waiting, saying she has been unwell. Then she leans forward in her chair and, in that upper-class voice of hers, says, "Mr. Johnston, I cannot express how much you bring to mind my boys at Scutari. Might I ask your age?"

"Nineteen on Friday."

"Just so. Torn from their mothers' arms. Brave, gentle boys. Most died uncomplaining."

She closes her eyes. It is awkward, since he is now completely covered up in cats. He finds himself petting one that has planted itself on his lap. After some minutes—he thinks she's dropped off—she opens her eyes, completely alert, and looks at the phonograph case between his feet.

"Is that it? The device? It's rather small, isn't it? I am doing this, you understand, for the Light Brigade. For the Relief Fund. For veterans living out their last years in poverty, forgotten by a shallow, ungrateful nation. I do this for them. You are Mr. Edison's assistant?"

Assistant to the assistant, he explains. Colonel Gouraud is Thomas Edison's "recording ambassador" in London; as his protégé, he is helping the colonel complete Edison's "London Celebrity" series. Would she care to see the phonograph, be shown how it works? Without waiting, he unlatches the instrument from its case, assembles it on the table in front of her. She shows a keen interest, asks questions, as if she is mentally disassembling and reassembling it, wanting to understand how it can pluck the human voice—patterns of vibration—out of the air and fix it, permanently, eternally, to a wax cylinder.

He reminds her that she will have exactly two minutes of recording time.

"What I have to say will take thirty-two seconds. Why wax?"

He explains Mr. Edison first tried tinfoil before finding beeswax did a better job.

"I should like to meet him, the first man to capture the human voice. Strange, it is the voice we first forget, after someone we love dies, even before his features. . . ." Her voice trails off. She glances at the portrait on the wall. A handsome man, thirty-five or so, a sweep of dark hair, large dark eyes. The idea of asking who it represents is beyond him.

"Just think of it, Miss Nightingale. Your voice will be heard by unborn generations."

"A little victory over death, isn't it, Mr. Johnston? Though memory, they say, only lasts three generations, and who would care to listen to my screeches, I have no idea."

He's begun to realize how wrong he'd been in his assumptions. Setting up the phonograph, making certain it is in working order, he helps her position herself before the wide end of the long black funnel and lean into its mouthpiece. Standing to the side, he is ready to turn the hand crank.

"Would you care to practice first, Miss Nightingale?"

"Not at all. Just say when I am to begin." She has no paper, no notes.

"All right, then. One potato. two potato, three potato—go."

When I am no longer even a memory, just a name, I hope my voice may perpetuate the great work of my life. God bless my dear old comrades of Balaclava and bring them safe to shore. Florence Nightingale.

Perfectly, precisely spoken, without a single mistake.

∾

Later on, he told Maud about his visit.

"Well, what did she say?"

The dance music was so loud, they were shouting into each other's ears.

"What was it she said into the phonograph?"

"I've forgotten. You know, Maudie, you're a sport."

"How so?" She leaned back in his arms, smiling.

"Pretending interest in my work." They had gone to sit at a corner table.

"Oh, but I am interested! Nearly every girl in my school fantasized about becoming a Nightingale nurse. For most of us, it was a passing phase, though I do remember one girl, Agnes Gatewood, smart, very shy, who applied to the Nightingale school over at St. Thomas's."

"She kept repeating it, you know. How I reminded her of the soldiers at Scutari—'her boys,' she kept calling them. She talked about the thousands, my age, killed by disease or in battle. I liked her lots, Maudie, despite her awful cats."

"Well, you should like her. She's only the most famous woman in England besides the queen. If the French have their saint, Jeanne d'Arc, we have ours."

Thrashing about in bed that night, restless, he found himself trying to imagine what she had looked like as a young woman. Whose portrait hung on her wall, and what was the story behind the ugly cross made from Russian shrapnel and musket balls? He should have asked about all that instead of letting her talk on about her cats. He wondered, too, if she had ever been in love. Suffered losses. Lacked hope. Failed. If she had ever been that uncertain, that human, once.

Acknowledgments

On a rainy London afternoon during the spring of 2013, I made my way to the Florence Nightingale Museum at St. Thomas's Hospital. In the dimly lit museum, I stood before each exhibit and, as was my habit, began taking notes and photos. That I happened to be the sole visitor at that hour added to the museum's solemn, haunted ambience. Standing before a framed, engraved portrait of Sidney Herbert, I was startled, ambushed by the raw conviction that I would one day write a novel about Florence Nightingale. Wandering the labyrinth of exhibits, reluctant to leave, I eventually made my way to the street, lugging copies of nearly every book, pamphlet, and postcard the gift shop offered for sale.

My Nightingale treasures traveled with me from Phoenix, Arizona, to my new home in Columbus, Georgia, where they waited until I completed another writing project. Finally, in 2018, I taped the postcards, mostly images of Florence and Parthenope, onto the walls of my study, hauled out the books and pamphlets, and began to read.

A novel is written in silence and privacy, but the novelist, if fortunate, is wreathed by encouragers, generous cheerers-on, who, in a hundred different ways, help bring the finished book into the physical world. It is these people I am indebted to and keen to thank.

Enormous thanks to my agent, Joy Harris. From the novel's earliest drafts, she offered a gracious, sustaining faith and gave suggestions so smart, they inspired me to ultimately transform the style and tone of the book. Deepest thanks to my publisher and editor,

Erika Goldman, whose intellectual rigor and uncompromising eye for literary quality pushed me beyond any temptation toward complacency and into the tough but exhilarating terrain of deep edits and revisions. Special thanks to Laura Hart, Joe Gannon, Carol Edwards, and Elana Rosenthal, Bellevue Literary Press's superb production team. And to Molly Mikolowski, finest of publicists.

Great thanks to readers of early and subsequent drafts: Peggy Richelieu Harris, Claire Ryle Garrison, Father Murray Bodo, OFM, Gyorgyi Szabo, Ph.D., and my beloved "sister," Elissa Hutson Reynolds. Thanks to Debra Hughes for cheering me on, to Joy Harjo for sharing my fascination with medicine and all forms of healing, to Lauren Green for her intuitively timed acts of kindness, to Ubiquity University for the opportunity to give a lecture on Florence Nightingale. Thanks to Barbara Dossey, Ph.D., R.N., friend and author of a superb biography of Nightingale. Grateful thanks to Luisa Materassi, who took me to see the bronze statues of Florence Nightingale and Sidney Herbert in Waterloo Place. Thanks to world-renowned photographers and friends, Carol Beckwith and Angela Fisher, for generously introducing me to Anthony Sattin. To Mr. Sattin, for his willingness to speak by phone to an American stranger and for his invitation to one day join one of his guided trips down the Nile.

Thanks to Mamie Willoughby Pound and the Wednesday-night writers' group in Columbus, Georgia. To the "Southern Om Ladies," my pre-COVID yoga classmates, especially our book-loving instructor, Judy Barnett, R.N. Loving thanks to my irreplaceable daughters, Noëlle and Caitlin, and my granddaughter, Juniper Skye, limber sprite, deep soul, born at nearly the same time I conceived of this novel.

To nurses and midwives everywhere. To my grandmother Augusta Duwe Brown, R.N., and my great-aunt, Lorna Duwe

Brown, R.N., sisters and nurses. To my grandfather Dr. Clarence J. Brown, surgeon and vice admiral, United States Navy, for organizing the overwhelming task of caring for all D-day casualties, transported by boat and train to the Royal Victoria Military Hospital in Southampton, England, a grand-looking, Italianate, nineteenth-century hospital Florence Nightingale once declared a catastrophe of inefficiency.

Endless gratitude to Dr. Philip Thomas Schley. You read every draft with your surgeon's eye for detail and historian's attention to accuracy, never once complaining about that weird, ink-stained creature you married, even as she wafted, absentminded specter, between two worlds. All love, always.

Recommended Reading

The following books provided vital facts and insight into Florence Nightingale's long, prolific life. They are the sources I found most helpful in creating a fictionalized portrait of one of the most extraordinarily complex and brilliant women to emerge from the Victorian era. Each book helped me transform a sentimentalized figure, remote icon, lay saint, and simplified legend, into the deeply human, relatable woman she was.

Nightingale's epistolary correspondence consists of thousands of letters; her journals encompass an immense collation of intimate thoughts. I wish to give additional credit to the books on this list, as well as to the British Library and other online library sources, for providing invaluable access to Nightingale's written tone, diction, and voice, as well as a greater awareness of the psychological and spiritual scope of her correspondence and private reflections.

If you are interested in delving more deeply into Florence Nightingale's life and writings, or into her time in Crimea, I unreservedly recommend these excellent books:

Bostridge, Mark. *Florence Nightingale: The Making of an Icon.* New York: Farrar, Straus and Giroux, 2008.

Crawford, Paul, Anna Greenwood, Richard Bates, and Jonathan Memel. *Florence Nightingale at Home.* Cham, Switzerland: Palgrave Macmillan, 2020.

Dossey, Barbara Montgomery, RN, PhD, AHN-BC, FAAN. *Florence Nightingale: Mystic, Visionary, Healer.* Commemorative edition. Philadelphia: F. A. Davis Company, 2010.

Goldie, Sue M., ed. *Florence Nightingale: Letters from the Crimea, 1854–1856.* Manchester, England: Mandolin University Press, 1997.

Goodman, Ruth. *How to Be a Victorian.* London: Penguin Books, 2014.

McDonald, Lynn. *Florence Nightingale at First Hand.* London: Continuum UK, 2010.

McDonald, Lynn, ed. *Florence Nightingale: An Introduction to Her Life and Family.* Vol. 1. *The Collected Works of Florence Nightingale.* Ontario, Canada: Wilfrid Laurier University Press, 2002–2012.

——— *Florence Nightingale's Spiritual Journey: Biblical Annotations, Sermons and Journal Notes.* Vol. 2. *The Collected Works of Florence Nightingale.* Ontario, Canada: Wilfrid Laurier University Press, 2002–2012.

Nightingale, Florence. *Cassandra.* New York: Feminist Press, City University of New York, 1979.

——— *Letters from Egypt: A Journey on the Nile, 1849–1850.* New York: Weidenfeld & Nicolson, 1987.

——— *Notes on Nursing.* New York: Fall River Press, 2009.

Nixon, Kirsteen. *The World of Florence Nightingale.*
London: Pitkin Publishing, 2011.

Reef, Catherine. *Florence Nightingale: The Courageous Life of the Legendary Nurse.* New York: Clarion Books, Houghton Mifflin Harcourt, 2016.

Sattin, Anthony. *A Winter on the Nile: Florence Nightingale, Gustave Flaubert and the Temptations of Egypt.* London: Windmill Books, Random House, 2011.

Soyer, Alexis. *A Culinary Campaign.* London: G. Routledge & Co., 1857.

——— *A Shilling Cookery for the People.* London: Routledge, Warne and Routledge, 1860.